REMEMBRANCE

Michelle Madow

DEDICATION

To my family and friends, for your constant enthusiasm and belief in my writing. This book wouldn't be what it is today without you!

AGKNOWLEDGMENTS

Thank you for picking up this book and reading it—I hope you love it as much as I loved writing it!

Thank you to my Intro to Creative Writing class, for reading the first chapter and encouraging me to complete this book. My best friends Kaitlin, Tiffany, and Alicia, whose enthusiasm for my writing kept me going, for being my constant cheerleaders, and for reading my first draft and letting me know it wasn't totally awful. To everyone who helped me edit this book—Mom, Dad, Steven, Aunt Barbara, Grandma Phyllis, and Grandpa Paul. This book wouldn't be where it is today without you all! A huge thanks to my agent Christine Witthohn, for her enthusiasm about this book from the first time I met her, for her confidence in me as a writer, and for her great advice. My agent-mate and friend Taryn Browning, for being a great critique partner. Taylor Swift, for writing a beautiful song, Love Story, and for creating a gorgeous video to go with it that helped inspire this book. If you're reading this, that's beyond awesome! Lastly, my parents and brother, for your belief in me and constant encouragement that I should go for my dreams. It means the world to me. I love you all!

PREFACE

It was at the Halloween dance that I got the first glimpse of my past life.

The gym was packed, and due to the masks and the dim lights, it was impossible to tell who anyone was. I looked through the crowd, trying to see who Chelsea was dancing with, but even her red dress blended into the darkness.

Then I felt a movement from behind.

"Your boyfriend won't mind if you dance with someone else?" a familiar voice whispered in my ear, barely audible over the loud, trancelike music. I turned around, disappointed to find that the black bandanna wrapped around his hair and the matching cloth mask covering the top half of his face made it impossible to see his features in the low lighting. But I knew it was Drew.

He pulled me closer before I could respond to the question. His arms wrapped around my waist, and I rested my head on his shoulder, closing my eyes and inhaling the sweet scent of pine coming off his skin. Jeremy *would* mind, but pulling away from Drew would be like trying to yank two magnets apart. It was dark, and we were in the back of the room, far enough from the main crowd in the center for anyone to notice. One dance couldn't hurt.

He must have figured that I wasn't going to try pulling away again, because he raised his hand to my shoulder and trailed his thumb down to my elbow, reaching my wrist and intertwining his fingers with mine. The palms of our hands connected, and I decided to enjoy the time we could be together, knowing that everything would return to the way it had been come Monday morning. The world spun to the beat of the music, and I let myself sink into it, clearing my mind of everything around me.

That was when the first flash came.

CHAPTER 1

Today was going to be different. I could feel it.

It wasn't because it was the first day of school, or that it was ten minutes after the time Jeremy agreed to pick me up. There was something strange in the air.

Or maybe I was just being ridiculous.

Tires screeched around the corner, and I looked down the street, recognizing Jeremy's red Jeep Wrangler speeding down the pavement. He pulled up in front of my house and I hurried to the side of his car, swinging the door open and hopping onto the hot leather seat.

"Way to be late for the first day of school," I said, pushing a few strands of hair off my face that had gotten out of place during my dash to the car.

He looked at me and smiled, his blue eyes hidden behind his sunglasses, and reached to tuck a loose curl behind my ear. "Liz," he calmly spoke his nickname for me. "It'll be fine. The teachers won't even care on the first day." He leaned back, the sunlight shining through the window glistening off his sandy hair. He looked like a model featured in a summer clothing catalogue; the pale colors of the blue and white striped shirt and khaki shorts he wore intensified his golden tan from his recent outdoor soccer practices.

"Not all of us have gym first," I pointed out. "Your teacher might not care if you're late, but mine will."

He shrugged and turned to look at me again. "Why didn't you straighten your hair today?" he asked, unhappy with my decision to let it dry naturally.

"I like it like this," I said, unsurprised that it didn't take long for him to mention it. I'd started to embrace my curls over the summer, which was easier than straightening my hair every day. It wasn't like they were springy and uncontrollable. They were loose and flowing, the kind of curls people cherished before the invention of flatirons.

"I like it better straight," he told me. "You look so young right now, you could pass as a freshman."

The words stung. I took a deep breath to calm myself, keeping my eyes focused on the road. "If I'd straightened it, we would have really been late to school."

He reached his arm across the gearshift and squeezed my hand. "I'm sorry, Liz. I meant it as a compliment. You look great when you straighten it."

I shrugged and pulled my hand out of his, looking out the window as my house disappeared behind us and blended in with all the others in the quaint New England neighborhood. The early September leaves were still green, and I soaked in the last days of summer, not looking forward to the weather getting cold. Even though I'd lived in Pembrooke—a town right outside of Manchester, New Hampshire—for my entire life, I still hated the winter. Whenever snow, sleet, or ice fell to the ground, I stayed in as much as possible. There was no point in going outside and freezing to death.

Jeremy stopped at a red light and reached over to turn on the stereo. The heavy pounding of an awful rap song filled the car; it was so loud that the floors vibrated with the bass. The old man in the rundown truck next to us glared and shook his head in disapproval.

"When did you start listening to this kind of music?" I asked, lowering the volume.

"Some guys on the team got me into it." He grabbed his iPod off the dashboard and handed it to me. "Check it out, it's pretty good."

I glanced at it before putting it back where it was, uninterested in the other songs in the album. "You know," I said, looking back over at him, "I just realized we don't have a song."

The words sounded stupid after I said them.

He thought about it for a second. "I guess we don't," he said, switching the stereo over to the radio. "Why don't you put on any station, and whatever comes on will be our song."

It sounded ridiculous, but I reached towards the tuner to change stations, closing my eyes before turning it.

AC/DC's "Highway to Hell" blared through the speakers, and I turned if off so quickly that I feared the knob might break off in my hand.

"Great pick, Liz," he said with a laugh, driving into the parking lot of The Beech Tree School—a private school for kindergarten through 12th graders that sprawled across a small campus. We drove past a variety of cars—everything from used Volkswagens, brand new SUVs, and even the occasional Lexus, BMW, or Mercedes—but Jeremy didn't turn to find a parking space. Instead, he pulled up next to the flight of steps leading to the entrance.

"How about I drop you off here so you're not late?" he asked, resting an elbow on the armrest and turning to look at me. I couldn't see his eyes behind the lenses of his sunglasses, making it difficult to tell if he meant it or if he was irritated at me for giving him a hard time earlier. But the offer was nice.

"Thanks," I said, forcing a smile I hoped looked genuine. Maybe he did care that I was upset about his being late. I grabbed my bag before hopping out of the car, swinging it over my shoulder and turning around to look at him again. "I'll see you in French."

The Jeep squealed against the pavement as Jeremy turned into the parking lot, and I ran up the steps, flinging the door open and scurrying through the commons where my friends and I usually ate lunch. Finally I made it to the main hallway. The light wood door leading to the European History classroom remained open, and I slid inside, not wanting to draw any more attention to myself than necessary.

"Just in time, Elizabeth," said Mrs. Wilder, turning her head in my direction. Her light grey hair was in a bun in the back of her head, and she wore a flowing brown skirt with a white button down blouse. She looked like she'd walked right off the prairie. She nodded for me to sit down, and I looked around the room to find an empty seat.

I spotted Chelsea sitting at the far end of the giant U-shaped table, her back facing the large paned windows on the opposite side of the room. Her straight, dark red hair cascaded over the edge of the chair, and her jean mini-skirt was paired with a dark purple top set off by a long golden necklace. She looked like she'd thrown her clothes on in the morning without a second thought. No one would have guessed that she didn't let me get off the phone with her the night before until she'd decided on the perfect outfit. When I sat down next to her, I knew that my dark jeans and light blue tank top I'd thrown on that morning looked plain next to her ensemble.

"Who would have thought that *you* would almost be late on the first day of school?" she snickered, keeping her voice to a low whisper.

"It wasn't my fault," I replied, leaning back in the plastic chair. "Jeremy was late picking me up."

I knew that his being late wasn't worth getting angry about, but my relationship with Jeremy was changing—and not for the best. He was constantly with his new varsity teammates, and while I knew it was normal for him to want to spend time with them, it hurt whenever he pushed me to the side. I couldn't help but hope that he didn't get elected co-captain, even though it was an awful thought to have. He'd tried introducing me to a few of his new friends' girlfriends, but I couldn't relate to them sitting on the bleachers analyzing every play on the field. While I did go to all of his games, kicking a ball around and barely scoring wasn't entertaining in the slightest—at least not to me.

I didn't realize that I was lost in my thoughts and hadn't heard a word Mrs. Wilder said about the beginning of the school year until the opening of the door brought my mind back into focus. I looked up in curiosity, wondering who else would risk being late on the first day.

The moment my eyes met with his, the other students in the room blurred into the background. My heart felt like it was pumping at a faster than normal rate, and my lips parted slightly as I took in the sight of the boy who looked so familiar, even though I couldn't remember where we'd met before. His spiky black hair was gelled to make it appear like he'd just rolled out of bed, although I had an image of what he would look like if it were a bit longer, with no gel. The midnight blue jeans, black shirt, and matching leather jacket that he wore seemed impractical in the summer heat, but I couldn't picture him wearing anything but dark, heavy clothes.

He yanked his gaze away from mine and scanned over the other students in the room, breaking the spell between us. Realizing that I'd been staring at him for longer that socially acceptable, I turned my attention down to my fingernails and pretended to be interested in the chipped pink polish. I tried to think of where we could have met before, but nothing clicked. It was like trying to recall a forgotten dream—each time I felt close to remembering where we'd met, the memories slipped away.

"You must be Andrew Carmichael," Mrs. Wilder stated the familiar name. I looked back up at him, but was still unable to figure out why I felt like I'd met him before.

He leaned against the door and crossed his arms over his chest, glancing around the room again. "I go by Drew," he said, sounding just as bored as he looked.

Mrs. Wilder ignored his attitude. "Please take a seat next to Elizabeth," she suggested, pointing to the chair next to mine—the last empty seat in the classroom.

Not wanting to be caught staring at him for a second time, I leaned down to grab a pen from my bag, trying to ignore the feeling of my blood pulsing faster through my body as he got closer. I was aware of his every movement, and it was impossible to act unaffected as he took the seat beside me. Goosebumps sprung up along my arms, and I inhaled the scent of new leather accompanied by a crisp trace of pine, reminding me of a campfire on a winter night. I tried taking shorter breaths in an attempt to ignore his presence beside me, but it didn't work.

Making sure not to look at Drew again, I readjusted in the chair, turning to Chelsea to see her reaction to him. She was looking at him, her eyes glinting with determination as she twirled a strand of hair around her finger, forming her mouth into what she probably believed was a seductive pout to try getting his attention. He must have not noticed, because an annoyed look crossed her face and she redirected her attention to Mrs. Wilder, who was walking around the room handing out the syllabus describing what to expect from the course that year.

I focused on the paper in front of me, shaking my pen back and forth between my index and middle fingers in the hope that I looked like I was deep in concentration. However, it was impossible to forget that Drew was sitting so close to me. My eyes kept drifting to the side, forcing me to see him in my peripheral vision. The pen wasn't enough of a distraction, so I dropped it on the table and gathered my hair over my shoulder, using it as a shield to block him from my line of sight.

Before I knew what was happening, the pen rolled off the side of the table, landing on the floor between us. I tried not to look at Drew when I leaned down to pick it up, but I was trying so hard to not acknowledge his presence that I didn't realize he had also reached to get it until the warmth of his fingers brushed against mine. A spark of electricity shot up my arm, and my breath caught in my chest at the sight of his dark brown eyes with a ring of golden flecks bordering his pupils. My mind grew hazy; everyone else disappeared around us, making it feel more like a dream than real life. I wondered if he felt it too.

The late bell shrieked through the halls before either of us could say anything, jolting my mind back into reality. He lifted the pen up and I smiled in thanks, making sure not to brush against his hand as I took it back. It was tempting to look at him to see if he felt the same draw towards me that I did towards him, but instead I gathered my hair over my shoulder again, re-creating the makeshift barrier between us. If I couldn't see him, maybe I would forget the strange attraction I felt towards him.

I also reminded myself that despite his recent change of attitude, Jeremy was still my boyfriend. Chelsea always gushed about how perfect Jeremy and I were for each other. My mom loved him, and she was best friends with his mom. Sometimes I wondered if they were already planning the wedding. Still, it took a concentrated effort to not look at Drew again—so much so that it felt like my struggle to keep my eyes focused on the front of the room must have been obvious to everyone else in the class.

The bell signaled the end of first period, and the only thing I could think about was getting out of the room so I could gather my thoughts. The best thing to do would be to get Drew out of my head, but it was impossible when I felt the energy pulsing off his skin, making me unable to ignore his presence as he gathered his books beside me. My heart thudded in my chest at a million times per second as I rushed towards the door, glad when I found myself amidst the bustling students in the hallway going to their next class.

"Lizzie!" Chelsea called from behind, making me stop in place. "Wait up!" We were both heading towards the language wing since I had French next period and she had Spanish, but apparently I was so caught up in thinking about Drew that I'd forgotten to wait for her in my dash out of the room. She bounced to my side, clutching her books to her chest. "So, how hot is Drew?" she asked, her eyes shining with enthusiasm.

I nodded and managed a small smile, hoping she would continue talking so I wouldn't have to reply. I was still trying to figure out why he seemed so familiar, and the last thing I wanted was for Chelsea to think I was interested in him.

She leaned in closer and lowered her voice. "He moved here last week from Manhattan," she said, glancing around to make sure no one was listening. "He lives on Lakeside Circle. I heard some people talking about him before you got here this morning."

I raised my eyebrows in surprise. The biggest, most elaborate houses in Manchester were on Lakeside Circle—the people who lived there were so rich that they didn't even need to work.

"Why would they move here?" I asked, wondering why someone would go from Manhattan to Pembrooke. Judging from Drew's lack of enthusiasm about being here, I figured there must be a story behind the move.

"I don't know," she said, her eyes wide with excitement. "But I'm going to find out."

"You do that." I laughed, doing my best to pretend not to care, despite the fact that I hadn't stopped thinking about Drew since leaving the classroom. "But we have to get to class. Meet you in the cafeteria for lunch?"

She smirked and stopped in front of the Spanish room. "Sounds good," she said, glancing at something in the distance before looking back over at me. "I'll let you know what I discover."

CHAPTER 2

Drew was the first person I noticed when I entered the French classroom. He didn't strike me as the first row type—that was typically reserved for teacher's pets who raised their hand after every question to show off their mastery of the material—yet he was front and center. He leaned back in his seat, not making an effort to talk to anyone.

His eyes locked with mine when I entered, and I paused in the doorway, wondering what would happen if I sat near him. However, his expression twisted into one of annoyance a second later, and he looked down at his desk, making me wonder why the idea had passed through my mind in the first place.

"Liz!" Jeremy called from the back of the room, breaking my train of thought. I saw him waving at me and walked over to join him, glad that he'd chosen a seat in back. "Mrs. Evans has assigned seating," he said as I navigated my way through the multiple rows of desks. "Which means you're all the way up there." He pointed to the first row.

I reached the empty desk next to him and widened my eyes, hoping he was joking. "Really?" I asked, looking at the front row with dread. Drew's expression when he saw me walk into the room made it clear that he didn't want me to sit anywhere near him, and the last thing I needed was for him to make it difficult for me to concentrate during another class as well.

"Really." Jeremy laughed, pointing at the piece of paper on his desk that said Jeremy Williams in black permanent marker.

"Great." I looked at the front row in agitation. "Now I'll be forced to participate."

I trudged forward to find my seat, my eyes traveling to Drew sitting with his back towards me, and then to the desk on his left. Andrew Carmichael ... Elizabeth Davenport. The seating was alphabetical, so I shouldn't have been surprised when I saw that mine was next to his.

Unsure if I should say hi or not, I took out my notebook and turned to the front page, writing 'AP French' on the top to stop myself from looking over at him. My hand started to shake and I concentrated on steadying it, not wanting him to think that I noticed him more than any other student in the classroom.

"This class should be easy," he broke the silence, his voice flowing with a warmth I didn't expect.

I looked at him to make sure he was talking to me, surprised to discover not only that he was, but that he was also leaning forward, like he was interested in my response. "Maybe," I said, trying to think of a way to continue the conversation. "I guess your old school had a good program?"

He chuckled, leaning back in his chair again. "You could say that."

I tilted my head in confusion, wondering if I was supposed to understand what he meant, but Mrs. Evans walked to the front of the room and greeted us in French before I could ask. Everyone quieted down as she handed out the book we would be reading for the semester and began going over the syllabus. We were only allowed to speak in French in the class, and I only caught half of what she said—partly because I didn't understand it, and the other part because I was too busy trying to act unaffected by Drew's presence next to me. I copied whatever she wrote on the board in the pretense that I knew what was going on, figuring she wouldn't call on me if I looked busy.

"*Élisabeth?*" she spoke my name, causing my pen to jolt to a stop on the paper.

I looked up in terror. "*What?*" I asked in French.

"*Would you care to tell the class what you did over the summer?*"

"*Okay,*" I began, trying to ignore the fact that everyone had turned to look at me, including Drew. "*I went to Pennsylvania. My dad lives there, and I stay with him every summer.*"

The vocabulary was simple enough, but my pronunciation was awful.

"What did you do when you visited him?" she prodded.

"I was a counselor at an art camp." I tried as hard as possible to speak with a proper accent, but the words refused to come out right.

Someone laughed in the back of the room, and I knew it was Jeremy before turning around. I narrowed my eyes at him before refocusing on my notes. I was already embarrassed enough—he didn't need to draw more attention to the fact that I had a difficult time speaking French, especially since he knew it was something I was self-conscious about.

Mrs. Evans moved on to ask Drew about his summer, and he replied flawlessly. I somehow managed to stop myself from looking at him. The class was easy for him, yet I stumbled over simple sentences, looking like a bumbling idiot. I started to regret not dropping down to the regular level French class. Then I reminded myself that AP classes looked good on college applications, and I didn't want to let my mom down by switching to the lower level class. She would tell me that it was fine either way, since she believed I was capable of making my own decisions, but she was proud that I was taking AP classes. I would just have to study really hard.

Mrs. Evans didn't call on me again for the remainder of class, and I managed to fill the sides of the page where I was supposed to be taking notes with senseless geometrical designs by the time the bell rang. Not wanting to deal with another awkward moment like the one in history class, I made sure to take my time gathering my books so Drew could leave before me.

"Nice job pretending you're awful at French," he said as he leaned down to get his bag, speaking quietly enough so no one else could hear but me.

I looked at him and raised my eyebrows. "Pretending?"

"Yeah," he said with a smirk. "And you did a good job of it. I think they all believed you."

I pressed my lips together, hoping he wasn't making fun of me, too. "What are you talking about?" I asked, trying not to sound as interested as I was.

He leaned in closer, holding his gaze with mine. "You *know* what I'm talking about."

"I honestly don't." I kept focused on him and tried to figure out what he meant, but there was no way to make sense of it.

Now he looked confused. "You mean you don't speak French?"

"Well, I'm decent at it," I answered in defense. "But it's not exactly my best subject."

His eyebrows furrowed as he looked at me, like he was trying to figure something out, or waiting for me to admit some non-existent fluency in the language. "Right," he said, pushing his chair back as he stood, the metal screeching against the floor. "I guess you just struck me as the straight A type."

"I like my other classes," I said, trying to lighten the conversation. "It's just French that gives me a hard time. I'm thinking about dropping AP and moving down to the regular level class."

"You'll do fine in this one." He shook his head and laughed, like he found my idea of switching into the other class ridiculous. "Trust me."

Before I could come up with a coherent reply, he turned around and walked out of the room. I looked at the door in shock. He had no reason to think I would do well in the class, especially after how much I'd messed up when called on to speak.

Jeremy approached my desk a second later, resting his hand on the back of my chair. "What was that all about?" he asked, staring at the place where Drew had just stood.

"I have no idea," I mused, leaning away from him to pick up my bag. Then I remembered what had happened earlier and looked back up at him, becoming irritated all over again. "But why did you laugh at me in front of everyone?"

He bit the inside of his cheek to keep himself from laughing. "You have to admit it's kind of funny that you sound like a clueless American tourist when you speak French," he said with a chuckle.

I glared at him. "Thanks, Jere."

"I didn't mean it like that," he tried to cover up the comment. "But maybe it wouldn't be a bad idea for you to switch out of AP."

His words made me freeze in place. "I'm not *that* bad at French," I defended myself, even though I'd said the same thing to Drew a minute earlier.

He picked the textbook off my desk and handed it to me. "Don't take it so seriously," he said, smiling as I took the book and shoved it into my bag. "It's just not your best class. And regular level French is at the same time, so you wouldn't have to change around your entire schedule if you switched. Plus, you would get an A."

"I'm staying in AP," I insisted, not in the mood to argue in the middle of the near-empty classroom. Mrs. Evans was speaking with another student at her desk in the corner, but she was still close enough to hear our entire conversation. "But third period's starting soon. I'll see you at lunch."

The entire way to my next class, I thought about the short conversation with Drew. It was no secret that French wasn't my strong point, and he had no reason to think otherwise. Still ... he sounded so confident. Maybe he was just being nice, but even though he had no reason to think I could do well in the class, it seemed like he believed every word he said.

CHAPTER 3

My next two classes, genetics and English, went smoothly, except I couldn't get Drew's dark eyes with the golden specks out of my head. It felt like he was everywhere I went. I spent most of third and fourth periods trying to figure out why he seemed so familiar, but every time I felt close to remembering, the thought disappeared. I wondered if I should ask him the next time I saw him, but I resolved not to say anything. It would sound so strange. I had no choice but to let it go.

A return to the normal routine of meeting Chelsea in the cafeteria before going to eat lunch in the commons seemed like the perfect way to focus on my life at school instead of my non-existent relationship with Drew. She waited for me like we agreed, but after we bought our food, Jeremy called my name from the center table in the cafeteria filled with his fellow varsity teammates. There was a huge smile on his face as he motioned us to join him.

"Looks like we have a new table this year," Chelsea said with a smirk, waving at Jeremy to let him know we were on our way. She started walking towards the long rectangular table, holding her head high as she strode through the crowd.

I wanted to sit with some of our other friends in the commons, but Jeremy and Chelsea both seemed happy switching locations, so I would have to deal with it for the day. When we got to the crowded table, I somehow managed to squeeze into a small space between Jeremy and the edge of the bench. Chelsea sat across from us. I crossed my legs in discomfort and looked around the table, which consisted of varsity athletes and their girlfriends. The guys were muscular from their workouts, and each one had a large amount of food in front of them, opposed to the salads on the girls' plates. They were all seniors except for Jeremy, Chelsea, and me.

"You know the guys on the team, right?" Jeremy asked me, a huge grin on his face. He seemed happy to move up in the world, if "the world" meant high school and "moving up" meant sitting in the center of the cafeteria.

"Yeah," I answered with a timid smile. I'd seen them around school and knew most of their names, but hadn't had a conversation with any of them before. Jeremy was aware of that, but he turned away to continue a conversation with one of the other soccer players, not attempting to make any further introductions. The other girls didn't make an effort to be friendly either, so I took a bite of my sandwich and listened to them talk about their summer vacations, doubting they would be interested in my experience as an art counselor at a summer camp in Pennsylvania.

"Drew just walked out of the cafeteria line with Danielle Parker," Chelsea said to me, stabbing a piece of cantaloupe with her fork. "I guess she's fighting with Brandon again and is using Drew to make him jealous. How typical."

I turned my head to look, and just as Chelsea said, Drew stood near the far wall of the cafeteria with the tall senior girl. He looked bored with whatever they were talking about, and he glanced around the room like he was looking for someone to save him from the conversation.

His eyes stopped when they reached mine. My head started spinning like it did the first time I saw him in history class, and the strange feeling of déjà vu refused to go away. But the far-out look in his eyes was different from earlier. He looked almost like he was in pain, opposed to his relaxed attitude from that morning.

"Oh my God, he's totally looking at me," Chelsea said, breaking the spell between us. When I turned back around, he was situating himself at a table by the wall with Danielle and her friends, not acknowledging the fact that he'd been staring at me a moment before. He didn't appear to be looking at Chelsea, either.

"Isn't that the new guy you were talking to at the end of French?" Jeremy broke into the conversation. "The transfer from New York?"

I looked down at my plate and moved a tomato around with my fork. "Yeah," I said, shrugging like it didn't matter.

Chelsea widened her eyes and leaned over the table. "You talked to him?"

"He just had a question about the homework," I lied, wishing she would let it go. "No big deal."

Jeremy laughed, looking at me in shock. "And he asked *you?*"

I paused, not knowing how to reply. It did seem unlikely that anyone would ask me for help in French, but Jeremy didn't have to announce that to the entire table.

He took a bite of his sandwich and resumed talking about the upcoming vote for co-captain with the guy next to him before I could say anything. Aware of the fact that the entire table had listened to our conversation, I sat back in my seat and tried not to look at Drew again. I doubted that he would ever embarrass me in front of everyone like Jeremy had just done.

Chelsea popped a grape in her mouth and rested an elbow on the table. "Since you know Drew, maybe you could introduce us," she said, looking over at him without bothering to be inconspicuous. "He's totally my type."

"Sure," I said sarcastically. "He asked me about the homework, and now we're best friends." I managed a small laugh, but her comment bugged me. She couldn't know if he was her type—she'd never even had a conversation with him. Then again, it wasn't like I knew him, either.

I spent the remainder of lunch trying to act engulfed in listening to Shannon Henderson, one of the senior girls, tell everyone about her month-long trip to Europe this past summer. She took full command of the table, speaking loudly and making huge gestures to get attention. Her stories were only vaguely entertaining, but her two best friends Keelie and Amber hung onto every word like she was giving a presidential speech.

At least listening to her talk provided an adequate distraction from Drew and prevented Chelsea from discussing him any further.

I checked my schedule at the end of lunch to see what class I had next, glad to find that it was drawing. Chelsea and Jeremy weren't in the class, and it probably wouldn't be one that Drew would sign up for either, since it tended to be mostly girls.

When I arrived at the art room it was only a quarter full, and I smiled when spotting Hannah Goldberg sitting by herself at one of the four tall tables. Her peasant shirt looked like it came out of the sixties, and she barely wore any make-up. She was a quiet girl— short, with mousy brown hair and a few freckles. She used to be best friends with Chelsea and me, but in the beginning of freshman year she started dating Sheldon, the star of most of the school plays, and the two of them started to isolate themselves from everyone else. I missed talking with her, but at least she seemed happy in her relationship.

I sat on the stool next to her, saying hi as I placed my bag on the ground.

"Hey," she said, smiling and placing her pencil on her desk. "Where were you at lunch today?

"Jeremy decided to sit in the cafeteria with the guys from the team, so Chelsea and I ate there today," I explained, hoping she didn't take it the wrong way. Last year we always ate together in the commons.

"Oh." She looked disappointed. I felt bad, since the only times we saw each other any more were during lunch or classes we shared, but at least we had drawing together.

We discussed what we did over the summer until our teacher entered the room and handed us all empty sketchbooks. He told us that by the end of the semester we had to fill them up however we wanted. It didn't matter what was in them as long as they were full, which wouldn't be a problem for me. I knew it would be easy for Hannah as well; she was an excellent artist.

Talking with her during class was a nice break from thinking about Drew, Chelsea, and Jeremy, but it was soon time for my final class of the day—trigonometry. I never found math interesting, but at least I shared it with Chelsea, which would reduce my boredom.

The classroom contained five small clusters of desks seating four students each. Chelsea sat in the back with her books on the desk next to her, and she moved them over when I walked into the room. I sat down and pulled my notebook out of my bag, glad that the day was almost over.

"You'll never guess what happened in chemistry," Chelsea said, tapping her pencil on her desk in excitement. Her eyes were wide and she leaned forward, looking like she was about to burst if she didn't tell me soon.

"What happened?" I tried to look enthusiastic, despite how tired as I felt. "I hope you didn't make something explode on the first day."

She rested her hands on her desk and took a deep breath in preparation to share the news. "I arranged it so I'm lab partners with Drew!" she squealed, a huge smile forming on her face. "Now we'll be working together every day for the rest of the semester."

Disappointment flooded my body, and I sat back in my chair, somehow managing to force a smile so she wouldn't get suspicious. "How'd you manage to do that?" I asked.

"Easy," she said with a smirk. "I sat next to him. When Mrs. Sullivan had us pick lab partners, I asked him to be mine. It's not like he knew anyone else, but all the other girls were totally jealous."

"That's great," I said, trying to muster up some excitement. "Mr. Roberts assigned us partners in my genetics class."

Mr. Barton, one of the math teachers at the school, walked into the room to begin class before Chelsea could continue. I tried to focus on trigonometry for the entire fifty-five minutes, but it was impossible to shake the image of Chelsea and Drew working together in chemistry.

At least she would be stuck wearing those huge goggles that left strange marks on people's skin afterwards.

The bell signaled the end of the longest first day of school ever, and I wanted nothing more than to go home and collapse on my bed from exhaustion. But since Jeremy drove me to school and he had soccer practice, I had some time to kill. The two-hour practice was at the same time for the varsity and JV teams, and I never minded going to the library to do my homework for the evening or read a book while I waited for him.

I walked past the lines of computers and aisles of books until reaching the back room. It was my favorite place to do homework. There were a few beanbags scattered around the space, and a large glass window overlooked the lake behind the school. Most students gravitated towards the desks in the center of the library, and the peace and quiet in the back was nice compared to all the commotion of the day.

I rummaged through my bag and searched for my planner, glancing at the short list of assignments and debating which to do first. I ultimately decided to read the first four chapters of *Pride and Prejudice*. I'd always wanted to read it, and it was one of the books my English class was reading for the semester.

I opened the small paperback and turned to chapter one. The first line caught my attention: "It is a truth universally acknowledged, that a single man in possession of a good fortune, must be in want of a wife."

My thoughts wandered to Drew. From what Chelsea had said earlier, he certainly was "in possession of good fortune," and it probably wouldn't be long until he had a girlfriend. Unfortunately, with the way things were going it seemed likely to be Chelsea.

I finished the first four chapters in under an hour, and despite wanting to read more, I had other homework assignments to complete. I placed the book on the floor next to me and took my sketchbook out of my bag. There was no better time to start filling it up than the present. I opened it to the first page and placed the tip of my pencil on the blank paper, beginning to draw.

The scenes from the book remained in my mind, and by the time 5:15 rolled by, I was staring at a half-completed sketch of a girl with long blonde hair in a high-waisted flowing ballgown from what I assumed was the early 1800's. Long satin gloves traveled up to her elbows, and a headpiece adorned her curls. Her hair flowed all the way down her back, just how I imagined mine might look if I grew it longer. She looked into a mirror, and it appeared like she was preparing to attend a ball much like the one described in the chapters that I'd just read in the book. It looked and felt so familiar—almost like I'd drawn it from memory.

I traced my fingers upon the image as I examined it, wondering what inspired me to draw someone who looked more like me than the main character, Lizzy. Her name was the same as mine—except for the slight variation of spelling—which could possibly explain why I merged us together, but I still couldn't quite make sense of it. She was the only figure on the paper besides the mirror, and I lifted the pencil again, beginning to sketch the background so it didn't look like she was floating randomly on the page.

More time must have passed than I realized, and the sound of the door opening interrupted my thoughts. I looked up to see Jeremy stride into the room. He still wore his brown gym shorts and white jersey with the number 12 on the back below his last name that was spelled in all capital letters. His hair was a little darker than its normal dark blonde because of sweat, and his cheeks were still red from practice.

I dropped my pencil in the crease of my sketchbook, disappointed to have to stop mid-way through the drawing. "Did you get co-captain?" I asked, trying not to get irritated about being interrupted while sketching. I could always finish when I got home from school.

"You bet I did!" he answered pumping his fist in the air in excitement. He walked over and joined me on the beanbag, slinging his arm around my shoulders. He was still sweaty, but I tried to ignore it as I rested my head on his chest, noticing that his arms were firmer than they were in the beginning of summer because of his intense workouts. "It was pretty much a given that I would get it," he continued, "but it's good knowing it's official."

"That's awesome, Jere," I said, looking up at him and smiling to show him I meant it. In that moment, he was back to the same Jeremy I knew growing up. Excitable, fun, and relaxed, he looked down at me with those blue eyes that were as familiar as the back of my hand. "I had a feeling you would get it."

"Thanks, Liz." He leaned closer and rested his forehead against mine, the sweat from his hair matting on my skin. The slight movement caused the pencil to roll out of the crease of my sketchbook, and it fell to the floor. "What're you drawing?" he asked, moving his hand down to the book in my lap. Despite knowing that I didn't like anyone seeing my drawings before they were completed, he grabbed it before I could respond and lifted it out of my reach.

"You don't want to look at that..." I pleaded, reaching forward to try getting it back. I was unsuccessful. "It's not even close to finished yet."

He ignored me and pulled it closer, examining the sketch. "This is different from your other stuff," he said, squinting as he looked at it.

"Different how?" I asked, even though I knew he was right.

"You normally draw scenery." He rotated the book in his hand, continuing to study the image. "Did you have some strange assignment to draw yourself in medieval clothes?"

"It's not medieval," I said, a little harsher than necessary. "It's what people wore in the early nineteenth century when *Pride and Prejudice* was written. It's the first book we had to read in my English class."

"Weird." He looked at me like I'd lost my mind and shut the book, handing it back to me before standing. "But anyway, what do you say we go to dinner to celebrate my victory?"

Even though I was tired, I smiled in agreement, allowing him to pull me out of the chair. I wasn't about to ruin his good day by whining about how terrible mine was, and my mom wouldn't mind if I went to dinner with Jeremy instead of eating with her. Unlike some of the other kids my age, I'd never been the type to get into trouble or make irrational decisions, so I was pretty much allowed to do what I wanted.

I packed my books in my bag and decided that for Jeremy's sake, I would pretend everything was the same as it had always been. It pretty much was, minus his recent attitude change and the new table at lunch. But it was impossible to deny the biggest change of them all—that no matter how hard I tried, I couldn't seem to get Drew Carmichael out of my head.

However, judging from his actions today, I doubted he felt the same.

CHAPTER 4

Drew ignored me for the next two weeks. Although maybe "ignored" wasn't the right term. Is it possible to ignore someone if you don't know them in the first place? It's not like one conversation meant we were friends. Still, I couldn't shake the feeling that he was going out of his way to avoid speaking to me. He always came to first period right before the late bell and sat as far as possible from Chelsea and me. It was the same in French class—he was always the last one there, rushing in before Mrs. Evans began the lesson. I lingered around Jeremy's desk and talked with him before class, walking to my seat just before the bell to avoid any unnecessary interaction with Drew. Well, it was more like a lack of interaction, since he didn't seem to notice my existence.

When I did sit in my assigned seat next to him, my skin prickled like it was absorbing a radioactive force emitted from his body. There were times when I felt like he watched me out of the corner of his eye, especially when I stumbled over my words when Mrs. Evans called on me to answer a question. When I walked around school or ate with friends in the cafeteria, I could always tell when he was near, like I was tuned into a frequency that picked up waves in his presence. I tried telling myself it was nothing but a high school crush and I would get over it, but I knew my feelings for him weren't something I could turn off like a light switch, no matter how hard I tried.

"In general, the quizzes were good," Mrs. Evans spoke in French as she walked around the room, handing back the pop-quiz she'd sprung on us earlier that week. *"The average was an A-, and most of you received grades in that range."*

She looked at me for a second longer than the other students before placing my quiz facedown on my desk. Slowly lifting the corner of the paper, I peeked at the grade written on the top. A bright red D stared back at me, laughing at my near-failure.

A slight movement on my right caught my attention, and I glanced over to catch Drew sneaking a quick look at my grade. I shoved the quiz into my bag so he couldn't see it, but the sunlight from the window shined through the paper, making the red ink visible from the other side. No one else cared enough to try to peek at my grade, but the concerned look in Drew's eyes let me know he'd seen it, and he turned his attention to the front of the room without saying anything. My cheeks flushed at the fact that he knew how poorly I'd done, and not wanting to be more embarrassed than I already was, I blinked away tears of frustration and prepared to focus on the lesson for the day.

"As you know, the reading from last night discussed vacations," Mrs. Evans began in French. *"So let's hear about some vacations you've been on and anything interesting you saw or learned."*

Lindsay Newman, a girl I'd only spoken to a few times who sat in the middle of the room, started the conversation by talking about a recent trip she went on to Italy. Just like the other private schools in the area, admission to Beech Tree wasn't cheap, and it wasn't unusual for students to vacation out of the country. However, instead of listening to people discuss their vacations, I thought about the quiz, trying to calculate how much it would affect my final grade in the class.

"Élisabeth." Mrs. Evans disrupted my thoughts, causing me to jump a bit in my seat. *"Have you ever taken a vacation to a foreign country and had an interesting experience while there?"*

I paused to translate the question in my head, catching the words "interesting," "experience," and "vacation." There were a few words in the middle that I didn't understand, but not wanting to embarrass myself by letting everyone know I wasn't paying attention, I decided I got the gist of it enough to answer.

"Two years ago I went to Hawaii." I spoke quickly, wanting to get the focus away from myself as soon as possible. *"We went on a helicopter ride and saw the volcanoes."*

Mrs. Evans looked baffled, and a few students began laughing—Jeremy included.

I looked around, confused. "What?" I asked in English, wondering what was so funny about helicopters and volcanoes.

"Hawaii's a state," Jeremy said, not making an effort to contain his laughter.

"Yeah," I said, still unsure what the problem was. "I know."

"But you just said your vacation to a foreign country was to Hawaii."

A foreign country—those must have been the French words I didn't understand enough to translate into English. The entire class looked at me like I was an idiot, and I glanced at Mrs. Evans for help only to find her laughing right along with them, although she tried to control herself when her eyes met mine.

"I just didn't know the French words for foreign country," I explained, hoping everyone believed me.

Jeremy laughed again. "Sure. Whatever you say."

I nearly threw my pencil at him in frustration. "I know Hawaii's a state," I said, crossing my arms over my chest. "I just misunderstood the question."

He smirked in disbelief, and I knew I wouldn't hear the end of this later. I was beginning to re-consider switching out of AP.

When class ended, I left without waiting for Jeremy. It wasn't long until he caught up with me.

"You never told us how your trip to the foreign country of Hawaii was," he said with a laugh, entertained by my embarrassment.

"You know I didn't actually think that." I looked at him in annoyance, pleading for him to let it go. Arguing about this was stupid.

"Sure you didn't," he drawled, leaning closer towards me. "Anyway, how'd you do on that quiz?"

I took a step back. "I did fine," I lied, not meeting his eyes.

"I got an A-," he jumped at the chance to brag about his grade. "But don't worry too much about what you got. It was one quiz. It doesn't matter that much." He stopped in front of one of the English rooms for his next class, which was on the way to the science wing where I had genetics. "I'll catch you at lunch," he said, seeming to have already put the Hawaii incident behind him.

I started to walk towards my next class, but didn't get far before hearing someone calmly say my name.

I recognized Drew's voice before I turned around. He leaned against the cement wall, both hands inside the front pockets of his jacket. "I know you don't think Hawaii's a foreign country," he said with a smirk, like he was proud of himself for being the only other person in the class who believed me.

I stopped walking, confused about why he decided to talk to me after pretending that I didn't exist for the past few weeks. "Really?" I asked, walking towards him and resting my hand against the wall. "Because everyone else seems to think I do."

"I believe you," he repeated, standing close enough to me that I could see the small flecks of gold in his eyes, made darker by the lackluster lighting in the hall. I waited for him to say more, but he stared down at me, waiting for a response.

"That makes you the only person who does." I shrugged, glancing at the ground before looking back up at him.

"I can help you with French," he offered, catching me by surprise. "If you want."

I paused, wondering if I heard him correctly. "Thanks," I said, playing with the strap of my bag. The offer was tempting, but Jeremy wouldn't be happy if he found out I was spending time with Drew. "But I think I might just switch out of AP."

"Come on." He leaned in closer, causing that whole electricity over my skin thing to happen again. "I know you're smart. If you practice a little, you'll blow everyone away."

I tried to focus on the conversation and not on how there were only inches between us, positive that my heart was beating loud enough for him to hear. "I'm pretty hopeless in French," I said, my voice steadier than I expected. "But if you want to try helping me, I'll think about staying in the class."

"You're not hopeless," he said, his eyes softening as he spoke. He hadn't looked at me that way since the first day of school. "And even though I probably shouldn't help you, I will."

I looked at him in confusion. "What do you mean that you *shouldn't*?"

"Just that Jeremy might not be happy," he said with a small smirk. "He seemed threatened when we talked on the first day of school. Not that I care about that, but

I wouldn't want to cause problems between the two of you."

I couldn't help but laugh. "I don't see Jeremy offering to help," I pointed out, feeling bad about the words the moment I said them.

"So," he said, a mischievous smile forming on his face as he leaned closer towards me. "When are you up for the first study session?"

We were standing so close that I could feel his breath on my cheek when he spoke, and I ran through my schedule in my mind. "Jeremy drives me to school on Fridays, so I'll be in the back of the library tomorrow until he gets out of soccer practice," I said, telling myself that there was nothing wrong with getting help outside of class. It wasn't like we were going on a date. It was just a tutoring session.

He looked at me quizzically. "You just wait around for him to drive you home?"

"Just on the days when he doesn't have workouts in the morning," I said in defense. "It's a good time to get homework done. Or to read."

"Whatever you say." The halls started emptying and he glanced at his watch, which looked more expensive than anything the other students had at Beech Tree. "I know you probably want a break from school after what happened in French, but as much as I'm up for ditching my next class, I'm guessing that's not your thing."

I jerked my head up in surprise. "How do you know I wouldn't be up for ditching?"

"Just a guess." He smirked. "If you're up for it, my car's outside."

I paused, considering what to do. I'd never skipped before, but my lab partner in genetics was also in my French class, and I wasn't in the mood to further defend my knowledge of world geography.

"Actually," he spoke without waiting for my response. "Forget I asked. You should go to class." Without waiting for me to answer, he started walking down the hall. "But I'll see you tomorrow," he called over his shoulder before turning around the corner.

"You'll never guess what happened in chemistry," Chelsea said, dropping her trigonometry book on the desk next to mine and sitting down. She always came straight to class to make sure she had enough time before the first bell to rehash the recent conversations she'd had with Drew. It was hard to smile and nod as Chelsea talked about him, but at least I was feeling better about the French quiz after Hannah helped me figure out how much the D would impact my final grade while we were in drawing. It wasn't as terrible as I'd thought, and as long as I started to do better on quizzes and tests, my grade shouldn't suffer too badly. I was also glad that Hannah believed me when I told her I didn't think Hawaii was a foreign country.

"Let me guess," I said, returning to Chelsea's question. "It has to do with Drew?"

"We're going to the movies on Saturday night!" she squealed, leaning forward in excitement.

I dropped my pencil in shock. "He asked you?"

"Well...I asked him. And I sort of said I was going to the movies with you and Jeremy and didn't want to be a third wheel," she sneaked in, fidgeting in her seat. "You'll come, right?"

"Sure," I said, keeping my voice level. "I'll have to ask Jeremy, but it shouldn't be a problem."

She barely let me finish my sentence before speaking again. "This will be so much fun!" She beamed. "Thank you so much. Next time you need me to do anything, I'm there. Not that I wouldn't be otherwise, but you know what I mean."

"Anytime," I said, the word sounding strained as I spoke it. Out of all the guys in school, of course Chelsea had to go for Drew. She was clueless about my feelings for him, but it was impossible to not be irritated.

I picked up my pencil and started doodling on an empty page of my notebook, trying to clear my thoughts of everything involving Drew and Chelsea.

"Are you okay?" she asked. I must not have been doing a good job at hiding my feelings.

"I'm fine." I smiled in a way that I hoped was convincing. "I just got a bad grade on my French quiz, and it's bothering me a bit."

"One bad quiz grade won't destroy your average," she assured me, shaking her head like it wasn't a big deal. "It was only a quiz, and you're really smart. I know you can do well."

The guilt hit immediately. "Thanks," I said, knowing she meant it.

For the rest of the class, I couldn't forget the conversation I'd had with Drew earlier in the day.

Technically I wasn't doing anything wrong by having him tutor me, but it felt like I was going behind Chelsea and Jeremy's back. And I still couldn't figure out why he offered to help me in the first place. Perhaps he wanted to ask about Chelsea, since our being friends must have come up in one of their conversations. However, I doubted that was the case—Drew didn't seem like the type to fish for information when he was interested in a girl—he would probably just go for it.

So what if he was doing that, but with me instead of Chelsea?

CHAPTER 5

Drew would be arriving in the library soon, and I debated bringing up the double date planned for tomorrow night. I leaned back in the beanbag and took a deep breath, telling myself not to worry. There was no need to make this complicated. When Jeremy got out of soccer practice, I would just let him know about the plans. We'd gone on double dates with Chelsea and whatever guy she was seeing at the time many times before. The big difference this time was that she would be there with Drew, who I couldn't seem to get out of my mind.

Glancing out the large window, I attempted to refocus by taking in the colors of fall. The late September leaves looked like a pointillist painting with the various colors of reds, oranges, and yellows, and I took out my sketchbook and colored pencils and began drawing the scene outside, concentrating on the trees as I tried to represent them to the best of my ability.

"I didn't know you were an artist." Drew's now familiar voice caught me by surprise. I must have been so involved in drawing that I didn't hear him enter.

Placing my pencil down in the crease of the book, I turned to look at him as he clicked the door shut. The temperature had dropped enough in the past few weeks that his leather jacket no longer looked out of place, and his dark eyes focused on me, the same way they had when we spoke in the hallway the day before.

"I like to sketch things sometimes," I said, shrugging and looking down at the drawing. "I'm not that good."

"Would you mind if I look?" he asked, remaining in place as he waited for me to respond.

"Sure," I said without a second thought. "It's just for class though. Nothing too elaborate."

Instead of waiting for me to get up and hand him the book, he moved to sit next to me on the beanbag, leaving only a few inches between us. It was impossible to think straight with him sitting so close, and I tried to stay calm, not wanting him to know the effect his presence had on me. Reminding myself that he'd asked to see my sketches, I pushed the book in his direction.

"It looks good," he said, comparing it to the scene outside. I didn't know if I was imagining it or not, but there seemed to be a trace of disappointment in his tone.

Maybe he didn't like scenery drawings.

"I have some other stuff, too," I said, flipping through the pages to show him the sketch from the first day of school—the one of the girl in the flowing dress.

He was quiet as he pulled the book towards him. My heart thumped in my chest as I watched him study it, wondering if he was silent because he loved it, or if he didn't like it and was trying to figure out what to say so it sounded like he did.

He grazed the paper with his thumb, taking in every line with his touch. "This is beautiful," he finally said, lifting his eyes to meet mine.

My cheeks flushed, and I looked back down at the drawing. "Thanks," I said softly, taking the sketchbook back and placing it on my lap. "Jeremy hated it. I'm glad to know it isn't completely awful."

"Jeremy's wrong," he said, his eyes becoming darker than their normal shade of chocolate. "He must be completely blind."

I shrugged. "He just likes my sketches of scenery better. And when I draw him playing soccer."

He glanced at the sketch again. "This is more interesting than Jeremy playing soccer."

"I have a few more like it," I said, surprised at my willingness to share the drawings.

"Can I see?" he asked, waiting for my response instead of grabbing it like Jeremy had on the first day of school.

He made an effort to not brush against my hand again when I handed it back over, and I lowered my eyes, trying not to show my disappointment.

My palms became clammy as he examined each drawing, surprised by how he appeared to appreciate each one of them. I viewed each one along with him—the first being the girl who resembled myself in what I'd discovered was a white morning dress from the early nineteenth century. She ate breakfast on a wooden porch overlooking a grassy yard that disappeared into a forest. In the next she laid on a felt-cushioned sofa, reading a novel by a lit fireplace while the setting sun cast shadows on her face through the rectangular window in the back of the room. Many sketches came after this, consisting of letter writing, playing cards, and riding horses. Drew leafed through them wordlessly, studying each page with the same intensity as the last. I was afraid to breathe, scared that the slightest sound would break the spell of silence.

He reached the end and lifted his gaze from the book for the first time in several minutes. "Where did you get the ideas for these?" he asked.

"We're reading *Pride and Prejudice* in my English class," I explained. "I guess it inspired me."

He nodded in agreement. "It's a good book."

"Something about it seems so familiar," I said, trying to figure out how to explain. "I have such clear images of what everything must have looked like back then, and I can draw them so easily. It's like the scenes are right in front of me instead of only in my mind."

His gaze never wavered from mine as I spoke. The room was silent except for the soft cry of the wind outside, and I could feel electricity crackling in the air.

He looked at me in question, like he was seeing something he hadn't before and was trying to figure out what it meant. "That's the sign of a great artist," he said after a few long seconds.

"Thanks," I said, looking down at the book between us. "You can have one if you want." I moved my hand across the paper, grazing his in the process. The small bit of contact sent a rush of heat up my arm. I paused, pulling my hand back towards myself a moment later.

"I probably shouldn't take your homework," he said pulling his hand to his side as well. "Anyway, we should start going over French since the test is coming up in three weeks. From what I saw in class today, we've got a lot to cover."

"Right," I said, trying to ignore the heat lingering on my hand from where it had touched his seconds before. "Although like I warned you earlier, I'm pretty hopeless."

He got up from the beanbag that we shared and moved to the one next to me, pulling his French textbook out of his bag. "And like I said earlier, I doubt that's true."

I didn't refute his comment, but the chance of my doing decently on the upcoming test was as likely as winning the lottery. However, since he seemed determined to help, I decided to at least put forth the effort.

Focusing proved impossible, and my French didn't seem to improve in the slightest, despite Drew's words of encouragement. While I tried concentrating, all I could think about was the upcoming double date, and whether or not I should mention it.

"So," I said, looking up from my book. "Chelsea told me you were coming to the movies with us tomorrow night?" The statement came out as a question, and I cringed at what an airhead I must have sounded like.

"That's the plan," he said. "Unless you don't want me to come?"

"No," I stammered. "I do. I mean, Chelsea does."

"I would hope so." He laughed. "Since she asked me."

I couldn't think of a response, and not wanting Jeremy to walk in during the study session, I looked at my watch to see how much longer there was until soccer practice got out. We had fifteen minutes, but I wanted to play it safe. Jeremy wouldn't react well if he walked in the library and discovered Drew and I sitting close together on beanbags in the back room speaking in French to each other.

"Jeremy will be here soon," I said, disappointed that the study session had to end.

"I would stay until he got here, but we wouldn't want to give him the wrong idea." Drew winked, leaning back in the beanbag.

I stared at him, shocked at the implication. "He wouldn't care," I lied.

"Sure." He smirked, not sounding convinced.

"Are you jealous?" I asked, amused by his reaction.

"Of Jeremy?" Drew laughed. "Never."

His response surprised me, and I had no idea how to reply. "I guess I'll see you tomorrow then," I said, closing my French book and packing it into my bag.

"Goodbye, Elizabeth," he said, grabbing his bag and swinging it over his shoulder. "I'll see you tomorrow."

I said bye and watched him walk out of the room, finally able to think clearly once he was gone. *Drew isn't interested in me,* I reminded myself. *He's interested in Chelsea.*

Still, I couldn't help but wonder if I was wrong. It would have made sense for him to say something to get me to talk about Chelsea if he was interested in her, but he didn't mention her at all.

Looked like I would just have to wait and see how he acted with her on the double date tomorrow night.

CHAPTER 6

"Should I wear blue or pink?" Chelsea's voice sounded distant over the phone, and I assumed she put it on speaker so she could walk over to her closet to figure out what to wear to the movies.

I rolled over on my bed and looked at the ceiling, putting the light blue princess phone I'd had since I was six back up to my ear. "Whichever you're in the mood for," I replied, stifling a yawn. "But pink always looks good on you."

I winced after my suggestion. Blue was Chelsea's best color.

"I think I'll go with black," she decided, even though it wasn't one of the original options. "Drew seems like the type to like black. He's always wearing it."

Wrong, I thought. *He likes when girls wear white.* I tilted my head a moment later, wondering why I'd thought that. It was just an assumption—he'd never mentioned it to me.

So why did it feel like the truth?

Chelsea must have finished changing, because the line became clearer, meaning it was off speakerphone. "I'm so nervous," she said, lowering her voice even though no one else could overhear. "Drew's so different from other guys I've dated. I might actually like him. More than I've ever liked anyone."

"Don't be nervous," I reassured her, despite the guilt that washed over me at her comment. Even though nothing happened between Drew and me in the library during the tutoring session yesterday, I couldn't help but feel like I was lying to Chelsea by not mentioning it. "He seems like he's really into you."

"Yeah," she said. "Otherwise he wouldn't have agreed to come to the movies."

"Right," I said, sitting up and leaning against the wall. "But I have to finish getting ready. I'll see you soon."

She said bye, and I placed the phone back in its blue cradle, standing up and looking at myself in the mirror. I debated changing out of my favorite faded jeans, since Chelsea told me she was wearing a short skirt tonight, but I decided to stick with them. They complimented the white spaghetti strap top that showed off the remainder of my summer tan, and the shimmery eyeliner I'd applied earlier enhanced what Jeremy called my "natural good looks." Happy with my outfit, I ran my straightener through my hair again—the brisk

September air stopped my hair from frizzing, and it now stayed in place when straight.

The honking of a horn blared from outside, and I walked into the hall to look out the front window, seeing Jeremy's Jeep parked next to my house. The rap music blasting from his car was so loud that I could hear it from inside, and I hoped he would turn it down—or off—when I got in the car. I ran back into my room to pick up my lightweight white jacket from its resting spot on the back of my vanity chair and did one last mirror check before grabbing my bag and heading out of the house.

"What took you so long?" Jeremy asked when I opened the door, turning the volume down as I hopped inside the car.

"I was finishing getting ready," I told him, trying not to get annoyed at the fact that he hadn't bothered to say hi.

He was silent for a moment. "You look beautiful," he finally said, leaning his elbow on the steering wheel.

"Thanks." I brought my hair over my shoulder and looked up at him, surprised by the compliment.

"I miss hanging out just us," he whispered, leaning forward so his breath was hot in my ear. "How about we ditch the movie and stay in tonight?"

"I promised Chelsea we would go," I insisted, the lack of electricity between us obvious compared to how I felt around Drew. "It won't be that bad. We used to go on double dates with her all the time."

"Fine," he glowered, like a child whose mom told him he couldn't have any dessert after dinner. He pulled away, putting the car into drive and slamming his foot on the pedal. The engine revved into high gear, and the tires of the Jeep squealed as they fought with the pavement for more speed. A car heading in our direction flashed its brights, signaling him to slow down, but Jeremy ignored it and went even faster.

"Jere," I said, gripping the armrest for support. "Slow down. You'll get us killed."

He accelerated the car more. "Relax, Liz. It's time you got over your little fear of speed."

I held the armrest tighter and glanced at the speedometer, watching the needle go past seventy. "Seriously, Jeremy. Stop," I said, breathing slowly to keep my voice steady. My heart started pounding in my chest, the sound filling my head and blurring my vision. I closed my eyes and tried to block the sights of the houses flying by so quickly that they blended together in a stream of grey. The wind whistling through the windows made it impossible to forget how fast we were moving, sending my stomach swirling with nausea.

"Geez, Liz." Jeremy snickered, slowing down so he was now going the speed limit. "You need to lighten up. What's wrong with driving fast?"

I leaned back on the headrest, not in the mood to have the conversation again. "I just don't want to get in an accident," I repeated the same thing I'd always told him.

He took his focus off the road for a moment to look at me. The deep blue of his eyes were the type that would render most girls speechless—as they used to do to me— but lately I'd noticed that I was completely unaffected.

"You don't trust my driving?" he asked, offended. "Come on, you know I wouldn't risk wrecking the Jeep."

"I know. Just not when I'm in the car, okay?"

"Fine," he said, pulling up to the movie theater. I breathed a sigh of relief that we had arrived alive.

He draped his arm around my shoulders as we walked through the parking lot, but his feet fell into a different rhythm than mine, making it difficult to walk. "You owe me for this one," he joked in my ear. "You should give some of the girlfriends of the guys on the team more of a chance. Like Shannon and her friends. They're not as bad as they seem."

"Okay," I agreed. "I'll try, but I don't see Shannon and I becoming close anytime soon. I don't know if you listen to her at lunch, but she always talks about her supposed 'friends' when they're not there."

"She's a little judgmental," he said, "but it's not in a mean way. Just because you take everything so personally doesn't mean everyone else does."

"So Shannon says nasty things about people and *I'm* the one with a problem?" I asked, not bothering to hide my irritation.

He shrugged it off. "I never said you had a problem."

"You said I take everything too personally."

He laughed. "Yeah, and you're doing it now."

I tried to calm down, not wanting to ruin the night before it even started. "Let's just drop this, okay?"

"There's nothing to drop," he said. "But whatever you say."

He opened the door to the movie theater and I walked through, spotting Chelsea and Drew standing near the concession stand. Chelsea laughed at something Drew said, and she leaned into him, taking a sip of what I assumed was a diet soda. To any outsider they would have looked like a couple that had been together for a while, and they were so involved in their conversation that they didn't notice us in line as Jeremy bought our tickets. I made sure not to meet Drew's eyes when we reached them.

"Hey guys," Chelsea greeted us. "Thanks for agreeing to see the horror movie. It looks really good—and totally scary."

Drew looked at Chelsea. "I was surprised you wanted to see it," he said with a smirk. "You didn't strike me as a horror movie type of girl."

"Liz just loves horror movies," Jeremy joked, giving my shoulder a squeeze. "I'll never forget when you called me at midnight after that one we saw in middle school because you were convinced there were invisible ghosts in your room."

"I just felt bad for the ghosts in the movie," I said, embarrassed that he'd brought it up. "Their lives ended so badly, but they were trapped in between worlds and couldn't fix what happened when they were alive."

Jeremy laughed. "Sounds like they needed to get a life and move on."

"Maybe." I fidgeted with the strap of my bag. "But it would have been nice if they had the opportunity to change things. Or if they had a second chance."

"Who's to say that the second time wouldn't end up just like the first?" Drew said, surprising me by jumping into the conversation. His voice was sharp, and his eyes focused on me. "Maybe it would be best if they moved on so they wouldn't have to experience that pain all over again."

"But they could never find out unless they tried," I pointed out. "Otherwise, what's the point of having a second chance?"

"You guys totally lost me," Chelsea said, looking back and forth between Drew and me. "Let's go in, or we'll be stuck with awful seats."

She started walking towards the entrance to the horror movie and slipped her hand inside of Drew's, pulling him closer towards her. The top of her head reached the height of his shoulders, and I grimaced at how good they looked together, especially when he whispered something in her ear and she laughed in response. Combined with the stately way they both walked, her deep red hair against his dark brown resembled how I imagined Mr. Darcy looked when he was with Caroline in the beginning of *Pride and Prejudice*. Maybe Drew felt the same way towards Chelsea that Mr. Darcy felt towards Caroline— completely disinterested. However, I doubted that was the case.

"Scared for the movie?" Jeremy asked as we walked up the steps inside. The previews had just started, but the theater was mostly empty. So much for being stuck with awful seats.

"Not really." I looked at him in question. "Why?"

"You seem tense. But don't worry; I'll protect you from your imaginary ghosts."

"I don't mind the ghosts anymore," I said, shifting away from him as we walked. "Now it's the jump scenes that get me."

He swung his arm around me and pulled me closer. "Then feel free to jump on me."

He meant it to be protective, but it felt like he was invading my space. I tried to not let my irritation show.

Chelsea approached a row she liked in the middle and walked to the seat in the center. Drew sat down next to her, leaning back and placing his feet on top of the unoccupied seat in front of him.

Jeremy motioned for me to enter the row and take the seat next to Drew. "After you," he said, holding out his hand so I could pass. "I'm going back out to get popcorn. Do you want anything?"

I shook my head no and sat next to Drew as casually as possible, making sure that my eyes looked in every direction except where he sat on my left. I hoped I didn't look awkward, and I tried to ignore the warm tingling in my left arm from being so close to him.

Jeremy returned when the previews ended with a large tub of popcorn. He offered some to me, but I wasn't hungry. The movie started, and while it was interesting, trying to ignore Drew sitting next to me proved harder than expected. My body remained alert for every small movement he made, warming when he was closer and cooling when he moved away. Bringing my hair over my shoulder, I attempted to create a barrier between us like that first day in class, since it made a good shield for stopping my eyes from wandering in his direction.

Once involved in the plot, I concentrated on doing my best to prepare for the jump scenes so I wouldn't embarrass myself by screaming in the theater. Thumping background music clued viewers into the fact that someone—or something—would jump out of the shadows at any moment. I wrapped my arms around myself and tried not to anticipate the scene too much, since it would only lead to a more intense reaction when whatever lurked in the shadows finally popped out.

Then an ear-piercing scream rattled from the sound system, accompanied with the flash of some sort of pale, deformed human-monster creature. My hands flew away from each other and into the air, grasping for something solid to hold onto. The first thing my hand went for was Drew's, which lay on top of the armrest like he barely registered the jump scene at all.

I was about to pull my hand back towards me when he rotated his around mine, connecting our palms and tracing the side of my index finger with his thumb. His hand wrapped around mine so perfectly; it was like he'd held it many times before, triggering a familiarity I couldn't place. It was the same feeling as when I first saw him in history class, and all I could focus on was Drew's hand in mine, surprised when he made no effort to move it away.

I glanced over at him, freezing in place with what I saw. He didn't look at me at all—his eyes still faced forward, leading anyone else in the theater to believe that he was deeply involved in the plot. He sat as still as a statue, yet his hand remained soft and warm, continuing to brush against mine.

Jeremy crunched on a handful of popcorn, bringing me back into reality. I pulled my hand away from Drew's, cursing myself for thinking that Chelsea and Jeremy wouldn't notice, at the same time grateful that neither of them did. I crossed my arms to prevent my hands from falling into Drew's again and leaned to the right, reminding myself that I was there with Jeremy. Chelsea wanted to spend time with Drew, and that didn't include him holding my hand in the movie theater, regardless of how short the moment lasted.

Jeremy thrust the bag of popcorn in my face, the buttery smell filling my nose. "Want some popcorn?" he asked. "It'll take the edge off."

I shook my head. "No thanks," I whispered.

I tried focusing on the movie again—not on Drew sitting so still next to me, or Jeremy crunching on the other side. I wondered if Drew would mention what had happened between us. Even if he did, it meant nothing. He wouldn't be there with Chelsea if he wasn't into her.

However, no matter how hard I tried to forget about it, the place where Drew's hand connected with mine felt warm for the rest of the movie. He didn't look at me again after that, and I wondered what he was going to say to me about the moment between us in the theater— if he planned on mentioning anything at all.

CHAPTER 7

Drew refused to look at me when we got out of our seats, and Jeremy held my hand as we walked down the steps—the same one that Drew had held only an hour before.

"What'd you guys think of the movie?" Chelsea asked as we walked outside.

"It was alright," Drew replied, not going into any more detail. I looked at him, and he held his gaze with mine for a second before turning back towards Chelsea. Neither Chelsea nor Jeremy noticed.

"There could have been more jump scenes." Jeremy laughed.

"There were enough," I answered quickly, looking at the ground so my eyes wouldn't wander in Drew's direction again.

"You looked scared to death in there." Jeremy laughed again. "Almost as much as when I drive fast."

Drew turned to look at me, surprised by Jeremy's statement. "You're scared of speed?"

I pressed my lips together and narrowed my eyes at Jeremy for bringing it up. "Yeah," I said, looking away in the hope that they would get the hint that I didn't want to talk about it.

"It's really funny," Chelsea said with a smirk. "Don't speed in a car with Lizzie, or she'll totally freak out."

Drew remained silent and looked out into the parking lot, like he wasn't listening to a word she said. It was the same distant look in his eyes that he'd had during the movie—like he was trying to remove himself from his surroundings by concentrating on something far away.

"So," Chelsea said, trying to regain Drew's attention. "Are you guys up for ice cream? That really good place where you can pile on the toppings is around the corner." She looked at me after asking, her eyes begging me to say yes.

"Sure," I agreed after a few seconds. It wasn't like she gave me any other choice.

She smiled and looked at Drew, excited to spend more time with him. At least that made one of us. It wasn't that I didn't want to be around him—it was actually quite the opposite—but I still didn't know what to say to him after the incident in the theater. It would be best to forget it ever happened.

Jeremy's iPhone started blasting the most recent rap song before he could respond, and he pulled it out of his pocket, looking at the screen. "Hold on guys, I need to take this," he said, bringing it to his ear and walking a few feet away.

"That movie scared me so much." Chelsea attempted to fill the silence. "I was totally freaking out every time something was about to pop out. I'm surprised you liked it, Lizzie," she said, looking over at me. "I thought horror movies scared you."

"I was fine," I said, wishing she would stop talking about the movie. It wasn't helping me forget about the incident in the theater. I looked at Jeremy as he paced back and forth while talking on his cell, wondering what was taking him so long.

"I'll be there," I overheard him say to the person on the other end of the line. "See you soon." He ended the call and rejoined us. "It's time for the new members of the team to be initiated," he said, his eyes shining with excitement.

"But you're co-captain," I pointed out. "Wouldn't you have known in advance?"

"I'm still a new member," he explained, slinging his arm around my shoulders. "And the fun part's how we don't know when the initiation's gonna be until it's time. You'll be fine getting a ride home with Chelsea and Drew, right?"

Drew glanced at me and took a step closer to Chelsea. "I've got no problem driving home two beautiful girls," he said.

Jeremy nodded, squeezing my shoulder to pull me closer towards him. "Hey, man. Liz is all mine."

"I'll remember that." Drew's voice was edgy.

Chelsea looked from Drew to Jeremy and back again. "How about that ice cream?" she asked, clapping her hands together to regain everyone's attention.

Jeremy ignored her and looked down at me, cupping my cheek in one of his hands. "I'll let you know how it goes," he said, pressing his lips against mine right in front of Chelsea and Drew.

I pulled away a second later, guilty that Drew had to see that. But the feeling was unreasonable. Jeremy was my boyfriend—not Drew.

"Have fun," I said, despite my annoyance that Jeremy ditched me again for the team. At least he was there for part of the night, which was better than nothing.

He threw his keys into the air, catching them in his other hand. "Don't worry, I will," he said, turning around with a small hop to make his way to the Jeep.

Chelsea turned towards Drew, twirling a strand of hair around her finger. "I bet you can't guess my favorite flavor," she challenged, smiling in a way that she probably thought was seductive. I thought she looked overly animated, but guys fell for it all the time.

He paused, unprepared for her question. "Rocky Road?" he guessed, his lazy tone giving me the impression that he didn't care one way or the other.

"No way! I'm totally a chocolate girl," she said, laughing. "Now try and guess Lizzie's."

"Strawberry," he said without a second thought.

Surprise flashed across Chelsea's face. "Lucky guess," she said, looking at me in annoyance. She seemed to get over it a second later and returned her attention to Drew. "I bet yours is ... coffee. Since you're a New Yorker and all. But let Lizzie try, too."

"Vanilla," I went with my first instinct. A moment later I realized that I should have guessed something that I knew couldn't be right so I wouldn't irritate Chelsea, but it was too late.

He looked at me, showing no emotion. "You've got it."

Chelsea scrunched her nose in distaste, like I did something wrong by guessing correctly. "I'm actually not hungry anymore," she said, looking at Drew. "Do you want to come over to my place after we drop off Lizzie?"

He shoved his hands in the pockets of his jacket and paused. Chelsea looked worried, and I suspected he might turn down her offer. I hoped he would.

"Sure," he said, focusing on Chelsea like I wasn't even there.

"Cool." She smiled and looked at me, her eyes sparkling with happiness. But I must have looked as upset as I felt, because her features softened with concern. "Are you okay?" she asked.

"Just upset that Jeremy left so quickly," I lied, saying the first believable excuse that came to my mind.

"He's excited about his new team," she said gently. "And you heard him—it's not like he had a choice."

"You're right," I agreed, not wanting to make a bigger deal about it than it was. I looked at Drew, who was silent through the entire exchange, surprised to find him watching me intensely as I spoke. He turned his attention back to Chelsea before she noticed, removing his keys from his pocket.

"Are you girls ready to head out?" he asked, twirling the keys around his finger.

Chelsea turned in the direction of the parking lot, excited to get out of there. "Let's go," she said, looking up at Drew.

He didn't look at me again as we walked to the car, and Chelsea had a smile plastered on her face for the entire drive, like she didn't have a care in the world. I supposed she didn't; it seemed like everything was working out perfectly for her.

If only I could say the same for me. All I knew was that I couldn't forget the feeling of Drew's hand wrapped around mine in the theater, and judging from the way he looked at me when we were talking, I doubted he could either.

I couldn't help but wonder what he would say the next time we were alone together.

CHAPTER 8

I didn't want to know what had happened between Chelsea and Drew after they dropped me off. I imagined them sitting close together on the couch, laughing about something funny Drew said, while Chelsea threw herself all over him until he couldn't resist her anymore. It made me upset to think about it, and I spent all day on Sunday reading *Pride and Prejudice*, trying to worry about Lizzy and Mr. Darcy's problems instead of my own.

Chelsea and Drew sat together in history on Monday morning, and there were no empty seats near them. I sat next to Hannah's boyfriend Sheldon, who was in the middle of the room talking with Shayna, a girl who was in the school play with him. He smiled when I sat down but went back to his conversation with her a second later, so I took out my sketchbook to pass the time before the beginning of class.

"We're doing something different today," Mrs. Wilder said upon entering the room. "I've noticed that a lot of you don't feel comfortable speaking up in discussions. In order to change this, I've devised a ten minute exercise to do in class so we get to know each other better." She removed a stack of papers from her desk, handing them to a girl sitting in front who started passing them around. "Take a few minutes to read the directions and then we'll begin."

When the papers arrived in front of me, I took a copy and passed them along. The assignment was that for ten minutes we were to write about a turning point in our lives. It had to be a specific event—no generalizations—and we were supposed to write everything we remembered about it and how it changed who we are and our outlook upon life. When time was up we had to share what we wrote, saying as little or as much as we wanted.

"Does everyone understand what you're supposed to do?" Mrs. Wilder asked after giving us a few minutes to read the instructions.

The class nodded unanimously.

"Then you may begin."

I held my pen over the paper, contemplating what to write.

When Drew walked into the room on the first day of school, I thought, shaking the idea out of my mind a second later. There had to be something more significant in my life than meeting Drew, but I knew that the moment we first saw each other was a huge turning point in my life. The connection I felt with that one glance was more than I'd ever felt with anyone, and even though it didn't make any sense, there was a strange emptiness in my chest when we were apart.

I ultimately decided to write about the day when Chelsea and I became friends, and didn't stop writing until the ten minutes were up.

I'll never forget the day that Chelsea and I became friends in third grade. The two of us had never spoken before—she had tons of friends on the playground who surrounded her during recess, whereas I was shy and always built sandcastles with Tracy Summers. Tracy and I were "default friends"—the type who only spent time together because we were too afraid to talk to anyone else.

Then Chelsea was absent from school for an entire week, and our teacher explained to us about her mom passing away. I tried imagining how I would feel if the same thing happened to me, but couldn't begin to comprehend the pain that Chelsea must have been going through. I'd always envied Chelsea's extraversion and how easily she made friends, but then I realized that she could be as fragile as the rest of us.

When she came back to school the next week, her friends seemed awkward around her. They didn't know what to say and treated her like a china doll that would shatter with the lightest touch. Tracy was home sick the day of Chelsea's return, and Chelsea walked over to me building a sandcastle by myself and asked to join. I was shocked that she even knew who I was, and that she was more interested in building sandcastles than playing house with her usual friends on the jungle-gym.

That was the best recess I'd ever had. We created an entire world revolving around the castle we built—taking place in England when people lived happily ever after, attending balls and not having to go to school. It seemed like the perfect life, and we laughed the entire time. We had perfect husbands who were Kings of the land, and the two of us were both Queens. Technically there could only be one Queen, but we allowed two because we didn't want one of us to be a higher rank than the other.

I was the only one who treated her like an actual person and not "that girl whose mom had just died," and she helped me open up to others. From that day on, sandcastle building became the most popular activity at recess, and I met so many more friends, including Jeremy, who played the part as King of the castle after "marrying" my make-believe Queen. Ever since then, I've known that whenever I needed a true friend, Chelsea would always be there for me, just as I would always be there for her.

"Ten minutes are up," Mrs. Wilder said, interrupting my train of thought.

I dropped my pen on the desk and looked at everyone else in the room. Most people were looking over what they had written, and a few of the shyer students were fidgeting in their seats, looking worried about sharing their pieces with the class. Mine wasn't as personal as what I'd imagined some other people wrote about, but talking about something life changing in front of people that I didn't know very well was still a strange concept.

"Who wants to go first?" Mrs. Wilder asked, looking around for volunteers.

A blonde girl named Lara raised her hand and shared her first experience riding on a roller coaster. It didn't sound like a life changing experience to me, but I decided not to judge what other people wrote, since that defeated the purpose of feeling more comfortable with the other members of the class. After Lara finished, Mrs. Wilder told the boy next to her to go, and we continued going around in a circle from there.

Just as I expected, Chelsea wrote about her mom passing away. Her voice quivered as she spoke, and she mentioned how our friendship helped her through the mourning process. Chelsea wasn't one for sharing emotional moments, and I nodded in encouragement, afraid that she was going to start crying in front of the class. She refused to look at anyone when she finished, and I saw Drew's hand squeeze hers under the table. My chest tightened at the affectionate gesture.

"Thank you, Chelsea," Mrs. Wilder smiled. "Drew, it's your turn."

He hesitated before speaking. "Mine's when I moved here," he said, not going into any more detail. His eyes flickered to mine, and I wondered if he was just as affected by meeting me as I was from meeting him. Then he looked away, and the hope disappeared. I tried convincing myself that I was just imagining he felt the same way. It could never work out between Drew and me, so there was no reason to get my hopes up. Chelsea and Jeremy created too many complications.

It got to my turn and I shared what I wrote, leaving out the part about not having any friends before meeting Chelsea. I leaned back in my chair when I'd finished summarizing what I'd wrote and looked around to see the reaction of the class. Most of them looked bored, but Chelsea smiled in encouragement, the same way I had to her earlier. Drew looked disappointed—I wondered if he'd hoped that I would write something about him— and he smiled for a second before looking away, pretending that the tiny interaction didn't occur at all.

"Aren't you curious about what happened with Drew after we dropped you off from the movies?"

I turned around, surprised that Chelsea was talking to me instead of walking to the language wing with Drew.

"Sorry about not returning your calls yesterday," I apologized, preparing to recite the excuse I'd already planned. "I forgot to charge my phone, and didn't realize until this morning."

"It's fine." She shrugged before continuing. "But in case you were wondering, we had lots of fun. We watched a movie, but didn't end up watching much of it, if you know what I mean."

I looked around at the other students walking through the hall, not wanting to hear any more. "Sounds great," I managed to say. My voice sounded fake to me, but she didn't appear to notice.

"I'll tell you more in trig," she said, turning around on her heal and practically floating towards the Spanish classroom. She looked over her shoulder a second later and added, "And remember to charge your phone from now on!"

I smiled until she turned around again. Luckily she wouldn't be able to talk with me about the rest of the night during lunch since she sat with Drew at a table by themselves in the commons, so I wouldn't have to hear her gushing about him until later that day. He didn't like sitting at Jeremy's table in the cafeteria. Not that I could blame him—I didn't like it either, but it wasn't like I had much of a choice.

I sat down at my desk in French class and was disappointed to find Drew's seat empty. Maybe he was skipping. I took my books out to get ready for class, and a minute later he strolled into the classroom, refusing to look at me as he sat down.

"Hey," I said to him, placing my elbow on the table and resting my chin in my hand.

A look of annoyance crossed over his face. "Hi." He glanced at me before turning away, making it clear that he was done talking to me.

My heart felt like it dropped into my stomach at how cold he was being, and he didn't seem to care. "I'm sorry about what happened on Saturday night," I said in a rush. "The movie caught me by surprise. I don't know why ..." I felt my cheeks turn red, and I started fiddling with the pen that I'd laid on my desk. "I don't know why I jumped like that."

He refused to look in my direction. "Don't worry about it," he finally said, the coldness of his voice feeling like tiny daggers piercing my skin.

I dropped my pen on the desk. "I don't get why you're so angry about it," I said, leaning back in my seat and crossing my arms over my chest in frustration. "I didn't do anything besides … guessing your favorite ice cream flavor. There was Friday in the library, the movies on Saturday night, and now you don't want to talk to me." The boldness of my words surprised me, but the entire situation was ridiculous.

"I'm not mad at you." His face softened for a second, returning to the hard stare a moment later. "But I think we should stop the French sessions. You'll pick it up without my help."

I huffed in annoyance. "Fine. I don't know why you wanted to help me so badly, anyway. I'm hopeless in French."

"You're not hopeless," he insisted. "You're smart. I mean it when I say you'll do fine without my help."

"Right." I shrugged, not wanting him to know how disappointed I was about his canceling the French sessions.

"Anyway," he started, turning to face me. "Chelsea invited me to the soccer game on Saturday."

"Okay…" I said, not quite sure where he was going with this.

"Just wanted to let you know." He glanced at the door when Mrs. Evans walked in. "I'm guessing you're going, too. Although you don't strike me as the type to enjoy watching soccer."

"I don't mind it," I lied. I hated watching soccer.

He smirked. "I'm sure you find it fascinating."

I shrugged, glad when the bell rang and the class started to quiet down. He shook his head in disbelief and turned to face the front of the room, not looking over at me for the rest of class.

The fact that he was going to the soccer game that weekend made me dread it even more than normal. I should have known that Chelsea would invite him. However, he didn't make it sound like he'd agreed to go, so maybe there was hope that I wouldn't have to sit through the entire game dealing with him being there with Chelsea instead of me.

Because I wasn't sure if I could handle that.

CHAPTER 9

Drew didn't make an effort to talk to me again for the rest of the week, and I was stuck listening to Chelsea gush about him every day in trig. When the final bell rang on Friday afternoon, I was looking forward to the time alone in the library to work on filling the sketchbook for my drawing class.

My pencil danced across the page, and all I could see were the images flashing through my mind that my hand ached to bring to life on paper. The current one filling my thoughts was of a glittering mask meant for an old-fashioned ball, and I tried replicating it to the best of my ability, focusing on each detail as I drew. I rested the sketchbook on my knee when I finished, examining what I just created.

The gold wiry lines of the mask slithered around each other like snakes, pointing downwards until the tip of the nose to accentuate the upward tilt of the eyes. The wires twirled around in a final circle at the ends adorned with silver and gold gems, and a silver stone hung below each eye like a tear mid-fall. It was beautiful, and I knew I had to purchase something similar to it for the Halloween masked dance at the end of the month. It was only the beginning of October, but if I wanted to get the mask custom made, I would have do it soon so it was ready in time.

Jeremy burst into the room after practice. His sudden entrance sent my pencil skidding across the page, resulting in a thick black line upon the drawing. "You excited for the game tomorrow?" he asked, not waiting for me to answer before continuing. "We're gonna beat Derryfield so badly that they won't know what hit them."

I closed my sketchbook, figuring I would fix the drawing later. "I'm guessing practice went well?" I asked. I hoped it did—Manchester Prep slaughtered them in a game two weeks earlier, and Jeremy was still waiting for Beech Tree's first win with him as co-captain.

He walked towards me and held out a hand to help me get up. "That's an understatement," he said, his blue eyes flashing with excitement. "They don't stand a chance."

"Awesome," I said, shuffling my feet to stand. "I also kind of wanted to talk to you about something. We haven't spent much time together just the two of us in a while, and our three-year anniversary is coming up on Sunday. I was thinking we could do something to celebrate?"

A smiled crept onto his face. "How does Alfonzo's on the Lake sound?" he asked. "I've already made reservations, so I hope it's okay."

I widened my eyes at the mention of my favorite restaurant. "You really thought to make them before I asked?"

"Of course." His eyes filled with intensity, and he pulled me closer, pressing his lips against mine. A drop of sweat trickled from his hair onto the bridge of my nose. "I've missed you, Liz," he said, his breath hot against my face.

"Jere," I said, spotting some freshmen watching us through the glass door. "We're in the library."

"Let's go back to my place then."

"Aren't your parents home?" I asked, glad to have the excuse.

He rested his forehead against mine, his sweaty hair matting onto my skin. "So what if they are?"

"I just don't think it's the right time."

He slammed his hand against the wall, and I jumped at the sound. "It's never the right time," he said, leaning back to look at me. "Geez, Liz. You need to lighten up."

I ducked under his arm, grabbing my backpack from its resting spot next to the beanbag. "Just drop me off at home," I told him. "I've got a lot of homework."

"You always have a lot of homework."

I crossed my arms over my chest. "Now you're mad because I care about doing well in school?"

"I'm not mad," he said, walking past me to yank open the door. "Let's just go."

"Sounds fine to me." I stomped after him, glaring when he turned his back to me.

Both of us remained silent on the walk to his car, and we didn't speak for the entire first half of the drive.

"Shannon, Amber, and Keelie want to go to the soccer game with you tomorrow," he finally broke the silence.

I looked at him like he'd lost his mind. "They want to go to the game with me?" I repeated, making sure I'd heard him correctly.

"I mentioned it and they didn't seem to not want to go with you."

"I'm sure it'll be a blast." I rolled my eyes. "You know how much I love Shannon's company."

"Her friend Amber's not that bad."

"Only because she's had a crush on you for a year," I pointed out. "So she's nice to you. Not so much to me."

"She's jealous of you."

I looked at him like he was crazy. "Maybe."

"Of course she is." He snickered. "You've got me."

"Right," I said, not wanting to inflate Jeremy's ego any more by continuing the conversation.

"Anyway," he said, trying to change the subject. "I gave Shannon your number. She said she'll give you a call tomorrow to let you know when to meet up, or whatever it is you girls do before the game."

"Great," I said, glad when we reached my house. The gabled windows with open gray shutters welcomed me home, and I couldn't wait to relax after the exhausting week. Maybe I could "forget" to charge my phone and miss Shannon's call. However, that would mean missing the game, and even though things weren't great between Jeremy and me, I still needed to be there to support him.

The screen of my cell phone lit up at noon the next day, letting me know I had a new text message. I didn't want to be interrupted from reading *Pride and Prejudice* for the second time, but I rolled over to see what it said.

We'll pick you up at 4:30.

It was simple and to the point, and judging from the unfamiliar number, I assumed it came from Shannon. If not, I would see who came by my house at 4:30 and go with it. Maybe it would be Mr. Darcy coming to pick me up in an extravagant horse-drawn carriage, but I couldn't picture Mr. Darcy using a cell phone.

Chelsea told me that Drew agreed to go with her to the game, and not wanting to feel like a third wheel with them, I texted Shannon back saying I'd be ready soon. Shannon and her friends wore jerseys to every game, but not wanting to freeze to death on top of being bored and stuck with the cheerleader wannabe's, I opted for a comfortable purple sweatshirt on top of a white long-sleeved shirt. Shielding myself against the cold weather was more important than showing school spirit. I let my hair hang loose over my shoulders, since it would also help protect my face against the wind.

"Elizabeth!" my mom screamed from downstairs. "Your friends just pulled up!"

"Alright!" I yelled back, unsure if she heard. I did one last glance in the mirror before grabbing my bag and heading out of the house.

Pop music blared from the open windows of the silver Lexus SUV, and Shannon sat in the driver's seat, smearing brown war paint in thick lines on her cheeks. The school colors of brown and white were unfortunate; it looked like she grabbed fresh mud and splattered it all over her face. Amber sat in the passenger seat, her face painted in a similar way.

Keelie stuck her head out the back window. "Where's your school spirit?" she asked, her hair blowing in front of her face from the wind. Just as I'd expected, the three of them wore brown and white jerseys over long-sleeved shirts, which I doubted would keep them warm. My purple sweatshirt would stick out like a grape in the dirt.

"I'm wearing white under my sweatshirt," I said, hoping they would drop it.

"We can wait for you to change," she said. "We're early, anyway."

It was more of a command than a suggestion, and not worth the energy to argue. "I'll be back out in a few minutes," I told her over my shoulder, turning around and heading back inside.

My brown jersey was in the back of my closet, and I managed to dig it out and throw it on top of my shirt, hoping the sun would stay out so the temperature wouldn't drop too much during the game. There wasn't much room for jackets on the cramped bleachers—you either had to wear it or put it near everyone's feet.

If it did get cold, perhaps I could leave early in the pretense of catching hypothermia.

Once changed, I trudged out of the house and into the car, sitting in the back next to Keelie. She was applying face paint in thick lines on her cheeks to match Shannon and Amber. The brown matched the color of her hair, so she didn't look quite as ridiculous as they did.

"Do you want some paint?" She held up the tube and squeezed some onto her finger, preparing to smudge some on my face. I was about to say no, but remembering how Jeremy wanted me to try being friends with them, I nodded and allowed her to smear two mirrored lines along my cheekbones. I felt like an Indian at a pow-wow.

"How come I've never seen you at the games before?" she asked, twisting the cap on the tube and tossing it in her bag.

"I usually sit in the back of the bleachers with Chelsea," I answered.

"Oh." She seemed at a loss of words, although I was glad she was trying.

"They better win," Shannon announced, turning the music down so we could hear her. "I don't want Warren getting upset like he did after the Manchester Prep game."

The three girls talked for the rest of the car ride, so all I had to do was nod and laugh at the appropriate moments. The conversation revolved around hoping the guys would win the game, and Shannon and Amber arguing over which team members were the most attractive. Shannon insisted it was Warren, but Amber disagreed. She wasn't the least bit hesitant in sharing her opinion that Jeremy was the best catch of them all.

CHAPTER 10

A group of freshmen clustered in the front of the bleachers, so Amber led the way up to the third row, making sure to pick a spot in the center for prime viewing of the field. Keelie, Shannon, and I followed her in, and once seated, I looked behind me to see if Chelsea and Drew had arrived yet. There was no sign of them. Not wanting to think of the reasons why they could be late, I wondered if they'd changed their plans.

At least not having to see them together would be one less thing to worry about during the game.

We stood up when the players entered the field, and Shannon and Amber cheered and clapped until I thought they would permanently damage their vocal chords. Keelie was calmer than the two of them. She reminded me a bit of myself, and even though I didn't know her very well, I thought there was a chance we could be friends.

A breeze blew through the air, and I wrapped my arms around myself to stay warm, unsurprised that the thin shirt I'd thrown on while leaving didn't guard my arms from the brisk October weather. I regretted changing out of my comfortable sweatshirt. Then music blared through the speakers, signaling Jeremy and Warren to lead the team across the field. Jeremy had a huge smile on his face, and he scanned the bleachers, waving when he spotted me.

"Jeremy looks good," Amber said, taking a sip of her diet soda.

"He does," I agreed, reminding myself that Jeremy had no interest in her. She was just trying to get a reaction out of me. And I wasn't going to give her one.

The crowd quieted as the game began, and everyone took their seats. Only one goal was scored by well into the second half, and the point went to Derryfield, causing the crowd to groan in disappointment. Nothing else happened for a while after that. Soccer had to be the most boring, slowest game ever. It would be much more interesting if every so often, the ball spontaneously exploded.

I missed sitting in the back with Chelsea, the two of us talking about everything from what colleges we wanted to look at to her boyfriend of the month. Unfortunately, this month it was Drew. Hearing her talk about him made me upset, and I couldn't help but wonder what it was that I did to make him dislike me so much.

Before I could contemplate the reason behind Drew's sudden change in attitude, the crowd erupted into cheers, and I clapped my hands in the pretense that I was paying attention. "What happened?" I asked Shannon, since she sat on my right.

"Warren scored a goal," she said in annoyance, returning her attention to the field after speaking.

Leaning back in my seat, I watched Jeremy on the field, since the whole point of my being there was to support him and the team. The scoreboard changed to read 1-1, and the crowd calmed down as the game continued.

"So," Keelie said, resting her elbows on her knees and leaning forward. "Do you know what you're wearing to the Halloween dance?"

"I'm not sure," I replied, rubbing my arms with my hands as another chill swept through the air. "I have an idea for the mask, but haven't thought about the dress yet."

"That's okay," she said, pushing her hair behind her ears. "I'm going shopping for mine next Saturday. Shannon and Amber already have their dresses, so you can come with me if you want."

"Alright," I said, smiling at the unexpected invitation.

I was about to ask if Chelsea could join us and considered asking about Hannah as well, but Shannon interrupted the conversation before I could say anything. "There's only five minutes left," she hissed. "Stop leaning over me so I can watch."

Keelie snickered and sat back in her seat. Not that I could blame Shannon for being annoyed. We *were* hovering over her, and I leaned back to give her some room.

Pulling my sleeves over my hands, I began focusing on the game, hoping someone would score so it wouldn't go into overtime. A player from Derryfield ran the ball towards our goal, preparing to kick it in. Then Warren stole it back and headed in the other direction, progressing down the field towards Derryfield's goalie.

Each team continued to steal the ball away from each other, and a sense settled over me that someone was watching me. I rubbed my hands over my arms as goosebumps traveled up my skin. A soft rumble came from the sky, and I looked up to see storm clouds in the distance. They were far enough away that the game would end before it started raining—if it didn't go into overtime.

Another minute passed, and the feeling of someone watching me remained. *It can't hurt to look*, I told myself. I turned my head and glanced up the bleachers, my eyes traveling to the spot where Chelsea and I typically sat. My instinct was right. Drew sat in my usual seat, his eyes directed straight at me. The chattering of the crowd lowered to a mere hum, and everything around me fell into the backdrop. The goosebumps remained on my arms, but not because of the cold. I couldn't even feel the cold anymore.

Before I could figure out why he was paying this bit of attention to me, his eyes shifted towards Chelsea, who sat next to him talking on her cell phone. He didn't look at me again. I turned around to watch the game, but it was impossible to focus. He was probably just looking at me because I was looking at him. But no matter how many times I tried to tell myself that, I knew what I saw. He was definitely watching me first.

The crowd broke into cheers, snapping me out of my thoughts. I stood to clap along in the pretense that I knew what was going on, hoping it would be easy to figure out what had happened.

"Jeremy's such an amazing soccer player!" Amber beamed, her over whitened teeth almost as fake as her bleached blonde hair. "You're so lucky to be dating him."

I smiled and continued to clap, trying to think of a subtle way to get her to tell me what I'd missed. It obviously involved Jeremy, and she would surely tell him if she noticed I wasn't paying attention and missed a big play.

"I know, right?" Keelie filled the silence. "I can't believe he made the winning goal right before the game ended." She winked at me a second later while Shannon and Amber reached to get their purses from under their seats. I would have to thank her when they were out of earshot.

I refocused on the field to try finding Jeremy, spotting him standing in the center of the swarm of brown and white, slapping high fives with every member of the team. And despite the fact that the game bored me to tears, and that it wasn't something I would choose to watch on my own, I was happy to see him succeed in something that he loved so much.

"Let's go congratulate them," I said with a smile, grabbing my bag off the ground.

Shannon shoved past me to get to the aisle. "I'm already there," she said, flinging what she could of her short hair into my face. I took a deep breath, convincing myself not to walk past her and "accidentally" push her down the stairs on my way out.

Keelie linked her arm with mine, the action reminding me of something Chelsea would do. "Don't let her get to you," she said when Shannon was out of earshot. "She's not so bad once you get to know her."

The comment struck me as something that Jane Bennet, Lizzy's older sister from *Pride and Prejudice*, would say. She was always trying to see the best in people. It was tempting to roll my eyes or say something about how obnoxious Shannon was, but I opted against it. "You realized I wasn't paying attention to the game, didn't you?" I asked as we walked into the aisle, hoping I was right and not making an idiot of myself.

"Of course." Keelie laughed, glancing around and lowering her head to talk so no one could overhear. "You were looking at the hot new guy."

I wouldn't have chosen the word "hot" to describe Drew—"devastatingly gorgeous" was more appropriate— but I tried to not let my feelings show on my face. It would be humiliating if Keelie knew she was right.

"I was just checking to see if him and Chelsea were having a fun time," I lied, saying the first thing that came to my head.

"Or checking him out!" She laughed, hopping off the stairs after me and onto the grass field.

"He *is* my best friend's boyfriend," I said, attempting to stay neutral. Keelie was more observant than I'd given her credit for. "I should find Jeremy," I told her, scanning the crowd standing on the field.

"I'll see you at Warren's later?" she asked. "He always has a party to celebrate when we win."

I was taken aback that Keelie cared if I was coming to the after party, but I reminded myself that she wasn't like Shannon and Amber. She seemed to want to be friends with me.

"Yeah," I said, even though large parties weren't on the top of my favorite things to do list. "I'll see you there."

Keelie ran over to Amber and Shannon, and I spotted Jeremy still surrounded by tons of people on the side of the field. I was about to head over to join them, but my phone vibrated in my bag, and I took it out to read the text message.

Hey Lizzie...it's Hannah. Call me back when you can.

I checked my missed calls to see if anyone else had tried contacting me during the game, surprised to find four of them—all from Hannah. Something big must have happened. I called her back, since it seemed like an emergency, and Jeremy appeared busy celebrating the win. He wouldn't notice if it took me a minute longer to go congratulate him.

Hannah answered on the first ring. "Lizzie?" Her voice sounded shaky.

"Hey," I said, glancing back over at Jeremy to make sure he was still talking with his teammates. He was. "What's going on?"

She paused before answering. "Sheldon broke up with me," she managed to say, bursting into tears a second later.

"What?" I asked, my mouth opening in shock. "Why? What happened?"

I could hear her sobbing on the other end of the line, and she waited to calm down before speaking. "He's with Shayna now," she said, gasping for air between each word. "They're the leads in the school play, and apparently they've been seeing each other for the past two weeks. Behind my back. I can't believe he would do something like that to me."

"Wow." I couldn't think of what else to say. "I'm so sorry. Is there anything I can do to help?"

"Can you come over?" she asked, her voice weak from crying.

I glanced back over at the clump of people surrounding the team, catching eyes with Jeremy as he waved me over. He looked irritated, but I couldn't ignore Hannah's request. She needed a friend. She was content with only spending time with Sheldon since they began dating, and I was all she had left.

"Sure," I said, trying to figure out who could drive me to her house, since Hannah was a few weeks away from getting her license. The party at Warren's was south, closer to town, and Hannah lived thirty minutes north of school. Shannon was going to Warren's, so there was no way she would drive me back home. It wouldn't be fair to ask Jeremy to miss an hour of the party, so Chelsea was my only option. "I'm at school right now, but I'll be there as soon as I can, okay?" I said, hoping Chelsea would be able to drive me back. If she couldn't, I would figure something else out.

"Okay," she said, her voice steadier. "Thanks, Lizzie. I appreciate it a lot."

We said bye, and I hurried to where Jeremy stood surrounded by a few remaining members of the team. There was no easy way to tell him that I couldn't go to the party to celebrate the win, but I had to do it. I wasn't about to leave Hannah by herself when she was so upset.

He turned away from his teammates when he saw me running towards to him, a huge smile forming on his face.

"Great job!" I mustered up some enthusiasm, jumping up as he scooped me into his arms.

He swung me around in a circle so my hair flew behind me, placing me back on the ground a moment later. "Thanks, Liz." He smirked knowingly, since the entire team probably already told him how awesome the play was. He looked down at me, and a look of confusion crossed his face. "What's wrong?"

"I know Warren's having a party," I started, clasping my hands in front of me as I continued, "but I was just on the phone with Hannah—she called four times during the game, and I had to call her back." I paused to take a deep breath before telling him the next part, hoping he would understand. "Sheldon broke up with her."

"Wow." He took a step back, seeming just as shocked as I was.

"She was freaking out," I said, dreading what I had to say next. "She asked if I could come over."

"And you said yes?" he asked, surprised.

"Of course I did," I told him. "If the situation were reversed, she would do the same for me in a heartbeat."

"But what about the party?" He frowned. "We just beat Derryfield—I scored the winning goal! Don't tell me you're gonna skip it like it doesn't matter."

"I have to," I said, glancing at the ground before looking back up at him. "I can't be in two places at once, and Hannah needs someone to talk to."

"And *I* need you to come to the party." He widened his eyes and placed his hands on my shoulders, trying to convince me to change my mind. I would have given in a year ago, but things were different now.

"Jeremy!" Warren yelled from across the field. "We're leaving soon!"

"Be there in a sec!" he shouted back. He looked down at me again, his eyes flashing with irritation. "Are you coming or not?"

"I can't," I said, steadying my voice so I wouldn't cry. "I promised her."

"Fine." He scowled, taking a few steps back. "I have to go to the party though. We'll talk about this tomorrow." He turned his back to me, running towards where Warren and a few other guys waited for him without even bothering to ask how I was getting home.

CHAPTER 11

Walking to the main parking lot by myself was strange. It felt like someone was watching me, but everyone else was probably too consumed with their own plans to worry about why I wasn't with a group of people, piling into a car to head over to the party. I scanned the area, confirming that I was right. Everyone was too worried about leaving before it rained to bother looking in my direction.

I flipped my phone open and pressed the number four, followed by the green send button. Chelsea was fourth on my speed dial, preceded by my dad's cell, mom's cell, and home number. Jeremy was number five. The phone rang three times, and I quickened my pace, nervous that she wouldn't pick up. She probably drove to the game with Drew, but an awkward car ride with the two of them again was better than being stuck at school with no way of getting home.

I listened to the phone ring, looking up at the sky as the storm clouds I spotted earlier passed over the sun. A flash of lighting shone overhead, followed by a rumbling thunder. I ran a hand through my hair in irritation. The last thing I needed was to be stuck in the rain without a jacket.

"Hey Lizzie." Chelsea finally answered the phone. "Are you going to Warren's party?"

"No," I said, pacing in a small circle as a louder burst of thunder growled through the air. I brought her up to speed on everything that happened as quickly as possible, hoping the rain would hold off. A few drops fell on my arm and I opened my palm, confirming the imminent storm.

"Jeremy left without making sure you had a ride home?" she asked when I finished, even though that was what I had just told her.

"Yeah." I gathered my hair over my shoulder, which was starting to frizz in the humidity. "I was actually wondering if you could drive me home so I can get my car. Shannon drove me here and she went to the party, so I'm stuck at school."

"I would," she started, "but I'm on the way to my grandparents house, and I'm already late because of the game. It's their fiftieth anniversary, so they're having a party to celebrate."

I bit my lip, looking up at the darkening clouds. "No problem—I can just call my mom."

"You know I would come get you if I could," she said, pausing in thought. "There's no one else there to give you a ride?"

I glanced around the parking lot again, double-checking to see if anyone was there. The last of the players were heading to their cars after showering, but everyone else must have left after the game to escape the storm. "Only some players from the team, but they're going to Warren's," I answered, ducking under a nearby tree as the rain came down a bit harder. "Don't worry. I'll figure something out."

"I'm sorry I can't help," she apologized. "But call me when you get home."

A flash of lighting split the sky in two as I snapped my phone shut, followed by a long roar of thunder. Buckets of rain started falling from the sky a moment later, and in only seconds my hair was so wet that if I'd told someone I'd just gotten out of the shower, they would have believed me. I put my phone in my pocket and sprinted towards the front of the school where the roof covered the sidewalk, soaking the bottoms of my jeans in the process. Once under cover, I leaned against the brick wall and took out my phone again to dial my mom. She didn't answer at home, so I tried her cell, hoping she'd remembered to charge it the night before.

She picked up after two rings. "Lizzie?" she questioned, sounding confused about why I was calling.

I gave her the short version of the story, and she listened without interrupting. "Can you come pick me up?" I asked when finished.

She took a moment to absorb what I'd said. "I'm at dinner in town right now..." She paused in thought, clicking her tongue against the roof of her mouth before continuing. "But we're waiting for the check. I can be there in a little over a half hour. Is that okay?"

"I guess," I said, squeezing my hair to get rid of the excess water. Thunder boomed through the air again, much louder than before.

"Is that thunder?" she asked, her voice ringing with concern. "Can you go inside so you're not waiting in the rain?"

I knew the doors to the school were locked, but didn't want to worry her. "Yeah," I said, figuring the white lie wouldn't hurt anyone. "I'll see you soon."

It wasn't long before the wind picked up, blowing the rain sideways and under the covered area where I was standing. If there was anything worse than regular rain, it was sideways rain. The best umbrella couldn't defend against it, and neither could the overhanging roof. I sat on a bench as close to the wall as possible and pulled my legs towards my chest in a futile attempt to shield myself from the downpour. It was hopeless, and my jeans became so drenched that they looked like they were a few shades darker than their original medium-blue color. The freezing rain felt like thousands of tiny razor blades cutting into my skin at once, and my entire body shook from the cold.

Trying not to cry, I looked down at the sidewalk, which brought back a memory from middle school when Chelsea and I drew hopscotch boards with sidewalk chalk while waiting for our parents to arrive in the carpool line. Then I realized that as much as I didn't want to be, I was angry with Chelsea. Every time I passed Drew and her walking down the halls of school, I wanted to tell her to get her hands off him. It was irrational, but ever since the first day I'd seen Drew, none of my thoughts made sense. My entire world had turned upside-down, and I had no explanation why.

The honking of a horn filled the air, and I lifted my head at the sound, surprised that my mom got to the school in such a short amount of time. However, it wasn't my mother's sandstone Chrysler Pacifica SUV pulling up to the curb. It was a metallic black BMW with tinted windows, making it impossible to see who was inside.

But I'd been in that car once before when he drove Chelsea and me home from the movies, so I knew it was Drew before he rolled down the window. I stared at him from my spot on the bench, wondering what he could want. He was clear enough when he let me know he didn't want to spend time with me. He had no reason to care about me sitting alone freezing in the rain.

"Do you need a ride home?" he asked. The offer sounded forced.

"I'm fine," I replied, curling up tighter as a gust of wind blew through the air.

"Just get in the car," he said, gripping the steering wheel in frustration. "You'll freeze if you stay out here, and your house is on the way to mine anyway."

Deciding it was too cold to stay out in the rain anymore, I texted my mom to let her know I got a ride home and walked towards the BMW. Drew leaned across the passenger seat and opened the door before I could reach the handle.

"Thanks," I said, hoping my wet jeans wouldn't ruin the black leather seats as I sat down.

His eyes filled with a concern that I wasn't expecting. "I wasn't about to leave you sitting in the rain," he said, holding his gaze with mine before turning to look out the windshield.

I put the seatbelt on and he pressed his foot to the pedal, sending the car into a smooth acceleration. "Why are you still here?" I asked, leaning my elbow on the armrest. "The game ended twenty minutes ago."

"I left my jacket at the field and had to get it," he answered without a second thought.

I looked at his dry clothing. "And you managed to avoid the rain?"

"I have a good umbrella." He chuckled, glancing at me before returning his focus to the road.

I tilted my head in confusion, knowing he couldn't be telling the truth. "But it's sideways rain."

He raised his eyebrows. "Sideways rain?"

"Yeah," I said, realizing that not everyone knew my term. "When the wind blows the rain sideways. It gets under the umbrella." I motioned at my wet clothing. "But you're dry."

He held the steering wheel tighter, his knuckles turning a pale shade of white. "Fine," he admitted. "Chelsea left to go to her grandparents house. Some people were telling me about Warren's party, and then I saw you walk towards the parking lot without Jeremy. I wanted to make sure you got home without freezing to death."

The explanation caught me by surprise. I leaned back in my seat, unsure of how to respond. "Why do you even care?" I finally asked, shaking my head in confusion.

He glanced over at me, his now gentle gaze convincing me that he really was concerned about making sure I got home okay. I wondered if he felt the same draw to me that I felt towards him, but told myself not to get my hopes up.

"You're my girlfriend's best friend," he said simply.

The words felt like darts thrown at my chest, and I looked out the window, hoping he didn't notice how much the statement hurt me. Still freezing, and needing a distraction, I re-adjusted the vents in front of me to blow hot air in my direction. It only helped a little—the freezing rain that soaked my clothes felt like it went straight to my bones, and I reached forward to turn on the seat-heater in hopes that it would help me warm up further.

Apparently Drew had the same idea, because his hand collided with mine, sending a spark of electricity over my fingers. My hand was cold from the rain, but his touch warmed it up in an instant.

He pushed the button, refusing to look at me as he pulled his hand back to the steering wheel. "How come Jeremy left you out in the cold?" he asked, keeping his eyes focused on the road as he waited for me to answer.

"I was supposed to go to the party at Warren's with him, but my friend Hannah had an emergency and needed me to come over," I explained. "My mom said she would pick me up, but she wouldn't have been here for another twenty minutes. I just texted her to let her know I got a ride."

"Jeremy didn't bother asking how you were getting home?" he asked, each word radiating with anger. "He ditched you in the rain?"

"I told him Chelsea was driving me home," I said, not wanting to discuss it any further. "He didn't ditch me."

He shook his head. "It looks like he did."

"He was excited about the celebration," I said in defense, realizing that it wasn't much of an explanation. "He made the winning goal."

Drew paused before responding. "Clearly that's more important than you."

I looked over at him in shock. "You can't just not talk to me for two weeks and then start criticizing my relationship with Jeremy," I spurted, unable to contain my frustration.

"From what I've seen of your relationship, there's nothing *not* to criticize." His words were like ice.

"That's not true."

He glanced over at me, anger imminent in his eyes. "Really? Because that's what it looks like. You deserve a whole lot better than Jeremy. Someone who doesn't leave you freezing in the rain while he's out partying with his friends."

"Someone like you?" I asked, matching his earlier sarcasm. "Because pretending to be nice to me and then acting like I don't exist is just *so* much better."

His eyes flashed with pain. "You think I was pretending to be nice to you?"

"So you were pretending to not want to talk to me?" I asked, taking a breath to calm myself.

"Trust me," he said tightly. "It's not a good idea for us to be friends."

"I can decide who I want to be friends with."

He was silent for a moment. "And do you believe we could manage to just be friends?"

The question caught me by surprise. I knew the answer, but couldn't bring myself to say it out loud. So I slowly shook my head no, looking out the window as the car rolled to a stop in front of my house.

"That's what I thought." He turned his body towards me, his eyes blazing with intensity. "It's better that we stay away from each other. That way no one will get hurt."

My head spun with confusion. "What if that's not what I want?"

"Do you want to hurt Chelsea? And Jeremy?" He sneered at his name.

"No," I resolved, knowing he was right. "But can you answer one question?"

"Fine. One question."

"The other day in class during the writing prompt, you said the moment that changed your life was when you moved here." I took a breath, and he looked at me to continue. "Why?"

"Easy," he said, holding his gaze with mine. "I met you."

I tilted my head in confusion, repeating the words in my head to make sure I heard him correctly. "So how come you say we can't be around each other?"

"You said one question." He smirked. "That's two."

"It's the second part of the same question."

He laughed, looking out the windshield again. "Either way, it doesn't matter."

"It matters to me," I insisted.

He didn't answer, instead shrugging out of his leather jacket and handing it to me. "Wear this inside," he instructed, looking at me as he held it out for me to take. "It'll protect you from the cold."

I didn't look at him as I put on the jacket, which was still warm from his body heat. "Thanks," I said, knowing from the determined look on his face that he wasn't going to tell me any more. "And thanks for driving me home."

"Hopefully that's the last time I'll have to," he said. "Goodnight, Elizabeth."

I ran towards my house and opened the door, hearing Drew's car drive away once he made sure I was inside. I knew in my heart that school on Monday would resume the same way it was until that car ride, and I couldn't help but feel like I was saying good-bye forever.

CHAPTER 12

Drew's cryptic words in the car made my head spin, and when I got inside I almost forgot to call Hannah and tell her that I would be at her house in about an hour, since I needed to dry off and take a shower first.

"Lizzie?" my mom called my name from her downstairs office as I entered the house. Her hair was wet as well. She was able to take the highway back from town, so she must have gotten back a few minutes before me.

"Hey," I said, trying to act as normal as possible.

She swiveled in her chair, concern passing over her face the moment she saw me. I shuffled my feet, dripping water onto the carpet and realizing how disastrous I must have looked. My jeans were soaked, my hair was a frizzy disaster, and Drew's jacket hung loose around me, the largeness of it making me look tiny in comparison.

"What on Earth is going on?" she asked, looking at me like I was an animal in a zoo. As a psychiatrist it was her job to know when people needed to talk, and I supposed it was obvious from looking at me that something was going on.

I summarized what had happened, telling her everything except the fact that Jeremy didn't bother making sure I had a ride home and that Chelsea didn't know about Drew driving me back. She seemed to question the story, but I reminded her that Hannah was expecting me soon. She nodded in understanding, asking me to let her know how it went when I got back later that night.

"Just wondering," I said before heading upstairs. "Who were you out with at dinner?"

"A friend," she replied, not looking up from her desk when she answered.

Getting the hint that she didn't want to discuss it, I trudged up the stairs to my room, hugging Drew's jacket close around me. The sweet scent of pine still clung to the leather. I wondered if I should bring it back to school for him on Monday, but decided not to, since Chelsea and Jeremy would probably ask how I got it in the first place. I put it on the back of my vanity chair and walked into the hallway towards the bathroom, looking in the mirror to see how awful I looked.

My reflection was worse than I'd expected. The freezing rain turned my cheeks bright pink, the rims of my eyes looked puffy like I had been crying, and my normally bouncy hair matted to my head like a dogs fur after it comes in from the rain. The room filled with steam as the water heated up, fogging the mirror and blurring my features together.

The shower warmed me up instantly, and I scrubbed my body clean, as if doing so could erase everything that had happened over the course of the evening. There was one part of the night, however, that I didn't want to erase. I still couldn't believe Drew's answer to my question in the car. It was like I'd caught him unaware, and his words replayed in my head like a broken record.

Easy. I met you.

Those four words confirmed that I wasn't going crazy—the bond I felt with him was mutual. Our connection was like a hidden force pulling us towards one another, and resisting it took a strength that I didn't know I could keep up for much longer.

Everything would be so much easier if it weren't for Jeremy and Chelsea. I shivered after the thought, angry at myself for thinking it in the first place. Jeremy wasn't a bad person, despite the fact that he'd changed in the past few months. He still had a good heart; he was just confused about how to balance spending his time between his teammates and me. Then there was Chelsea. She would be devastated if Drew broke up with her. But it hurt me every time I saw them together, like someone ripped out my heart and left an empty cave in my chest, and I didn't know how much longer I would be able to handle it.

Then came the stream of tears. It was unexpected, like lava bursting out of a volcano and spilling everywhere, not stopping until it had destroyed everything in its path. I rested my shoulder on the tiled wall and allowed them to flow, not bothering to fight them anymore.

The image of Drew's dark eyes popped into my head; they were so soft and understanding, yet sad at the same time. Perhaps if I tried harder I could get him to open up to me again and we could be together like I knew we were supposed to be. The thought made me smile, and I envisioned a perfect world where I was happy with Drew and still friends with Chelsea and Jeremy. But that could never happen.

I knew what I had to do. I would go over Hannah's and sit with her while she cried about Sheldon, doing the best I could to listen and be a friend to her when she needed support. Then tomorrow night I would apologize to Jeremy at dinner and do my best to move forward. He was annoyed earlier, but I knew him well enough to know that he would be happy if we left the fight in the past and talked about other things instead.

Then there was the issue of what to say if asked how I got home. Letting Chelsea and Jeremy know that Drew had been the one to drive me would cause too much drama. But no one would question me if I told them my mom had picked me up from school, so that's what I would have to say. Most importantly, I had to convince myself to listen to what Drew said in the car. It probably *would* be better for everyone if we stayed away from each other. And it's not like there weren't other things I could do besides sit around and pine over the fact that nothing could ever happen between me and Drew. I wasn't going to be pathetic like that. Jeremy wanted me to spend more time with his friends, and Keelie mentioned going shopping for dresses next Saturday. Maybe it would be fun.

I could pretend as much as I wanted, but deep inside I knew that no matter how hard I tried to let my interest in Drew go and proceed with my life as before, the charade couldn't continue forever.

CHAPTER 13

The plan to keep everything as close to normal as possible worked for the next week. Jeremy and I had our anniversary dinner at Alfonzo's, and just as I predicted, he was glad to forget about the fight and me not going to Warren's party after the game. I called Hannah every night to make sure she was doing okay, and the two of us met in the library after school to work on our sketches for class. It helped keep her mind off Sheldon and mine off Drew, who continued ignoring me in school. At least I didn't have to worry about returning his jacket—he wore an identical one on Monday. Perhaps he had a collection of them in his closet.

Keelie made an extra effort to be nice to me at lunch, and I was looking forward to joining her on Saturday to look for dresses for the Halloween dance. Chelsea agreed to come with us, and Keelie seemed to welcome the idea of spending more time with her. I invited Hannah to come as well, but she decided not to go to the dance—she still wasn't up to seeing Sheldon with Shayna, which was perfectly understandable.

"That one's perfect!" Keelie gushed as Chelsea spun in a circle in the dressing room, the short green dress swirling behind her.

Chelsea stood sideways and examined her reflection in the mirror. "Are you sure it doesn't make me look fat?"

"Nothing can make you look fat." I assured her.

"I don't know." She turned around to look at her reflection from the other side. "This just isn't the one. It needs to have more sparkle."

"Alright." Keelie smiled, opening the door to go back into the department store. "So let's look at some more."

I reached down to grab my bag, which was heavy from the sketchbook that I'd shoved inside before leaving the house. "Do you guys mind if I meet up with you later?" I asked. "There's a store in the mall that makes custom masks, and I want to check it out. It's getting near their closing time, but you two should keep looking for dresses."

Chelsea placed her hands on her hips. "But you still haven't found one."

"I'll find one another day," I promised. "But I've got a particular idea in mind for my mask, and I want to show it to them to make sure they can get it done in time."

She hesitated, and finally said, "Okay. If that's what you want."

"It shouldn't take long," I said. "I've already drawn it out, so I just have to show it to them."

We agreed that I would call them when heading back to the department store, and I walked into the mall, referring to a nearby map to point me in the right direction. It wasn't hard to find.

Alistair's was an eclectic antique store at the end of the mall, specializing in both new and old costumes, paintings, jewelry, and masks. The inside was small and dark, with items packed together as tightly as possible. It even smelled old, like a fur coat after it's removed from a storage box full of mothballs. Exquisite masks and paintings lined the walls, elaborate costumes hung on racks in the back, and dark wooden tables displayed small, somewhat kitschy items in the front. I walked up to a table and ran my fingers over a golden horse pulling a coach, the small sculpture smooth to the touch.

"Can I help you?" a gruff voice asked from behind an antique desk in the back of the room. There was a computer on top of it, and it looked foreign amongst the other items in the store—like someone had brought it back in time.

"Do you make custom masks?" I asked, even though I already knew the answer.

"Sure do. Anything particular you had in mind?"

He didn't appear to be making an effort to stand, so I walked closer to him until I stood in front of the desk. "I sketched something out," I said, placing the sketchbook on the table and opening it to the bookmarked page. "But I don't know if it's possible to make. It's for the Halloween dance at my school in three weeks."

He placed a pair of spectacles over his eyes, leaning forward to take a closer look. "Interesting..." he trailed, bringing his face so close to the drawing that it looked like he was trying to smell the paper.

I played with the shoulder strap on my bag, wondering if that meant he could recreate it or not.

Half a minute passed before he looked up. "Did you copy this from a book?"

"No." I shook my head. "I just thought it up and drew it. No book."

He looked at it again, like he was searching for something hidden within the sketch. "It's remarkably accurate..."

"Accurate of what?"

"The style of mask that English ladies wore to masquerades in the Regency times. But surely you knew that already."

"I didn't," I told him. "It just popped into my mind, and I drew it."

"Hmm." He looked conflicted, and he studied me for a moment longer, like he was making sure I was telling the truth. "Okay."

"So you can make it?" I asked, smiling in excitement.

"All I have to do is weave the gold. It's like magic." He winked. "It should be ready in two weeks, so you'll have it a week before the dance."

"Great." I beamed, relieved by how easy that was.

"Now, for the rest of your outfit..."

I tilted my head in question. "What?"

"You need a dress to go with your mask. Unless you've already purchased one?"

I shook my head no.

"Perfect." He walked to one of the long racks in the back of the shop and rummaged through the draped clothing falling from the hangers. "Because I've got just the right dress for you. It's somewhere..." he trailed, pushing through the tightly packed clothing. "Ahh. Here it is."

I gasped upon seeing what he pulled out from the depths of the rack—a modern version of the first dress I'd drawn in my sketchbook, clearly meant to accompany the mask. It was sleeveless, with an empire waist defined by threads of gold, allowing the rest of the material to flow until just above the knee. A few days ago I'd resolved to not try finding something similar to the sketch, because a custom dress was out of my budget and I figured it would be impossible to find one like it. But here it was, like someone copied the one from my drawing and transformed it into a style that was perfect for current day.

"Do you like it?" he asked, raising a bushy eyebrow.

"It's perfect," I replied, clasping my hands together and walking closer to further inspect it. It was off-white—not as bright as the one I'd created while drawing, and it came accompanied with a matching hairpiece that was similar to the one in the sketch. I brushed my fingers over the material of the dress, surprised at how light the sheer fabric felt in my hand. It looked like it was the right size as well. "How much is it?"

I yanked my hand away when he told me the price. There was no way my mom would allow me to purchase it, and my heart sunk at the realization that I would be unable to wear it to the dance.

"I'll tell you what," he said, examining the dress and looking back at me. "I'll give you a good deal. Fifty percent off."

"Thanks." I smiled, taking a step back. "But you really don't have to..."

"The dress wants to be yours," he interrupted before I could finish. "I can tell this sort of thing."

I contemplated the offer. It was tempting.

"You never did tell me your name." He posed the question as a statement.

"Right. Sorry." I stumbled over the words. "It's Lizzie."

"Short for Elizabeth?"

I nodded.

He scurried toward the register, laying the dress on the counter before opening a miniature cabinet behind him and removing a small item from the dusty interior. The cabinet looked like it hadn't been opened in centuries, and the hinge creaked when he closed it. "I'll even add this in for free," he tempted, placing the object on top of the dress. "I picked it up in England last year, and it'll go perfectly with the outfit. It's a fine piece—you don't find them like this anymore."

Curious, I examined the glittering object on top of the dress. It was a necklace that looked like it would lie perfectly on the collarbones of the wearer. Thin silver strands dropped from the front with three stones lined up with about half an inch between them. The strands were all different lengths, forming a triangle with the longest one dropping straight in the center. The stones were clear and brilliant—they had to be fake diamonds.

"It's beautiful," I said, bringing my hand up to my neck in the place where the necklace would fall if I wore it. Even though it was on the table, I could practically feel the cold crystals upon my skin.

He chuckled. "I knew you would like it."

"I might be done with my shopping for the dance after this." I laughed.

He bowed like in an old movie, his silver hair shining as it caught in the light. "I'm glad to have been of service," he said, handing back my credit card and the bags for the outfit. "If you need any more assistance, my name is Alistair." He pointed to a business card perched on the counter. "Don't forget to come back in two weeks to pick up the mask."

"I won't forget." I smiled, picking up one of the cards and tossing it into my bag. "Thanks so much for everything."

My cell buzzed like crazy when I left the store.

"What've you been doing?" Chelsea's voice called from down the hall. She shut her phone when she saw me and jogged to where I stood, her cheeks flushed a light shade of pink. Keelie trailed close behind, busy texting on her cell phone.

"We've been looking for you everywhere," Chelsea said, tossing her phone in her bag. "Didn't you get any of my calls?"

"I guess I didn't have service in the store." I shrugged. "But I did find a dress for the dance."

"Let me see!" she squealed, reaching forward to grab the bag from my hand, all irritation about the missed calls forgotten.

I moved it away before she could touch it. "Hold on." I laughed. "I'll show it to you later. It's packed all nicely, and I don't want to mess it up in the middle of the mall."

"Fine." Chelsea pouted.

"Shannon's having a party at her house tonight," Keelie piped in, sticking her phone into the back pocket of her jeans. "Why don't the two of you come? Bring Jeremy and Drew."

"I'll ask Drew," Chelsea replied. "But don't count on it. He's not a big partier."

Keelie looked over at me. "You in?"

"I need to study for a French test." I grimaced, even though I was glad to have the excuse. The double date to the movies had been awkward enough—I didn't need to go through that again. At least not anytime soon.

"Please don't tell me you're studying on a Saturday night," Chelsea said in annoyance.

"If I don't do well on this test, I won't pass AP," I explained.

She shrugged. "Then move down to the regular class."

"I thought about it in the beginning of the year," I said. "But now it's too late, so I have to do well."

"Fine, be lame," she muttered like a spoiled kindergartener.

"You're still coming to the Halloween dance though," Keelie joked. "No staying home to study?"

"I wouldn't miss it for the world."

CHAPTER 14

"Most of you did well on the tests," Mrs. Evans said in French as she returned them two weeks later, walking down the aisles and placing the papers face-down on the desks. I focused on my hands in my lap as I played with my fingernails, careful to not look at Drew in his seat next to me. He hadn't spoken to me since he drove me back from the soccer game. I knew I should get over whatever feelings I had for him, but it was easier said than done.

Mrs. Evans arrived at my desk and placed the test down in front of me in the same way as the others. I touched the edge of the paper, scanning the classroom to make sure that no one was looking over to try to see my grade. Jeremy flipped through the sheets of his test, shoving it deep into the crinkled mess of papers in his backpack. All of the other students focused on their grades as well. I finally arrived at Drew, and my lips parted in surprise when his gaze locked with mine. It was the most he'd acknowledged my presence since he drove me home after the soccer game.

A flash of cold passed over his eyes before he looked away, his features taking on the same statuesque hardness that I'd grown used to seeing over the past two weeks. A sharp pain shot through my chest, like someone had taken a knife and shoved it into my heart, and I looked back down at my desk. Trying to shake it off, I lifted the edge of the paper, gaining the courage to look at my grade.

A large A stared back at me, written with a huge red marker.

I gasped in surprise, flipping over the test to make sure I'd seen it correctly. The grade stayed the same.

I flicked the tip of my pen against the desk, wondering how I managed to do so well. Drew might have helped a little, but one unsuccessful study session a month beforehand couldn't have made that much of a difference. So what did? I tapped my pen harder on the table, like the drumming could pound the answer out of my mind.

"Stop that," Drew whispered through gritted teeth, pulling the pen out of my hand and placing it on my desk. "It's annoying, and Mrs. Evans's head looks like it's about to explode from the noise."

I looked up and sure enough, if Mrs. Evans had been in a cartoon, there would have been steam erupting from her ears. I couldn't help but chuckle at the image. Looking back over at Drew, I rested my chin in my hand, disappointed to discover that he'd reconstructed the imaginary wall between us.

"*Élisabeth.*" Mrs. Evans glared at me, like she suspected me of cheating. Even though I knew I hadn't, I wouldn't blame her if she did. I had no idea how I managed to do so well on the test, either. *"Please describe to the class—in French—the ideal place you would like to live in ten years. Include details."*

An image formed in my mind, and I didn't miss a beat. *"I've never been there before, but I would like to live in England,"* I said, sitting up straighter in my seat. *"It would be in a small town, but close enough to a city that it wouldn't be boring. The house would overlook a field ... it would have two floors with a small attic, a chimney, and white wooden panels. Moss will have grown over it from age, and there would be a lake in the back and a swing in the front yard—one of those old rope swings that hangs from a tree, because the house would be quaint, like it came right out of the 1800's..."*

I paused and realized that everyone was silent; no one chuckled from behind me like I'd grown accustomed to. Instead, my classmates stared at me with wide eyes and mouths hanging open, looking like they'd seen a ghost.

"What?" I asked in English, glancing around the room in confusion. No one responded. I shifted in my chair, re-crossing my legs and waiting for someone to break the silence.

"Nice use of vocabulary." Mrs. Evans spoke in English, a confused look on her face. "I can see you've been studying."

Then it hit me that everything I'd said had been in French. The foreign tongue felt natural—I didn't have to think about it any more than when speaking in English. It was like I'd been able to speak French for my entire life, and while I did study hard, there was no explanation I could give her for the major improvement

I nodded, not knowing how else to reply, and sat through the remainder of class in stunned silence. I tried to come up with a logical explanation for what had happened, but I couldn't think of anything. It didn't make sense. People didn't magically learn how to speak foreign languages in a month ... did they?

Jeremy sauntered towards my desk after the bell rung. "How'd you manage to pull that one off?" he asked, lifting my bag from the ground and holding it out for me to take.

"I guess studying paid off." I shrugged, not believing my own words.

"Maybe it's a good thing you didn't drop AP," he said distantly. "But I can't believe you did better than me on the test."

My head shot up. "You saw my grade?"

"I sneaked a peak from the back of the room," he admitted. "You seemed so shocked that you forgot to hide your grade. It's fun to see what other people get."

I played with the strap of my bag, wondering how many other people tried to get a glimpse of my grade.

At least this time I didn't get a D.

"I just don't get how you did that," he mumbled. "It was like someone possessed your body who was fluent in French."

"Sure." I rolled my eyes. "A French speaking spirit now lives in my body. That makes perfect sense."

He chuckled. "It's not a bad theory!"

"I'll keep it in mind."

"You do that," he said, studying me for a moment before shaking his head in disbelief. "Well, I've gotta get to class. I'll see you at lunch."

I turned to walk towards my next class and saw Drew standing near the wall, appearing to be waiting for someone. He watched me intently, and I marched towards him, recalling his puzzling words from the beginning of the year.

"How did you know I would get better in French?" I asked when I reached him, not bothering to say hi.

"I didn't know." He smirked and leaned against the wall. "It was a lucky guess."

"Yes, you did know," I insisted, not in the mood to put up with the way he twisted conversations.

He leaned closer to me until I could feel the heat radiating from his face. "Do you think I'm psychic, Lizzie?" he asked, his eyes blazing with intensity as the golden flecks in them sparked to life. "Do you think I can see your future?"

I looked down at the ground, embarrassed by how ridiculous he made it sound. "Maybe," I mumbled. "I don't know."

He backed away, leaning against the wall again. "Well, I hate to break it to you, but I can't."

"Then how did I do that in class?" I looked back up at him, determined to not let this one slide.

"Do what?" he asked, putting his hands in the front pockets of his jacket.

"Speak in French," I said, not allowing my gaze to waver from his. "Perfectly. It wasn't ... well, it wasn't normal."

He paused, his eyes softening before returning to the hard stare. "You've always been able to, Lizzie. You just blocked it before."

I shook my head in confusion. "I have no idea what you're talking about."

"Good," he said, standing straighter in preparation to go to his next class. "But here are some hints for the future. Remember to mess up a little in class. Forget a word or two; mix up your tenses. You don't want Mrs. Evans to get suspicious."

I raised an eyebrow. "And how are you the expert on this?"

"Just do it," he instructed. "Or people will start asking questions."

I stepped back, unable to figure out what he meant. "I'll pretend in class," I said, since while I didn't want to admit it, he made a good point. "But I'm not dropping this."

He took a step forward. "There's nothing to drop."

"I don't believe you," I challenged.

He smirked, amused by my stubbornness. "Do you believe I want what's best for you?"

"Drew..." I trailed, his name catching in my throat. "I honestly don't know what you want."

He held his gaze with mine as he struggled to find a response. The sound of the last students scrambling to class faded into the background; all I knew was that while he didn't want to admit it, Drew cared about me, and I for him. But I couldn't love him—I barely knew him. I loved Jeremy. This thing with Drew ... it was just a fascination. It would pass.

I was lying to myself again, and I knew it. My feelings for Drew couldn't just disappear. They were ingrained within every fiber of my being, and I needed them just the same as I needed air to breathe. Even though we'd only had a few conversations, I couldn't shake the feeling that I'd known him for my entire life.

"I want you..." His voice was hoarse, and my heart pounded in my chest. "To stay away from me. Nothing good can come from this. I'm with Chelsea—not you. Just give up already."

He yanked his hand back to his side, his eyes as hard as a serpent's, staring down at me like I was his prey. Then he turned around to go to his next class, not even bothering to look back at me. Every muscle in my body ceased to work; my blood felt like it stopped flowing through my veins, and my head pounded with an empty numbness at his words. It was like he'd shattered every bone in my body with a sledgehammer, and this time, I believed him. Drew Carmichael wanted nothing more to do with me.

The realization caused a golf ball sized lump to form in my throat, and I took a deep breath, praying when I sprinted to the restroom that I didn't start crying in the middle of the deserted hall. Luckily the bathroom was empty, and I looked into the mirror, red-rimmed eyes staring back at me. It looked like I'd trudged through a desert in the middle of a sandstorm, and I ran the faucet, splashing cold water on my face to cool down. I glanced back up and saw black lines smeared down my cheeks from my mascara, like a fresh painting left outside in the rain. There was no way I could go to class ten minutes late looking like this—my teacher would probably send me to the guidance counselor.

I leaned my palms against the sink and contemplated what to do. I would never skip school without permission, but it wouldn't be a lie if I went to the nurse and told her that I didn't feel well. She could easily write me a note to go home.

With that decision, I picked up my bag and walked to the student health office, reminding myself that each step was one closer to being home in bed where I could begin the process of forgetting that Drew ever existed.

However, I had a sinking feeling that while he seemed to mean it when he said he wanted nothing to do with me, trying to forget about Drew and my feelings for him would be impossible.

CHAPTER 15

I fell asleep as soon as I got in my bed, but my cell phone rang at 3:15, jolting me awake. My first hope was that it was Drew calling to apologize and tell me he didn't mean anything he'd said to me in the hall, but it was just Jeremy making sure I was okay. Chelsea called fifteen minutes later with the same question. Once I convinced her I was fine, she let me know that she was coming back from school and driving past my house. It was on the way to hers, and she needed to talk to me about something important.

I walked down the hall to look out the front window—her dark blue Volkswagen Jetta was already parked on the street next to my driveway. I was still in a daze from what had happened earlier and my eyes were puffy from crying, but I was supposed to be sick, so she most likely wouldn't think much of it.

"You're so lucky you missed trig today." She sunk into my bed after coming upstairs, making herself comfortable amongst the blue pillows perched against the wall. "You missed the most boring lecture about triangles."

"I wasn't feeling well," I said, pulling my knees up to my chest. Even if it wasn't the full story, it was still true. "But I'm fine now."

"Good." She smiled, eager to jump to the next subject. "So here's the problem I was talking about earlier. Drew told me at lunch that his grandparents decided to visit his dad in New York. They're coming on Halloween, and he wants to see them. But now he can't make it to the dance next weekend. I'm totally bummed that he's missing the biggest event of the fall, but his grandparents live in England, so he barely sees them. He said he wants to go to the dance, but family comes first." She paused, clasping her hands together and leaning forward before continuing. "That's why I love him."

I took a sharp breath inwards. "You *love* him?" I asked, even though I knew I'd heard correctly. The idea that Chelsea could love Drew seemed ridiculous. They hadn't even known each other for over two months. "Don't you think it's a little soon for that?"

"I think I do." She giggled. "But I haven't told him yet. I was thinking of saying it at the dance, but now I can't since he's not going." She pouted, pausing in contemplation. "Maybe I should before he leaves? It would be so romantic, like out of one of those old movies where they're standing in the rain about to say good-bye

... except we're only saying bye for the weekend, so it won't be sad and all."

"You should wait," I said quickly. "You'll probably want to hang out afterwards and talk. But if you do it that way then he'll leave right after and he might ... forget when he comes back. It won't be fresh in his mind."

The reason sounded lame. But there was no way he loved her back. Was there?

"I guess you're right." She twirled her hair in thought. "Do you think you and Jeremy can give me a ride to the dance? I was thinking we could get ready together like we did back in middle school, and I don't want to show up alone."

"No problem," I said, glad she'd changed the topic.

"Speaking of Jeremy," she said, "he told me about what happened in French today with the test and how well you spoke in class. How'd you manage to pull that one off? No offense, but last I heard, French wasn't exactly your best subject."

"I guess studying paid off," I repeated what I'd told Jeremy after class, trying to focus on the conversation and not on Drew possibly telling Chelsea he loved her back. "You should have seen Mrs. Evans's face when I actually knew what I was talking about. It was priceless. She looked like she saw an alien spaceship land in the middle of the classroom."

Chelsea forced a laugh, unsatisfied with the answer. "Jeremy was so confused," she continued, not seeming to buy my explanation. "I don't think he was happy you got a higher grade on the test than he did. He said something about it being a fluke, and he would do better next time."

I didn't realize it was a competition, but to Jeremy, everything was a competition.

"It's great to know that he has confidence in me." I paused, considering whether to bring up the problems between Jeremy and me. As my best friend, Chelsea was supposed to listen to this sort of thing. "This might sound weird," I started, picking up the stuffed teddy bear holding a pink heart that Jeremy bought me for Valentine's Day last year. "But do you think Jere's been acting different recently?"

She lifted a small pillow and placed it in her lap, playing with the edges. "I thought you two worked out the thing that happened after the Derryfield game," she said. "What'd he do now?"

"I don't know." I shrugged, holding the bear to my chest. "It's just the small things—like the new music he listens to and the way he talks to people. It's like now that he's co-captain of the team, he thinks he's better than everyone else." I watched her reaction, but only got a blank stare. "I guess I'm over-analyzing."

"Honestly? I haven't noticed that much of a change," she replied. "If anything, he seems more confident, which makes sense given the circumstances. I'm sure he'll chill out soon."

"I guess you're right." I shrugged. "It's weird though; I haven't felt the same connection with him recently. Does that make sense?"

She looked at the ceiling in irritation. "Come on, Lizzie," she said, returning her focus to me. "You guys are like, *the* couple of the school. You're the Romeo and Juliet; the Mr. Darcy and Elizabeth. You'll be together forever."

Forever. The words made me dizzy, and the walls in the room felt like they were closing in from all directions, making it hard to breathe.

"Maybe." My voice wavered, and I focused on breathing evenly to calm down. "But in case you forgot, Romeo and Juliet didn't have a happy ending."

"Whatever," she said, throwing the pillow in the air and catching it. "You get what I mean. The thing with Jeremy will pass. Trust me."

"Since you're the expert on long-term relationships," I joked, deciding to let it go. "But you're right—I'm probably overreacting."

"Of course I'm right," she said. "But anyway, you never did show me your dress for the dance."

Glad for the change of subject, I hopped off the bed and opened my closet where I hung the dress after coming home from the trip to the mall two weeks ago. I brushed my hand against the light material before lifting up the hanger, taking in the sight of the white dress and accompanying headpiece.

Chelsea walked closer to the dress to inspect it, nodding in approval. I brought the necklace out of my jewelry box and she widened her eyes as she took it in, running her fingers over the small stones. Since the mask wouldn't be ready to pick up for two days, I showed her the sketch. She loved it as well.

The whole time I was showing her, all I could think about was how I wanted Drew to see me in the outfit. It would be like in Cinderella when the prince sees her dressed up at the ball, knows that she's the one he loves, and they live happily ever after.

But it was time to realize that I wasn't Cinderella, and no matter how hard I wished it were true, life wasn't a fairy tale where everyone lives happily ever after.

CHAPTER 16

The following week passed faster than expected, and it was finally the night of the dance.

"How does it look?" Chelsea spun around in the center of my room, puffing her knee-length red dress to reveal black lace underneath. She caught sight of herself in the mirror and stopped to admire her reflection, smiling and switching from one pose to another like she was a model on a photo shoot. "Do you think people will know what I am?"

"Anyone who's seen *Moulin Rouge* will know," I replied. "If they don't, they'll just think you look hot."

"Well, I can't complain about that." She laughed, leaning closer to the mirror and smudging her purple eyeliner, which made her green eyes pop more than they did naturally.

I sat down at my vanity in preparation to fasten the gold headpiece into the up-do hairstyle that took an hour and a half to get right. Doing my own hair was difficult, and my hand now displayed three small burns caused by run-in's with the extra hot iron while trying to define my curls—something Chelsea insisted I do to even them out. She took over with the iron after the third burn, helping me pin up the back pieces and wind the front ones to form a makeshift crown out of the twists of hair so the headpiece could wrap around them.

I picked up the headpiece and looked at it, amazed by how similar it was to the one in my drawing. It was thin and had sparkly gems along the top, and the pale yellow color blended with my hair. It would look like interwoven jewels when worn, but while I could draw it effortlessly, putting it on was harder than acing an exam in trigonometry.

"I'll put it in," Chelsea offered. A few bobby pins later and it was set in place, the gems sparkling with the slightest of movements.

My breath caught in my chest when I looked into the mirror, surprised at the reflection staring back at me. Cinderella must have felt the same way when seeing what she looked like when she wasn't covered in soot and ash. For the first time in my life, I didn't feel outshined by Chelsea's inarguable beauty.

The final step was the mask, which Alistair made exactly how I'd imagined. It looked like a piece of artwork, and I lifted it out of the box, feeling every detail of the twisted metal with the tips of my thumbs. I unraveled the strings on each side and Chelsea helped me tie it around the back of my head. She made sure not to mess up my hair, which I feared would fall flat by the end of the night.

The Venetian mask wasn't effective in hiding my identity, but when I looked into the mirror, it was like I was seeing a completely different person.

Tonight was going to be different. I could feel it.

Looking around the gym, it was hard to imagine that it was the place where I'd been tortured in my first two years of high school by gym teachers trying to show me how to accurately throw a ball into a hoop. The floor was covered with black tarp so the non-rubber soled shoes wouldn't scratch the wood, and black curtains draped across the walls, creating a dark, mysterious atmosphere. A DJ booth lined up against the side of the longer wall with two large speakers on each side, thumping so hard that the bass resonated throughout the room. Atop each speaker were revolving lights sending flashes of colors in every direction, obscuring people's faces from view.

"Can you tell who anyone is?" Jeremy whispered in my ear, his arm intertwined with mine like he was escorting me to a real ball held by nobility hundreds of years ago. The metallic edge of the sword from his Zorro costume brushed against my bare knee and I flinched away, surprised by the flash of cold.

"There's definitely a lot of people I don't recognize," I said, checking out the crowd. I stopped at someone who didn't bother concealing her identity. "But Shannon's not hard to miss." Instead of a mask, she smeared the area around her eyes with dark silver shadow, drawing attention to herself as she strutted onto the dance floor dressed as a black angel, wearing barely-there undergarments, fluffy wings, and a halo.

I took a minute to look around at all of the other outfits. A group of vampires stood in the corner—such a typical Halloween costume—and opposite of them were the witches; yet another cliché. There were comic book characters, lots of girls dressed as various animals, and I even smiled at the irony of a white-masked Phantom holding onto a Christine. Unable to spot a Raoul, I concluded that those two had a different opinion as to how the famous Broadway musical should have ended. I wondered if Drew would show up, but even in the rare chance that he did, the dim lighting would make it difficult to spot him in the large crowd. Also, much like Mr. Darcy, he didn't strike me as someone who enjoyed large parties and dancing.

Someone tapped my shoulder, and I turned around, coming face-to-face with a modern day masked Cleopatra. "You guys look amazing!" Keelie revealed her identity. "I know Jeremy's Zorro, but who are you?"

"A current day Elizabeth Bennet from *Pride and Prejudice*," I said the first thing that came into my mind.

"It's so hard to tell who anyone is around here," she said, glancing around the gym. "I know we're not supposed to recognize each other, but do they have to keep it so dark?"

"It adds to the mystery of it all," Jeremy said with a grin, swinging his arm around my shoulders.

"Whatever you say, Zorro." She laughed.

"I loved the outfit you helped Chelsea pick out," I told her, knowing she would appreciate the compliment.

"Thanks!" Keelie said, her eyes widening in enthusiasm. "*Moulin Rouge* is one of my favorite movies. But it's so sad how Satine dies in Christian's arms at the end ... it makes me cry every time. I like to pretend they somehow got another chance. Or else I just stop watching before she dies and pretend it ended differently." She looked around the dance floor, squinting as she tried to make people out in the flashing lights. "There's Chelsea," she said, pointing into the crowd.

I turned to look in the general direction, catching sight of the bright red costume amidst a sea of darkly clothed boys dancing to the pop music blaring throughout the room.

"Come on, Liz." Jeremy leaned closer towards me and squeezed my shoulder. "Let's go out there."

Before I could respond, Keelie grabbed my hand and dragged me out towards Chelsea. Jeremy followed behind, and Chelsea smiled when she saw us, widening the circle to make room for the three of us to join. It felt strange dancing to the synthesized voice of the pop star of the month while in an outfit resembling one worn in the early nineteenth century, and I chuckled at the image of Elizabeth Bennet and Mr. Darcy getting down to current day music; it was like a scene out a spoof movie.

Chelsea nudged me with her elbow. "Are you okay?" she asked, loud enough to be heard above the music.

"Why wouldn't I be?" I asked, feigning surprise at the question.

She shrugged. "You look bored."

"It's just the heat," I said, taking a small step out of the circle. "I think I'll take a break and get some water. Do you want some?"

"I'm fine. Just don't be gone for too long!"

Jeremy opted to stay on the dance floor, and I pushed through the crowd to get to the back of the room, where a few people sat in the chairs lining the wall. They were scowling like they were in prison instead of at a school dance, but the majority of my classmates were on the dance floor, moving to the music like they didn't have a care in the world.

The pop song ended, and a slow rap song started to pound through the speakers, the thumping music sounding like a steady heartbeat. The lights dimmed, making the gym as dark as a deep cave with a few slits of sunlight shining through. I looked through the crowd, trying to see who Chelsea was dancing with, but even her red dress blended into the darkness.

Then I felt a movement from behind.

"What's the beautiful Elizabeth Davenport doing standing by herself in the back of the room?" a husky voice interrupted my thoughts before I could turn around. My heart raced in my chest; even though Drew said he wasn't coming, I knew his voice anywhere. A few tendrils of hair fell in front of my eyes as I turned to face him, and I forget that the whole reason I walked over there in the first place was to get a drink.

It was impossible to make out his features in the low lighting, especially given the black bandanna wrapped around his hair and the matching cloth mask taking up the top half of his face. Only a small skull pendent hanging from a leather cord around his neck clued me in that he was dressed as a pirate, if he was dressed as anything in particular. I'd never seen the necklace before, but just like anything he wore, he pulled it off flawlessly.

"I thought you went to New York for the weekend?" I asked, taking a step closer to see if it was really him.

He leaned forward, his cheek radiating heat upon mine. "Why would I be in New York?" he asked, his breath warm against my ear. "You must have me mistaken for someone else."

I bit my lower lip in confusion, trying to lean back to look in his eyes that were visible only through the small slits in his mask. The golden flecks would give away his identity, but he wrapped his hand around my arm, pulling me closer and not allowing me to look up and see. But even though I couldn't say for sure, I knew it was Drew. His touch felt like electricity running over my skin, reminding me of the first time we met, the time when our hands touched during the movie, and the car ride after the soccer game.

"Your boyfriend won't mind if you spend one dance with someone else?" he whispered in my ear, his voice barely audible over the loud, trancelike music.

His arms wrapped around my waist before I could respond to the question, and I rested my head on his shoulder, closing my eyes as I inhaled the sweet scent of pine coming off his skin. Jeremy *would* mind, but pulling away from Drew would be like trying to yank two magnets apart. We were in the back of the room, far enough from the main crowd in the center for anyone to notice. One dance couldn't hurt.

It was so easy to get lost in the music. He must have figured that I wasn't going to try pulling away again, because he loosened his grip around my arm and trailed his thumb down to my wrist, intertwining his fingers with mine. The world spun to the beat of the song and I let myself sink into it, clearing my mind of everything but soaking in those few precious minutes.

That was when the first flash came.

The gym swirled in my mind, distorting and transforming into a room far more spectacular that could have only existed centuries ago. My head spun with dizziness and it felt like I was floating, watching the haze twist into the shapes of people who looked like they were dancing. After a few seconds the images grew sharper, revealing a ballroom that was much more extravagant than the setup at the gym. Gilded carvings climbed the two-story walls towards the ceiling, and marble tiles lined the floor. Instead of a DJ, a full orchestra played a classical song. The music was so familiar, yet I couldn't wrap my mind around the name.

Couples danced in a line, and one of them in particular stood out, the two focused only on each other. The girl looked like me—the one from my drawings. She was even wearing the same dress. Golden curls flowed down her back, and her partner had hair as dark as

Drew's, but slightly longer. It seemed like the love between them filled the entire room.

The orchestra stopped playing, and when my eyes snapped open I was back in the school gym, listening to the quick beats of a pop song. The flashing lights grew brighter as they picked up speed, and I blinked a few times to reorient myself. If I didn't know any better, I would have thought I'd been transported out of the gym and into the ballroom. But people didn't just flash back into a different time. That was impossible.

"Your boyfriend's looking for you." Drew's voice brought me out of the trance. "I better leave before he sees us together."

"Wait..." I said, my head still spinning from whatever had just happened.

His lips brushed against my cheek, soft and warm upon my skin. "Have a good night, Elizabeth."

"Liz!" Jeremy called my name over the music. I spun around to look for him, catching sight of him emerging from the crowd. "Why are you back here by yourself?"

I glanced over my shoulder to look for Drew, discovering an empty space where he'd stood moments before. He disappeared as quickly as he'd arrived. I wondered if I'd imagined everything that had happened, but the sparks of electricity flickering on my skin proved otherwise, and the images of the ballroom haunted my mind.

"I was just getting a drink," I said, remembering my earlier excuse. "I think the heat's giving me a headache."

"Are you getting sick?" he asked, his eyes flashing with concern. "You're all flushed."

Guilt rushed through my body, and I took a step back. Despite Jeremy's recently raised ego, he was still my boyfriend, and one of my best friends. None of this was fair to him.

"I don't think so," I answered. "It's just the heat."

"Do you just want to leave then?" he asked, although the twinge of annoyance in his tone let me know he would be irritated if I said yes.

I shook my head no. "I'll be fine in a bit. We don't have to leave."

"Alright." He shuffled his feet and looked around the room. "We can sit down until you're ready."

"It's okay," I said, surprised that the dizziness had passed. "I'm actually feeling much better now."

Jeremy held out his hand and led me back to the center of the gym, rejoining Chelsea, Keelie, and some seniors they were dancing with. I tried to enjoy the rest of the night, but I couldn't stop wondering why Drew made an appearance at the dance, and why he was so insistent on concealing his identity. I wouldn't be able to get any answers that night, but if he thought I was going to forget about it and not bring it up at school on Monday, he was wrong.

He was there, and even if he didn't want to, I was going to get him to admit it.

CHAPTER 17

Drew's mysterious appearance at the dance distracted me all night. I'd asked Chelsea if she was sure he wasn't coming, but she looked at me like I was crazy, reminded me that he was in New York, and dropped the subject. The rest of the dance passed slowly, and I was glad when it was time to leave. My mom was asleep when I got home, so I went to my room and flopped onto my bed, more comfortable now that I had changed out of the dress and into warm sweatpants and a t-shirt.

Still, despite what Chelsea had said, I knew Drew was there. I'd tried thinking of who else it could have been—a senior I didn't know, a freshman who might have a crush on me, even someone who didn't go to our school. However, I kept returning to the same conclusion: Drew was at the dance. The problem was that if I were right, I could never tell Chelsea. It would break her heart if she knew that he'd shown up and hadn't bothered to tell her.

Then there was the bigger mystery of the night—the strange flash when we danced. It was more vivid than a dream, but there was no way I could create so much detail by myself, down to the composition of a classical song. It could have been a memory, but that was impossible. I'd never lived in that time period. Perhaps it was from a movie I'd seen that took place in the past.

That had to be it, because the only other explanation was that it was a *real* memory, which was ridiculous.

My curiosity got the best of me, and while the theory was far-fetched, I sat in front of my computer and typed "reincarnation" into the search bar. The fact that I was considering it made me laugh aloud, but maybe it was the reason I'd suddenly been able to understand and speak French.

Yes, it was impossible, but it couldn't hurt to do a bit of research.

None of the links mentioned anything I'd experienced, but I continued to look, even stooping to a cheesy "past life generator" that informed me I was a Saudi Arabian shepherdess in my past life. I closed the page, hoping no one took that site seriously.

Then I found one that convinced me that I might not be losing my mind. It said that a person wouldn't remember a past life without a trigger: a person, place or thing that the past self felt so strongly about that it instigated the memories to return. In my case it was a person, and that person was Drew. If the website were correct, then he must be having similar experiences to mine.

I continued researching for over an hour, and when my eyes started burning from staring at the screen, I decided to look into it more in the morning. I went to put away my bag that I'd brought with me to the dance, pausing when I spotted Alistair's card in the bottom where I'd tossed it after my first trip to the store. It seemed like a strange coincidence that he was able to help me with the entire outfit, but I wondered if he knew more than he told me.

It wouldn't hurt to ask.

The small door at Alistair's made the store feel more like a cave than the typical airy shops in the mall, and I walked inside, the wooden floorboards creaking with each step.

"Elizabeth Davenport," Alistair's scratchy voice greeted me from the back before I could start looking around. "I trust there was nothing wrong with your purchases?"

"Not at all," I said, walking closer until I reached him sitting at the desk. "They were perfect."

He smiled and removed his glasses, placing them down on an old book he was reading. "What are you looking for today then?"

I pressed my lips together, realizing that I should have planned how to start the conversation. How did one go about asking a storeowner if he had any knowledge on reincarnation? I shifted my weight from one foot to the other, contemplating how to begin.

"I just wanted to thank you for everything," I said, figuring it was as good of a start as any. "The mask was beautiful. So was the necklace, headpiece, and dress."

"You're very welcome," he replied, a knowing smile crossing over his face. "You're quite a talented girl to design such an exquisite mask."

"Thanks," I said, pulling the sleeves of my shirt over my hands.

He closed the book and placed it in a drawer inside the desk. "But I suspect there's another reason you're here?"

"Yeah," I said, searching my mind for how to begin. "This may seem like a strange question ... but the dress and necklace seemed so familiar. Do you know when they were from?"

"I had a feeling you would like them," he said. "The dress was inspired by the fashions of the Regency Era, and the necklace was from England. That one in particular was from Hampshire County. It belonged to a beautiful lady from around 1815."

"That's when *Pride and Prejudice* took place, right?" I asked, remembering discussing it in class.

"Jane Austen lived in Hampshire herself." He pursed his lips before continuing. "Speaking of Austen, a long time ago I purchased something very special with the inclination that someone might need it someday." He smiled and opened a drawer in the desk, lifting out a key that looked like it came out of the nineteenth century. The key fit into the lock of the wooden cabinet behind him, and he twisted it until it clicked open, revealing three books standing next to each other with light brown matching spines. He lifted them out of the cabinet and placed them on the desk, holding them as carefully as one would hold a newborn baby.

The textured covers were unlike anything I'd ever seen, and I looked up at him in question.

"*Pride and Prejudice* was three volumes long," he said, motioning to the books. "These were printed when Austen was still alive."

My eyes widened in shock. "Those are first editions?"

"They are," he replied, like it was the same as buying them from a local bookstore.

I took a step closer to examine them. "How'd you manage to get them?"

"The same way I get all of my items. I come across rarities, and trade or purchase them."

I wasn't an expert in antique books, but that sounded expensive. First editions of an Austen novel must cost thousands of dollars, if not more. I would have to look it up when I got home.

"I want you to have them," he interrupted my thoughts. "They're slightly worn, but only because the previous owner enjoyed them very much."

"Have them?" I asked. "As in for free?"

He laughed, crinkling the thin skin around his eyes. "Yes, that's normally what 'have them' means."

I waited for him to say that there was some sort of catch, but his encouraging smile led me to believe he was serious about the offer. Shifting my gaze back down on the books, I reached forward, brushing my thumb against the cover. Relief washed through my body when it didn't break or disintegrate, and I opened the third volume, examining the first page. The title stared back at me in bold capitalized font, and I looked at it in amazement.

"They're beautiful," I said, closing the book. "But why would you give them to me?"

He sat down again, taking a few seconds to contemplate the question. "I've been in this business since before you were born," he started. "I've purchased, traded, and sold many items. Most of the time the item is forgotten—separated from its original owner generations ago, or sold by someone who no longer wanted it. But on rare occasions someone like you comes into the store and connects with one or more of my pieces. That's why I entered the business in the first place—I want to match people with items that I feel belong to them. And these," he looked down at the books, pushing them in my direction, "belong to you."

I stared at them in wonder. "I do love them," I said, looking back up at him. "But how can you tell when an item ... belongs to someone?"

"For simplicity's sake, let's call it intuition." He winked, motioning to the books. "Please take them. No one will ever come around who is even half as deserving as you."

I opened the third book again and imagined what the tanned pages must have looked like fresh off the press, when they were a crisp white.

"Thank you," I said, giving in. "This is the best gift anyone's ever given me."

He packed the books up carefully to keep them safe for the drive to my house, and I wondered what I'd done to deserve everything he'd done for me. It was only when I arrived home that I realized I was so caught up in the books that I'd forgotten to ask about the flash from the previous night.

"How was the mall?" my mom asked when I entered the house, her eyes traveling to the bag in my hand. "I see you bought something."

"Just some books," I said, not wanting to tell her what had really happened. I barely understood it myself.

"You never did tell me about the dance last night," she prodded, pouring herself some water from the dispenser on the outside of the fridge. "How were everyone's costumes?"

I shifted the bag from one hand to the other, itching to run upstairs and examine the books. "They were cool," I said. "Jeremy dressed as Zorro."

"What's been going on with you and Jeremy recently?" she asked, taking a sip of water. "You used to never stop talking about him."

"That was when we first started dating." I shrugged, wishing she would let it go.

She held the glass in front of her and studied me. "Well, I'm glad everything's fine between you two." She didn't sound convinced.

"Yeah," I agreed, taking a step back towards the stairs. "Well, I think I'll put away the books. Let me know when it's time for dinner."

I hurried up to my room and placed the bag on my bed, my hands hovering over the package like a child about to open a Christmas present. I was careful when unpacking the books, afraid that one wrong move would break the ancient paper, despite the protective covers. Published in 1813, the books must have had many owners before me. I could picture someone reading one on a rocking chair on a porch overlooking grassy hills that extended into a forest. It must have been great to live back when people could relax and enjoy life, not having to worry about homework or exams.

I picked the first volume up from its place next to the others and sat on my bed, placing it in front of me and lifting the cover. I expected to see the same bold title as the volume I'd opened in the store, but folded pieces of yellow parchment lay pressed between the cover and the first page. I lifted the top one and unfolded it. It was a sheet of music, and the title on top said "Minuet" by Mozart. The rest of the papers completed the song, and I laid them on my bedspread, flattening the creases with my hands.

I studied the composition, and what I learned from middle school choir came back to me. I heard what the notes would sound like if played on the piano—each one crystal clear in my mind. I closed my eyes to listen, and the flash of the couple dancing in the ballroom reappeared.

I knew why the song felt so familiar. It was the same one I'd heard while dancing with Drew—or the person I suspected was Drew—at the Halloween dance.

There wasn't a piano in my house, but the school had one in the music room, which was left unlocked after school for anyone to practice. Nobody would mind if I attempted to play during that time, unless my attempts were awful, which they most likely would be.

Shaking my head, I realized that what I was thinking was impossible. The piece wasn't exceptionally hard to play, but piano students started with "Twinkle Twinkle Little Star" or "Mary Had a Little Lamb." No one walked up to a piano and started playing Mozart. There was no reason to think that I would be any different.

However, I decided it couldn't hurt to try. French wasn't my forté either, and I now spoke it like I'd known how to for my entire life. Sight-reading was something I never mastered in choir, but the notes popped into my head like magic. Perhaps it *was* magic.

It was ridiculous, but there was no other explanation.

I couldn't believe I was considering such a possibility. But resolving to keep an open mind, I stuck the sheet music in the back folder of my binder, just so it was there if I decided to try.

After all, given everything that had happened to me recently, the existence of magic didn't seem quite as impossible as it had before.

CHAPTER 18

Thoughts of how to approach Drew about the dance haunted my mind as I tried falling asleep that night. I was stuck in a tough situation. Asking him was the same as accusing him of lying to Chelsea. He clearly didn't want me to know he was there, otherwise he wouldn't have been so mysterious about his identity. I fell asleep before deciding what to do, but all of that time spent awake was unnecessary—his seat was empty when the late bell rang in history the next morning, and class ended without his arrival.

"So, where's Drew?" I asked Chelsea as we walked towards the language wing.

"He decided to stay with his dad in New York for the rest of the week since he hasn't seen his grandparents in so long," she replied, looking around the hall before returning her attention to me. "You don't think the girls in New York are prettier than me, do you?"

"No way," I said, since it was what she wanted to hear. "Just because they live in New York doesn't make them prettier than anyone else."

She breathed a sigh of relief. "Good point."

"A week's a long time to miss school," I said, trying to keep the conversation casual. "Won't he get behind?"

"He does well in French, English, and history," she said, counting them off on her fingers. "I'll catch him up in chemistry, but I don't know about calculus. He got a C+ on the last test, but he didn't study at all. I asked him to drop back a level into trig so he could be in class with us, but he didn't seem happy about the idea." She laughed. "Actually, he seemed repulsed by it."

I almost stopped in my tracks. *Because then he would have to have another class with me*, I thought, reminding myself to continue on pace with Chelsea so she wouldn't realize how much what she'd said had rattled me. After all, maybe he just thought calculus would look better on his college application. Everything he did didn't have to do with me, but as much as I told myself to forget about him, he continued to consume my thoughts. They were trapped inside my head, and it wouldn't be long until I couldn't hold them in anymore—my feelings for Drew and whatever they meant couldn't stay buried forever.

It would be an explosive mess when they finally came pouring out.

Trig felt like it lasted forever, and when the bell rang I hurried to the music wing instead of going to the library. One of the smaller rehearsal studios was empty, and I stepped inside, closing the door behind me. The room was tiny—only three feet were between the end of the piano and the door. A chart showing the notes on the piano hung in back.

For the next hour I experimented with the scales, using the chart as a guide. Even though I'd never taken a piano lesson before, it all made sense. I could see in my mind what keys corresponded to the notes on the staff, and I continued quizzing myself until I could pick one at random and play the scale with ease. The sheet music for "Minuet" still looked complicated, but at least I could make sense of the notes.

Looking at the clock hanging over the door, I saw that it was almost time for Jeremy to get out of soccer practice. He was sure to come looking for me in the library, so I gathered my belongings and closed the door to the room, figuring I would come back tomorrow.

Learning the basics was easy, and on the third day I decided to try the song. It wasn't too hard. If I played with just my right hand or my left hand it sounded decent, but combining them resulted in one hand getting off rhythm. But by the end of the week the notes were in harmony with each other, and it sounded similar to how I heard it in my mind. Almost like I had played it before, during some other part of my life.

Two hard knocks pounded on the door, and I lifted my hands off the keys midway through the song to open it. Jeremy stood there with his hand raised to knock again. His cheeks were still red from practice, and a look of surprise crossed over his face when he saw me.

"Hey Jere," I said, forcing a smile. "Did you get out of practice early?"

"No," he replied, twisting his head to look inside. "It's 5:30. I looked all over school for you. Why are you in here?"

I shrugged. "I was playing the piano."

His eyebrows knit together in confusion. "Since when do you play the piano?"

"Since Monday."

He stared at me like he was trying to probe some deep secret out of my mind. Before I realized what was happening, he stormed into the room like he was expecting me to be hiding something—or someone—inside.

"Why didn't you tell me you started playing the piano?" he asked after confirming that nothing too incriminating was going on.

"I was just playing around while you were at practice," I explained. "I'm not very good."

He placed his hand on top of my shoulder, his eyes blazing with an anger I didn't anticipate. "So stop playing around in here and come outside to watch me practice instead." He accentuated each word. "You can even sketch while you watch to get your drawing assignments out of the way."

"I'll try," I said, trying to think of an excuse. Sketching Jeremy and his teammates playing soccer didn't sound like much fun. "But it's cold outside. Maybe if there's a warm day."

"Shannon watches Warren," he said. "She brings a jacket."

"I know," I whispered. "I'm sorry."

He shook his head. "Sometimes I feel like I don't even know you anymore, Liz," he said, his voice soft with disappointment. "Something's changed since the beginning of the school year. I just want things to go back to how they were."

I nodded, unable to agree out loud. The only way for Jeremy and me to be like we were was to erase Drew from my memory, and I didn't want to do that.

"Let's just go," he said. "It's getting stuffy in here." He glanced at the piano, which took up half of the room. "By the way, you didn't sound half-bad."

He walked out of the room before I could thank him for the compliment, like he was embarrassed for even saying it in the first place. I couldn't help but wonder if Drew would agree, but given the fact that I didn't intend on performing for an audience—and that Drew wanted absolutely nothing to do with me—I doubted he would ever hear me play.

CHAPTER 19

Drew was already in his seat at the far end of the room in history class on Monday morning. His hair was shorter than normal—he must have gotten it cut in New York—and he wore his typical dark jeans with the black leather jacket.

I glanced at him before walking to the center of the room, but he held his gaze with mine, like he was daring me to sit next to him. Deciding to test his reaction, I lifted my head and glided across the floor to slide into the seat on his left, trying to ignore my heart pounding in my chest the entire time. He gripped his pen tight in his hand as I approached and shifted his eyes to focus on the door, refusing to look in my direction. For practically inviting me to come over, he sure wasn't welcoming. I leaned back in my seat and attempted to look relaxed, realizing I would have to be the one to start this conversation.

"Hey," I said, my voice surprisingly steady, even though it felt like it was going to crack at a moments notice.

He dropped his pen on the table and turned to look at me, his eyes dark with anger. "Are you trying to annoy me to death?" he asked, lowering his voice as he spoke.

Humiliated by his comment, I looked around the classroom to make sure no one was listening. It was early, and the only people there were Lara Foster and Lindsay Newman, who seemed involved in their own conversation.

"I know you were at the dance last week," I said, hoping that the confidence in my voice would make him more likely to admit what I knew was true.

He looked down at the table and snickered. "I was in New York."

"No." I shook my head. "You were there. All black outfit ... pirate skull necklace ... sound familiar?"

"I have no idea what you're talking about." He narrowed his eyes as he spoke. "But whoever you saw wasn't me. I wasn't in town last weekend."

I crossed my arms over my chest as other students started entering the classroom, my blood boiling with frustration. Chelsea arrived and sat on the other side of Drew, and we both said hi to her like the conversation we'd just had never happened, but I wasn't going to give up. He was at the dance. I just had to find a way to get him to admit it.

The rest of the day passed slowly, and after the final bell I hurried to the practice room to work on Minuet. I downloaded the music over the weekend to listen to, hoping it would help me play the song better, and it was time to see if it worked.

The heater in the room hummed at full blast, making it as hot as a sauna, and I opened the door halfway to allow some circulation so I wouldn't pass out from heatstroke. The room was far enough away from the entrance of the school that someone would have to walk out of their way to look inside. Hopefully no one would do that. My playing had improved in the past week, but I still wasn't ready for other people to listen.

When I began to play, it was like the music took over my body—each note rang in harmony with the others. I closed my eyes and didn't think about anything else but the song. It was like I had been practicing the piece for years. The last note echoed through the room, and I opened my eyes, realizing that I hadn't used the sheet music in front of me. It was as if I'd played it all from memory.

"That sounded good," an unmistakable voice spoke from outside of the room, and I turned to see Drew leaning against the frame of the door. "But I would work on the middle section. It was a little choppy."

"Thanks, Drew," I said, sick of his constant changes in attitude. Apparently we could only talk when he deemed it acceptable. That might work for him, but it wasn't okay with me. "But considering the fact that I'd never touched a piano before last week, I don't think it was half bad."

A small smile crept up his face. "Like I said, it sounded good."

"I'm breaking up with Jeremy," I said, taking my hands off the keys and placing them on the bench. The true meaning of the words pounded on my chest after I'd said them, but no matter how much the confession caught me by surprise, I couldn't take it back. "I don't care what you say. I know it was you at the dance."

He leaned against the wall, crossing his arms over his chest. "Let me guess—you're breaking up with him for me?" he asked, continuing before I could respond. "Not like it would be the first time I've had a girl break up with her boyfriend for me. It happened all the time back at home. We would get together, then I would get bored and find someone else. They would always crawl back to their ex's, begging for forgiveness. Sometimes the guys took them back, and sometimes they didn't. It's sort of sad when they're left alone, but it was their stupid decision to think they were special enough to keep my attention for more than two months to begin with." He shook his head in fake disapproval. "I thought you were smarter than that, Elizabeth, but it looks like I was wrong. How disappointing."

The cruelty in his voice felt like knives puncturing my lungs, and I had to remind myself to breathe. I remembered the dance—both the one at school and the ball I saw in my mind. He was so warm and gentle that night. He couldn't mean what he said.

"What about Chelsea?" I asked, gathering the courage to look at him again. Sadness passed over his eyes, but it disappeared a moment later, leaving me to wonder if it was even there to begin with. "You've been together for almost two months. Are you just going to ditch her, too?"

"The same way you're ditching Jeremy?" he challenged.

"I'm not ditching him," I said, the words hollow in my ears. "We've been growing apart. It has nothing to do with you."

"Sure it doesn't," he replied, rolling his eyes. "But why are you telling me? Is it because you think I'd want to be with you after you get rid of him? Because I wouldn't. Sorry, Elizabeth, but you're just not my type."

I swallowed back tears. "I don't know," I wavered, trying to stop myself from crying in front of him. If his goal was to make me feel like he took a knife and ripped me apart from the inside, then he succeeded. "Just leave me alone."

He didn't move, appearing unaffected by my words. I wondered if he would apologize and say he didn't mean it, but he turned around and walked out of the room, shutting the door behind him. I stared at where he'd stood and waited for him to come back, but after a few moments it was clear that he'd left and didn't plan to return.

I closed the cover over the keys of the piano and leaned down on it, pressing my eyes into my arms until I started to see swirling patterns behind my lids. My hair cascaded over my face like a protective cave, and I allowed the tears to run down my cheeks. The worst was that as long as I cried, it didn't make me feel any better. Every time it felt like the barrier between us was breaking down he would just put it back up again, and I didn't know if I had the strength to pull it down for good.

I could see a hazy outline of what I must have looked like, leaning against the old piano, crying so much that the tears threatened to stain the wood. The room spun around me and it was like I was in two places at once, both looking down on what was happening and living it myself. I envisioned Drew there next to me, wrapping his arms around me and saying it would all be okay. I could feel the warmth of his body and hear him whisper in my ear. A voice in the back of my head told me that he wasn't actually there, but I ignored it. It felt better to pretend.

The two scenes blurred together until they were both gone from my mind. None of it was real. My head felt light from lack of oxygen, and I took a few deep breaths inwards, managing to slow the tears.

Once back in control, I contemplated what I'd said about breaking up with Jeremy. It was so sudden, but it felt wrong to continue being with him when I couldn't stop thinking about Drew. It wasn't fair, and Jeremy deserved better than that. The spark between us was gone, and there was no way to go back to the way we once were.

The only thing I could do now was end it.

CHAPTER 20

It didn't feel like much time had passed before Jeremy knocked on the door, opening it without waiting for me to let him in.

"I thought I'd find you in here again," he said, pushing the door out of his way so it slammed into the wall. "I checked the library first, but you weren't there."

I lifted my head to look at him, knowing I looked like a complete mess. My eyes were wet with tears, and my cheeks splotchy from crying.

"Whoa," he said, taking a step back. "What happened to you?"

I swallowed to shrink the lump in my throat. "Rough day." I shrugged, gathering my hair over my shoulders and pulling off a few strands that were sticking to my drying cheeks. " But I don't want to talk about it here. I'll tell you in the car."

His body stiffened, and his eyes went as cold as a statue. "Okay," he said, walking towards me to help me gather my things. "Let's get out of here before anyone sees you like this."

Another tear threatened to fall, and I rubbed the corner of my eye, grimacing at the smudge of black mascara on my index finger. I reached into my bag to take out the sunglasses I left in there. It was rare for me to wear sunglasses, but hopefully it would hide the fact that I'd been crying.

The junior lot was five minutes from main building, and we didn't speak for the entire walk up to the car. There was no good way to break up with someone, especially when the relationship was as long as ours. I had no idea how to approach it. We drove in silence for a while, his face hard and angry as he waited for me to start the conversation. I stared out the window so I didn't have to look at him. It was like I was watching someone else's life, and I didn't know if I could follow through.

"Now do you want to tell me what's going on?" he gave in after five minutes, realizing I wasn't going to begin without him asking.

"I don't think we should be together anymore," I said, choking back tears at the words. The muscles in my body felt like rusted hinges that refused to move, but I somehow managed to force myself to turn in his direction.

His mouth was set in a straight line, and he remained silent, keeping the car moving at a steady pace. It was like any sudden movement would cause him to burst into a rage of anger.

"It's just that so much has changed in the past few months," I continued. "You've been so involved in soccer. I know co-captain is a big deal—and I'm really happy for you—but we're going in different directions. We barely even talk anymore, and whenever I try to say something, you don't listen because it isn't what you want to hear. I just ... I don't think I can do this anymore."

He jerked to a stop at a red light. "Wow, Liz," he said, gritting his teeth and flooring forwards when it turned green. "You're breaking up with me and you have the nerve to say it's my fault? Well let me tell you something. Ever since the beginning of the school year it's like you've become a completely different person. You've changed your drawing style, you're doing better than me in French, and you even started playing the piano without bothering to tell me. We don't talk anymore because you don't try to, and you don't care about anything going on in my life. I just found you crying by yourself, but it didn't even surprise me since lately you've been upset and irritable all the time." He revved the engine, the car lurching forward when the light turned green. "I don't even think I like this 'new you.'"

I sunk into the seat and closed my eyes for a second, taking in everything he'd said. My throat started to swell, and I knew that if I were to say any more, the words would be a mumbled mess of crying. A single tear escaped, and I wiped it away as quickly as possible.

"There you go again," he said, shaking his head. "You can't even break up with me without being pathetic about it."

He stopped in front of my house and I took in the sight of the familiar gabled windows, eager to get out of the car and run up to my room. Hopefully my mom wouldn't notice that anything was off. I would talk with her eventually, but right now I needed to think about everything that had just happened before I could talk about it with anyone.

Finally gaining the courage to look at Jeremy, I took a sharp breath inwards upon seeing the anger in his eyes. "You're right," I admitted, looking down at my hands in my lap. "It's not the same anymore. But I can't do anything to change it. I'm so sorry, Jere." I reached forward to touch the back of his hand, but he jerked it away and slammed it on the steering wheel.

"Just get out." He continued to face forward.

I tried to will him to look at me, but he stayed focused on the road. Realizing there was nothing more to say, I opened the door of the car and trudged towards my house, not looking back at the Jeep as it sped out of sight.

"How was school?" my mom asked when I walked inside, muting the TV so she could hear my answer. When she saw me her expression changed to one of concern—there was no way I would be able to go upstairs without giving her an explanation for why I looked so distressed.

I sunk into the reclining chair, not knowing how to start. "Jeremy and I broke up," I said, the words not sounding real.

"He broke up with you?" Her voice rung with alarm, and she sat up on the couch.

"No." I shook my head. "I broke up with him."

She was silent for a moment, absorbing the information. "Why would you do that?"

I looked at the ground, not wanting to see what was sure to be disappointment in her eyes. "We were just going in separate directions," I said, playing with my hands in my lap. "Ever since he was voted co-captain it's like soccer and impressing his new friends matters more to him than our relationship."

She scooted closer to me on the sofa. "Did you consider the fact that it might be a phase?" she asked. "I know you did what you thought was best, but sometimes people need time to adjust. And you know how much I like Jeremy. He really helped you break out of your shell."

"I think that was Chelsea," I said, placing my hands on the edge of the sofa and looking up at her. "Jeremy barely spoke to me until I became friends with her." I stood up, not knowing what else there was to say. "I'm actually not feeling well," I said, grabbing my bag from where I'd dropped it earlier. "I'm going to lay down in my room."

Walking up the stairs felt like climbing a mountain. When I finally made it to the top I entered my bedroom and collapsed onto my bed, falling asleep on contact. I wished I could stay there—not having to deal with Jeremy, Chelsea, or Drew—but I couldn't avoid school forever.

CHAPTER 21

My mom allowed me to stay home the next day, and I ignored all phone calls from Chelsea and Hannah. Even Keelie surprised me by calling once. Sick of hearing my cell ring every hour, I turned it off to stop it from reminding me everything that had happened.

The day after that my mom wasn't as forgiving, telling me I had sulked enough and had to go to school. Jeremy wouldn't be driving me that morning—or any morning ever again—so I rolled out of bed and made it outside to my bright blue Toyota RAV4. I drove as slowly as the speed limit allowed, not wanting to arrive any earlier than necessary.

Everyone stared at me when I entered the classroom—or at least that's what it felt like. I sat as close to the door as possible, trying not to look at anyone as I took out my books and placed them on the table. My eyes flickered to Drew's and instantly lowered, ashamed after what he'd said to me in the music room.

My throat constricted at the memory, and I felt like I was about to cry in front of the whole class, but I somehow managed to hold back the tears by concentrating my feelings to a pounding in my chest that was invisible to everyone else. It hurt so badly, and all I wanted was to close my eyes and disappear from the room and the questioning glances of everyone inside.

I caught Chelsea's eyes next, surprised to see the scowl and flash of anger on her face before she looked away. I shouldn't have been surprised. She was probably mad that I hadn't talked with her before breaking up with Jeremy. But I could never let her know the true reasons behind my actions, so I couldn't discuss the breakup with her.

I couldn't discuss it with anyone.

Focusing proved impossible, but since I was a naturally good student in European History, it didn't matter that I didn't pay as much attention as I should have. I spent the entire time looking down at my desk so I wouldn't catch Drew's eyes, attempting to lower the pounding pain in my chest to a dull roar. It felt like he was staring at me—even though he probably wasn't—and the only thing I could think about was that he was somehow aware of how hard it was for me to stop my eyes from wandering in his direction. Trying to be extra careful to not look at him only made me more aware of his presence, and after the bell rang I rushed out of the classroom.

I recognized Chelsea's quick steps behind me before hearing her speak. "Way to not tell me about breaking up with Jeremy," she said as she caught up with me.

I looked at her, cringing at her words. "I'm sorry," I mumbled, fighting back another round of tears. "I didn't plan it—it just kind of happened. He barely talks to me anymore, and when he does, it's either to brag about soccer or to criticize something I did. We couldn't stay together."

"You could have at least talked with me about it first." The anger didn't leave her tone. "You're *supposed* to be my best friend. I could have helped you make your decision before you went out and did something without thinking." She slowed down and lowered her voice. "He's upset, Lizzie. I've never seen him like this before. It's like he's pretending the breakup didn't happen. You should at least talk to him about it."

I looked away, not wanting to think about how much I'd upset Jeremy. "You're right," I said for her benefit. "Of course I'll talk to him. But I don't think it's something we can fix."

"Whatever, Lizzie." Chelsea shrugged off my words. "I'm going to Spanish. I'll see you later."

She turned and walked to her classroom before I could reply, leaving me standing in the hallway in a complete daze.

Drew didn't look my way once during French, and Jeremy sat in the back pretending to laugh and joke around with some friends. To anyone else he would have appeared unaffected by the breakup, but I could tell that every one of his movements was forced and robotic.

I drew in the margins of my notes through the entire class period, creating various intertwining circles, squares, and triangles. It helped me ignore the escalating pain in my head from sitting so close to Drew. When the bell rang I threw my pen and notebook into my bag, zipping it shut in preparation to dash out of there as fast as I could.

"Liz," Jeremy called from the back of the room, rushing to my desk before I could leave. "I need to talk to you."

I glanced at the other students packing up their stuff, knowing I couldn't walk away from him without everyone listening and thinking what a horrible person I was. "Okay." I nodded, watching as Mrs. Evans walked out of the room with a stack of papers. "But I have to get to genetics early to set up for a lab. We'll talk during lunch."

He stood in front of me, blocking my path to the door. "Let's talk now," he said. "Just for a second."

My hands started to shake, and I held the back of the chair for support. "I don't think this is the best time," I answered, my voice wavering. I tried not to look over at Drew, who was taking his time gathering his books in his seat next to me. I wondered if he was finding it entertaining to listen to our conversation. After what he'd said in the music room, I wouldn't put it past him.

Jeremy grabbed my wrist as I went to pick up my bag, stopping me from leaving. "I don't know what was up with you on Monday, but obviously you weren't thinking clearly," he said, looking down at me so intensely that it felt like he was trying to drill the words into my head. "We need to forget that conversation in the car ever happened."

"No, Jere." I tried pulling my wrist away, but he tightened his grip. "I can't forget what happened, because I meant what I said." I glanced around the room, embarrassed by the blatant stares from a few girls as they paused in front of the door. "You had to have noticed, too. It isn't working anymore." I barely managed to get the last words out, my voice catching in my throat.

"That's just what happens in relationships," he said. "Things change. I thought everything was going fine— obviously you're the one with the problem. But it's okay, because I'll help you fix it. We can be good again Liz, I know it."

I tried pulling my wrist out of his grip again. "You have to let me go, Jere," I said, wincing as his fingers tightened even more, threatening to cause bruises on my skin.

Another hand came out of nowhere, peeling Jeremy's fingers off my wrist and pushing him into the desk behind me. My mouth nearly dropped open in surprise when I saw Drew standing to the side, looking at Jeremy like he was challenging him to a duel. His dark eyes blazed with anger, daring him to retaliate.

"What was that for?" Jeremy demanded, leaning forward and clenching his fists.

"You were hurting her," Drew said with a surprising air of calmness, enunciating each word as he spoke. "I know she broke up with you—the entire school knows she broke up with you—but you don't have to give her a hard time in the middle of the classroom."

Before Jeremy could think of a response, Drew turned around and left the room to go to his next class. Jeremy's mouth was open in shock, surprised that anyone had the nerve to intrude on our conversation. I also stared at the area where Drew just stood, wondering why he involved himself with the fight between Jeremy and me after everything that he'd said to me in the music room the other day. None of it made sense. I had to remind myself to breathe so I didn't pass out in the middle of the classroom. Jeremy took a step towards me, and I snapped my head to look at him, grabbing my bag and backing away.

"I have to get to my next class," I told him before we could continue the conversation.

"Do me a favor and think about getting back together," he said, looking at the door and then back at me. "It's what's best for us. I know it, and I'm sure you do, too."

I shivered at the strength of the statement. "I can't promise anything," I said, unable to meet his gaze. "But I'll think about it."

"That's what I like to hear," he said, his tone warming. "I'll see you at lunch then." He strolled out the door, leaving me standing by myself. I didn't even tell him yes, but I couldn't shake the feeling that in his mind, he had won the conversation.

I turned to head in the direction of the science wing, but each step felt heavy, like I was dragging chains behind me when I walked. It was like I was stuck in a nightmare and couldn't wake up. My head felt like it was filled with cotton clouding my thoughts, and I knew that

I couldn't stay in school any longer. I contemplated what would happen if I just left, and the idea of skipping reminded me of Drew's offer from earlier in the year. I hesitated then, but if he asked now, I would say yes in an instant.

The school wasn't strict on keeping tabs on the students, giving us the freedom to come and go as we pleased, assuming we had enough self-discipline to know not to skip class. So no one noticed as I went to my locker, grabbed my belongings, and strolled out the front doors right before the late bell for third period rang through the halls.

My car came to life when I turned on the ignition, and I jumped back in my seat as the vents spewed icy air into my face, making it colder inside the car than outside. The thermostat read 47 degrees Fahrenheit, which didn't sound too bad, but the wind made it feel much colder. I moved the gearshift into reverse, but left my foot on the brake when catching sight of the kindergarten students running off the playground and toward the preschool building to go inside after recess. A blonde girl fell from a swing while getting off, and a taller girl with long, dark hair knelt to help her up. It reminded me of Chelsea and myself when we were that age, and the two of them ran inside, catching up with the rest of their class just outside the door.

The wooden playset was empty, and the four swings came to a stop, appearing to be frozen in time. I loved those swings when I was younger, always rushing outside to make sure I got one before anyone else. I could have swung forever if recess didn't have a time limit.

It would have been easy to leave school for the day, but I didn't know where I would go. I couldn't go home, and driving aimlessly didn't seem appealing. My thoughts were all over the place, and I feared losing concentration on the road and getting into an accident. So I pushed the gearshift back into park and pulled my keys out of the ignition.

Another gust of wind blew through the air, and I looked back at the empty swings as they swayed back and forth. Without a second thought, I stepped out of my car and ran down the hill towards the playground, going so fast that it felt like I was flying. Finally I reached the bottom and wrapped my hands around the cold metal chains of one of the swings, bringing it to a stop and sitting down on the flimsy rubber seat.

I pushed off the ground with my feet, lifting into the air and going so high that it felt like the swing would fly over the top of the set. The effort of staying in momentum kept me warm, and I don't know how long I swung back and forth thinking about everything that had happened since the beginning of junior year. My head felt like it was going to explode from confusion, and the back-and-forth motion of the swing proved soothing and calming. It was like the outside world disappeared and I was flying through the open air, leaving all of my worries behind. I leaned my head back and let my hair fly behind me, oblivious to anything but the crisp air and the cold wind on my face.

I could have stayed lost in my private world forever, but the sound of footsteps crunching from behind brought me back into reality. Hopefully it wasn't a teacher coming to get me in trouble for skipping third period.

I turned around, slamming my feet to the ground and forcing the swing to a stop when I saw who it was.

CHAPTER 22

Drew walked towards me, his black leather jacket open, revealing a matching colored shirt underneath. I didn't say anything as I watched him come closer, waiting for him to explain why he was there.

He leaned against the metal pole of the swing set and slid his hands into the front pockets of his jacket. "Hey," he said, acting like it was completely normal for him to talk to me like we were friends after what had happened a few days earlier. I remained in the same position, not bothering to move a strand of hair out of the way when it blew across my face. I waited for him to say more, but he seemed content to stand in silence, listening to the wind whistling through the bare trees.

"What are you doing here?" I finally asked. The past few days had drained all of the emotion out of me, and I held my gaze with his, waiting for an explanation.

"Chelsea couldn't find you in the hall between classes. She called you, but you didn't pick up." He glanced at my bag where I kept my phone. "She was worried about you."

I stared at him in shock. "That doesn't make any sense," I said, shaking my head as I tried figuring out what he meant. "I get that she was worried, but why did you come out to find me instead of her?"

"She had a project due next period," he started, like he'd already planned what to say. "I just had set design, and wanted to see if you were okay after what happened with Jeremy this morning." He looked away at the mention of the earlier incident in the French room, his words no longer sounding rehearsed when he returned his attention to me. "You did the right thing by breaking up with him. After what I just saw ... he doesn't deserve you." His eyes looked different than they did in the recent times we spoke. Before, he seemed to be in a constant battle with himself, always holding back. Now he looked sad; like something bad had happened that he couldn't fix.

I shook my head in disbelief. "I don't know what you're doing, Drew," I started, not bothering to contain my emotions any longer. "But you need to stop. You made it perfectly clear that you want to avoid me at all cost, but then you follow me out here and decide to strike up a conversation. It would be a lot easier for me to stay out of your path if you stayed out of mine. Then there's the Halloween dance. You can deny it all you want, and I don't understand what you're trying to hide, but I know it was you. We danced to that one song, and for the first time since the start of the school year, everything felt right." The words came spilling out, and I leaned against the metal chain of the swing to try calming the pounding in my head.

He stepped forward, grabbing the chain right above where I held it. "You're right, Elizabeth," he said, shaking his head like he wasn't sure if he should continue. "My grandparents came in a few days later than they originally said. I don't enjoy dances, but I decided to go. I thought I would surprise Chelsea. Then I saw you, and I realized that Chelsea wasn't the reason I was there. You looked so beautiful in that white dress, so similar to..." He paused, and I took a deep breath, wondering if the outfit looked familiar to him as well. "Like an angel," he finished. "It was so dark, and I don't know what happened. I should have walked right past you like I'd planned. But then, after we danced I couldn't tell Chelsea I was there, because you would have known it was me. So I decided to forget it ever happened. It was so hard to tell who everyone was, and I figured that if I said I wasn't there, everything that happened would disappear." His eyes were pained as he looked at me. "But I can't keep lying to you."

I stayed still as I processed everything he said. "What do you mean ... keep lying to me?" I finally asked, tilting my head in confusion.

"Tell me what you remember," he said. "From the dance."

"Well, I enjoyed dancing with you more than Jeremy," I said. "It felt right."

He looked away for a moment, disappointed. "Anything more than that?"

"This might sound strange," I began, surprised I was even considering revealing my thoughts, knowing it would sound far from sane. "But when we danced, it was so familiar. It was like it had happened before."

He nodded, encouraging me to continue.

"Have you ever met someone and felt like you've known them forever?" I asked, unsure how to phrase it.

"Only once." He sounded so confident, and I looked back up at him to find his dark eyes focused on me. "With you."

"Yes," I said, smiling at the fact that he'd felt it, too. "The first day you walked into our history classroom, it was like I knew you. And then the night of the dance..." Unable to say it out loud, I paused, contemplating how to continue. "It has to be impossible. Things like this don't happen in real life, right?"

He studied me before responding. "What did you see on the night of the dance?" he asked, ignoring my question.

"I closed my eyes when we were dancing," I said, picturing the flash in my mind as clearly as the first time I saw it, "And it was like I wasn't in the gym anymore. I saw us together, but it was in a different ... time." I shrugged, embarrassed by how far-fetched it sounded. "There was a ballroom, and 'Minuet' was playing. It felt so real."

He took a step closer. "What if it *was* real?"

I bit my lower lip, amazed this all was happening. "I thought about what else it could be, but there's no other explanation," I said, still trying to wrap my mind around what I was about to say. "We *have* met before. It was just … a long time ago."

"That's one way to put it." He laughed, his eyes lighter in the sun. "I thought it was crazy when I first realized it, too. I'd seen your face before, but it was too impossible to believe that you were real." He leaned forward, leaving barely any space between us. "I just don't get why you're still talking to me," he continued. "After what I said in the music room, you shouldn't want anything to do with me."

"You certainly tried to make me think that," I said, wishing I could forget everything he'd said to me a few days ago. "But it's not really what you want … is it? Everything's working out so perfectly, so why should we try to change that? It's like it's inevitable for us to be together."

"Not inevitable." His entire demeanor changed, his words sharp and jagged. He moved his hand back to his side, and his previously smiling lips formed into a straight line. "The only thing that's inevitable is death."

The lines on his face were harder than I'd ever seen. "What happened to you?" I asked, frustrated by how cryptic he was about all of this. "From what I remember, you were different. You wanted us to be together, and we were happy. Now we have the chance to be together again, and you're throwing it away. You act like you hate me!" Tears formed in my eyes, and I took a deep breath to hold them back, composing myself before continuing. "Why did you date Chelsea knowing she's my best friend?"

"I didn't make up everything in the music room," he said, lowering his eyes. "I can tell that you don't remember everything yet. But trust me, Elizabeth, I wasn't good for you then, and I'm not good for you now."

I took a step backwards, widening the space between the two of us. This Drew wasn't the one I remembered—the one who I felt happy with whenever we were together. All he did since we met was cause me pain. The harsh words, the lies, and the mind games were becoming too much to handle.

"You need to stop saying all of this," I said, unable to curtail my frustration. "Don't you realize that you're the only one who's been hurting me recently? It's hard enough with Jeremy and Chelsea. You say everything you do is 'good' for me, but you're making everything worse. Whatever exists between us is powerful enough to transcend time, but instead you ignore it, date my best friend, and act like it doesn't even matter!"

He studied me in silence. "Do you want me to leave then?"

"I don't want you to leave," I said softly. "I want to talk more about us. Don't you see how amazing all of this is? I want to be with you and learn about everything that's happening with us. But Chelsea loves you, and I can't go behind her back. You've made everything too hard by choosing to be with her."

He scrunched his eyebrows, perplexed. "Chelsea loves me?"

"Yeah, I think," I stammered, realizing from his reaction that she hadn't told him yet. It also appeared that he didn't return her feelings. I couldn't help but feel happy about that.

"Hmm." He took a moment to soak it in, smirking a second later. "I guess she just couldn't resist my charms."

I began to laugh, but stopped myself. "It's not funny," I said instead.

"It's kind of funny."

"Maybe," I admitted, trying not to allow myself to smile. "But if you don't love Chelsea, then why are the two of you together?"

"You *know* I don't love Chelsea," he said, serious again. "I just thought that if I were with her, it would prevent you and me from being together. I was right, wasn't I?"

I held onto the chains of the swing like the support could stop my brain from exploding inside my head. "I don't know," I said. "In every scenario I can think of, someone gets hurt. How do I choose between my best friend and..." I thought about what to call him, unable to find the proper words to describe our connection. "And everything we were and still could be?"

He was silent, and I knew he couldn't answer the question for me. All I wanted was for us to be together and not worry about the problems that would cause with Chelsea. But I couldn't hurt her like that. On the other hand, the connection I had with Drew was one of a kind. I couldn't just walk away from him like everything between us didn't matter at all.

Horrified that I'd considered betraying Chelsea's trust, I jumped off the swing and reached down to pick up my bag, swinging it over my shoulder. "I need to get out of here," I said, running a hand through my hair to move away the pieces blown into my face from the wind. "I can't think clearly when I'm around you."

"I understand how that is," he said, a flash of pain crossing over his eyes. "If I could think clearly around you, then none of this would have happened in the first place. I wouldn't have offered to help you in French, gone on that double date, driven you home when you were stuck in the rain, danced with you on Halloween, defended you to Jeremy, or even come out here to make sure you were okay. But I did, and it needs to stop. You can't keep remembering who we used to be. You won't like everything you're going to see, and I want you to spare yourself the pain."

I stared at him in shock—every sentence he'd said caused me to re-live the events of the past few months, until I was more confused than I was before. "I don't know what to do," I said, yanking my keys out of my bag. "But for now, I'm going to drive around for a while to get my thoughts together. This is too much to take in at once."

"Be careful," he warned. "Watch out for ice. The roads are slippery from the freeze last night."

"I'm pretty cautious when I drive," I said. "You know I don't like speeding."

"Of course." He nodded, understanding that I didn't want him to push it further. "But still be careful."

He wouldn't let me leave until I agreed, and when I turned away from him to walk up the hill to my car, I somehow resisted the urge to look back. It was hard—

each step felt like I was fighting against heavy weights on the tops of my feet—but I reached the parking lot and entered my car, enjoying the freedom as I drove off campus and away from everything that had happened at school.

I had to make the choice soon. Keep everything the same and remain friends with Chelsea, or tell Drew it was him I wanted to be with and that I didn't want to fight the bond between us anymore. The depth of our connection wasn't something that anyone could understand.

It was an impossible decision, and I would have to make it soon.

CHAPTER 23

Chelsea sat in the cafeteria with Jeremy on Thursday and Drew wasn't in school—so I went to the commons to sit with my old friends. I smiled when I saw Hannah happily chatting with a group of people. She started to reintegrate herself after the breakup with Sheldon, and I was happy she was forming some other friendships. I walked to join them, and Amy Gardner and Greg Collins, who I heard started dating mid-semester, watched me like I was descending from another galaxy. Greg scooted over on the couch to make room for me, and my hands shook as I placed my plate on the short round table.

"Welcome back, Lizzie," Amy said, narrowing her eyes as I sat down. Greg hadn't been shy in expressing his interest in me right before Jeremy and I started dating, and apparently Amy had yet to forget about that.

I eyed her up, pretending I didn't notice the contempt in her tone. "Thanks."

The rest of lunch didn't get any better, but Hannah insisted I sit with them again on Friday, which was just as uncomfortable as the day before. After ten minutes of awkward conversation with the group, Hannah told me to turn around, and I watched in surprise as Chelsea strutted into the commons, walking straight towards me. She was probably there to yell at me again for breaking up with Jeremy without telling her first. As much as I wasn't in the mood to deal with that, I did see her point.

"We need to talk in private," she said, hovering over the group sitting around the table and tapping her foot on the ground in irritation. "Let's eat over there." She glanced at a small round table near the sliding door to the deck. No one sat in that corner because the cold air seeped in through the door, but if I turned Chelsea down now I wouldn't hear the end of it later.

After apologizing to Hannah and telling her I would see her in drawing, I picked up my plate and followed Chelsea to the table. She plopped down onto the cold plastic chair and leaned back in her seat, crossing one leg over the other.

My heart thudded in my chest with the anticipation of what was coming. "What's going on?" I asked, hoping she didn't know about what had happened between Drew and me on the playground. Or at the Halloween dance, or after the soccer game ... I could go on forever. I'd been hiding a lot from her recently. I wouldn't blame her if she never wanted to be friends again.

She untwisted the cap of her Diet Coke, taking a sip before speaking. "It's about Drew."

I remained still, dreading what she was about to say. "What about him?" I asked, trying not to let the fear enter my voice.

"I've been getting a weird vibe from him since he returned from New York." She looked around, making sure no one was listening to our conversation. "He hasn't been coming to school, and he doesn't answer my calls. It's like he doesn't notice me or want to be around me anymore. When we do spend time together, he doesn't even talk to me. I have to monologue to keep the conversation going, and it's not fun."

I paused at the realization that this didn't involve me at all. "Have you tried talking with him about it?" I suggested, even though I knew it wouldn't do her any good.

"I have no idea what to say." She took another sip of soda, thinking. "I don't want him to break up with me. This is the longest relationship I've ever had. And normally I'm the one who ends it. It's so much easier that way."

The words stung, reminding me of when I ended things with Jeremy. "I don't know if it's 'easier,'" I said, sitting back in the chair.

"Your situation was different," she covered up her mistake. "You and Jeremy were dating forever. It's easier when you haven't been together for very long. Drew's barely talked to me this week, and it doesn't seem like he wants to hang out with me this weekend. He's acting distant, and I don't understand what's going on with him."

She pouted and waited for me to say something helpful, but I had no idea how to respond. Because when it came down to it, I wanted Drew to break up with her, and I doubted I was going to come up with anything helpful.

"I don't know, Chels." I shrugged, unable to deny the possibility of his breaking up with her. "Maybe it would be best if you just asked him what's going on? He might be having family problems, or maybe he got a bad grade on a test. I don't know."

"You're right." She twirled a strand of hair around her finger and sat back in her seat. "I'll call him when I get home. It's probably something stupid and I'm freaking out about nothing."

"Probably." I took a sip of water, trying to wash away the guilt I felt from not telling her the whole truth. Unfortunately, she would think that I'd lost my mind if I tried to explain what was actually going on.

"I still think you should consider getting back with Jeremy," she said, appearing content with her decision to talk with Drew. "You don't plan on staying broken up with him, do you? This was just you making a point so he would get back to normal?"

"No." I shook my head, frustrated that she wouldn't let it be. "I told you before—Jeremy's changed a lot since we first started dating. It's like he has this whole new life that I'm not a part of. His new friends don't even like me. Keelie's nice, but I don't know what to talk about with the others."

"I get what you're saying." She paused like she was wondering if she should continue. "But you've been acting differently, too."

I almost choked on my water. "What do you mean?"

"Well, it's not in a bad way," she said, shifting in her seat. "But you've been a lot quieter than normal. It's like you're thinking all these things, but keeping them to yourself. Maybe you could be friends with Shannon and all of them if you gave them a chance, but it's kind of obvious that you don't want to be around them. I know you're not doing it on purpose, but they could think you're snubbing them. And I know things weren't perfect with you and Jeremy, but you didn't even call me before breaking up with him. I didn't want to say anything more because I didn't want to make it harder for you than it was, but that hurt, Lizzie. I'm supposed to be your best friend, and you didn't want my opinion on what to do." Apparently finished saying everything on her mind, she sat back in her chair like a huge weight was lifted off her chest, waiting for me to respond.

"I'm sorry," I said, turning my eyes up to look at her. "I started mentioning it to you before the dance, but you shrugged it off. Then the other day when he drove me home after practice, it just happened."

"This is what I mean!" She threw her hands up in frustration. A few people sitting on the couches glanced over at us to see what was going on, returning to their conversations a moment later. "I've known you for eight years, and you've never done anything this impulsive."

"I know," I said, wishing she would let it go already. "But I just don't see Jeremy and me getting back together."

"Fine." She nodded, seeming content with my response. "But next time something big like this is happening, talk to me. That's what best friends are for, right?"

"Right." I gave her a small smile and took a bite of my sandwich.

She looked over at the table where Hannah sat with the group of our friends from last year. "It doesn't look like our old friends are going to be very welcoming," she said, shrugging like she didn't care. "And you can't go sit with Jeremy and all of them in the cafeteria without it being awkward, so you can sit with me and Drew when he gets back."

I somehow managed to force a small smile. I would rather deal with Greg looking at me like he wanted to ask me out again and Amy glaring at the two of us than sit with Drew and Chelsea. But the faraway look in Chelsea's eyes made it obvious that she was worried about what was going to happen between Drew and her, and every rational thought in my mind told me I had to stand by her.

Unfortunately, I knew it wouldn't be as easy to make that decision once Drew was back in the picture.

CHAPTER 24

That night I curled up in my bed with only my nightstand lamp on for light, continuing my second read of *Pride and Prejudice*. It was the paperback from school—not the valuable first edition given to me by Alistair. Last year I would have thought it was pathetic to sit by myself on a Friday night, but now I treasured my time alone.

A knock on the door jolted me out of the world of Jane Austen. "Lizzie?" my mom said from the other side. "Can I come in?"

"Sure," I answered, scooting up to lean against the bedpost. I hugged the book to my chest like it could protect me from what I suspected were more questions about Jeremy.

She entered carrying my bag. "You left this downstairs," she said, dropping it on the ground next to my desk.

"Oh." I placed the book facedown on my bed. "Thanks."

She walked over to my bed, sitting down on the end near my feet. "I wanted to talk with you," she said, her eyes flashing with concern. "I'm still worried about your decision to break up with Jeremy."

I took a deep breath, annoyed to be hearing this for the second time in one day. "It's not something I could have worked out with him," I said, surprised by how calm I was. "We're going in different directions, and I can't just ask him to change who he is. Well, who he's become."

She studied me like I was one of her patients. "Are you sure there's not something else going on? Another guy, perhaps?"

My mouth dropped open in surprise. How could she know about Drew?

"I do deal with this all the time," she explained with a knowing smile. "But tell me. Who's this new guy?"

"Just someone from school," I replied. There was no way I could tell her that it was Drew, since she knew he was Chelsea's boyfriend.

"Is he worth it for you to break up with Jeremy?"

I nodded, not needing to think about the answer. How could I compare three years with Jeremy to someone who I was bound to from a different time?

"That's what I thought," she said with a smile. "Did you know that I met someone else right before I married your father? Sometimes I wonder what would have happened if I'd stopped the wedding. Of course I'm glad I didn't—I never would have had you—but I still think about it from time to time." She paused, scooting closer to me on the bed. "What I'm saying is that if there's someone else, I don't want you to regret not doing anything about it because you're worried about hurting Jeremy so soon after the breakup."

I raised my eyebrows in surprise. "So you're telling me to see what happens with ... this other guy?"

"I'm saying you can't know if it will work out if you never try."

I took a second to contemplate what she'd said. "Thanks, Mom." I smiled, opting against telling her that the other guy was Drew. "I'll think about it."

She stood up, straightening the crease in the comforter from where she sat down. "You do that, and try not to spend the whole weekend alone. It's not good for you. Go out and have fun—it's what you're supposed to do at your age."

"It's just for this weekend," I promised, knowing I couldn't lock myself in my room forever.

"Good." She walked toward the open door, pausing before leaving. "And you know I'll want to hear about this new guy soon. You can't keep him secret forever."

"Right," I said, my voice wavering at the threat she didn't mean to make. "But I think I'm going to go to sleep. It's been a long week."

She said goodnight and closed the door, leaving me alone with *Pride and Prejudice* once more. I was at one of my favorite parts—when Lizzy had a run-in with Mr. Darcy at his house after he'd arrived home earlier than expected. It was a huge turning point in their relationship. He revealed a nicer side of himself, and Lizzy began to realize how much she loved him.

I sunk into my bed and opened the book to continue reading, but it was impossible to concentrate on the words. I kept replaying the conversation I had with Drew on the swings, wondering if I should listen to my mom's advice. After a few minutes of being unable to get through an entire paragraph without my thoughts interrupting me, I reached over to my nightstand to grab a bookmark from its spot next to my phone, deciding it would be best to go to sleep and worry about everything in the morning.

Then something clinked against my window.

I jumped and dropped the book on the floor, losing the place where I was reading. Attributing the sound to the wind, I reached down to pick it up, but another clink hit the glass before I could get it. It was louder than before. Annoyed, I got up and opened the doors to the balcony, trying to see what was going on. No trees stood near enough to the house to whip their branches against the glass, so I looked down, gasping at what I saw.

Drew stood on the ground below my room, the moonlight glowing off his dark hair and light skin. He looked better than ever. His arm was mid-throw, but he dropped it to his side when he saw me.

I rested my hands on the rail and leaned forward to get a better look at him, surprised by how warm it was for early November. "What are you doing?" I asked in the loudest whisper I could manage. I didn't want to risk my mom hearing and coming back into my room. It would be best if she thought I was asleep.

"Getting your attention." He grinned devilishly, causing my heart to do that pounding thing it did whenever I saw him.

I bit my lip to try to keep from smiling. "Couldn't you have just used your cell phone?" I asked, reminding myself not to smile. I was supposed to be annoyed with him.

"I tried," he said. "You didn't pick up. Besides, this is more fun."

I glanced at the bag that my mom had just dropped off in my room. My cell was inside it, still set on silent from school. "I left it downstairs," I explained, staring at the object in his hand to figure out what he was throwing. "Are those pinecones?"

"Yep." He tossed it in the air, catching it with his other hand. "I almost used rocks, but I didn't want to break the glass."

I laughed at his reasoning, watching a pale light spread across his face as the moon came out from behind the clouds. He looked up at me and smiled—a true, genuine smile that made his eyes glow. This was the Drew that I remembered, who danced with me at glamorous balls and listened as I played our song on the piano.

He tossed the pinecone from one hand to the other, preparing to throw it again. "Are you going to come down here, or will I have to come up and get you myself?" he teased.

I shook my head, still amazed that he was there. "I'll be down in a minute." I started to close the door but paused after it was halfway shut, leaning back out. "Stay there."

I changed into jeans and a zip-up sweatshirt, and put on sheepskin boots to protect my feet from the slight chill outside. After a glance in the mirror to make sure I looked decent, I tiptoed down the steps, making sure to be quiet when I passed my mom's room. The back door barely made a sound when I clicked it shut behind me.

I stepped onto the deck and looked at the spot below my balcony, smiling when I saw Drew standing there waiting for me, his hands in the pockets of his leather jacket like going to girls' houses in the middle of the night was an everyday occurrence. He walked towards the deck, stepping up to stand next to me. He was so close, and I stared at him in wonder, unable to figure out why he decided to drive to my house in the middle of the night.

"After the other day at the playground, I wasn't sure if you would want to talk to me or not," he said, his eyes serious. "What made you change your mind?"

"You were throwing pinecones at my door." I laughed at how ridiculous it sounded. "I should be irritated at you, but it was kind of cute."

"Well, 'cute' wasn't what I was aiming for." He chuckled and dropped the pinecone that he was holding to the ground. "But I'm glad it worked."

Worried that my mom might still be awake, I glanced at her window, glad to see that the lights were off. I felt guilty for leaving without telling her, but it wasn't like I was going any further than the backyard. It didn't count as sneaking out if I was still on our property.

"So, what's going on?" I asked, trying to hide my curiosity. A voice in the back of my mind told me to go back inside, but then I remembered the advice my mom had just given me. I wasn't about to throw away what I have with Drew and end up regretting it forever.

"I shouldn't be here." He reached forward to take my hand, but decided against it. "I know you're confused, and I'm not doing much to help. But I can't stand hurting you any more."

I didn't move a muscle, afraid that any movement would cause him to turn around and leave like he had many times before. "What changed?" I asked, tilting my head in question.

"Last Friday in the music room, every word I said felt like I was taking a knife to my own skin, cutting so deep that I thought I would never know how to not feel pain again," he said, his voice remarkably calm for such a strong statement. "The worst of it was knowing that in fighting us being together, I was still causing you pain. I can't do it anymore." He stood still, focused intensely on me. "Do you believe that we have the ability to change destiny?"

"I don't know," I answered, and my voice trembled, either from fear or excitement. "We'll never know unless we try. But I just don't understand what happened before that was so horrible. Were we unable to be together?"

"Something like that," he said, taking a step back. "But let's not worry about it right now. I want to show you something."

"Show me what?" I asked, intrigued.

He grabbed my hand, leading me off the deck and around the house. "It's a surprise," he said, "but I think you'll like it."

CHAPTER 25

His black BMW was parked on the road near my driveway, looking out of place in my neighborhood. At first I was hesitant about getting in—unlike talking in my backyard, driving somewhere with Drew definitely qualified as sneaking out. However, I wasn't ready to tell my mom about Drew just yet, and I was curious about the surprise he had to show me. Promising myself that it would be a one-time thing, I got into the car and tried to put the guilt in the back of my mind as he drove out of the neighborhood.

His house was only ten minutes away from mine. I'd been to Lakeside Circle a few times before, but the sizes of the homes sitting on what appeared to be two or more acres of land never ceased to amaze me. The road wound around in a big circle, since the houses sat around Pembrooke Lake, where the families kept their jet ski's, speedboats, and other water vehicles.

Halfway around the circle we pulled up to the largest of them all—a two and a half story grey-stone country estate on top of a hill, with a steep shingled roof that made it resemble an English palace. White columns surrounded the double door entrance, and bay windows extended from each side. The house was wide enough for four or more houses from my street to fit inside his one. Bare trees towered over the sides and back of the house, and a stone path went from the street to the front entrance, passing a fountain on the way up. He pulled up to the side of the house and parked in the four-car garage. Three other cars were inside—a black Hummer, a silver Mercedes convertible, and a dark grey Porsche Cayenne.

"That's a lot of cars for just you and your mom," I observed, standing up and looking around.

His car beeped when he locked it, and he glanced at the others in the garage. "We each have a sports car for when it's nice out, and an SUV for when the weather gets bad," he said, like having two cars was completely normal.

"Right." I nodded. "Of course."

Not seeming to want to discuss the cars any further, he walked towards the door on the inside corner of the garage, holding it open for me to enter. I stepped up onto the platform to go inside, and the first thing I saw was a straight hardwood stairway leading to the second floor. The narrow hallway continued further back, leading to a family room with a huge plasma screen TV hanging on the wall above the fireplace. Open paneled double doors were on the far side of the family room, revealing a billiard table inside a room with dark wooden walls.

I felt like an intruder inside the gigantic house, and he tugged my hand to direct me around the corner into a cherry wood kitchen with a granite-topped island in the center. Another open entrance on the other side of the kitchen led into a huge great room with an elegant French country sofa facing a pair of complimentary antique chairs. Peeking into the foyer, I saw another stairway, this one curved in a dramatic semi-circle across from the columned entrance.

"I'll give you the grand tour later," Drew said, walking towards the French double doors in the back of the great room and unlocking them. "But I want to show you something outside. Come on."

Disappointed to not be able to explore the rest of the house, but curious about what Drew wanted me to see, I followed him through the doors onto a huge wrap-around porch with thick wooden rails overlooking the lake.

"Did you buy this place right before moving here?" I asked, feeling like an insect next to the hugeness of the house.

"We built it as a vacation home when I was a kid." He leaned against the railing, waiting for me to follow. "We would come here every summer. All of my friends had summer homes in the Hamptons, but my mom grew up around here and she insisted we come back every year."

I walked to where he stood, shaking my head in amazement. "How many houses *do* you have?" I laughed, trying not to be too intimidated. Pembrooke had a good amount of people who were well off, but the Carmichael's were in a completely different league.

"Four." He chuckled again, glancing up at the house towering above us. "There's this one, the condo in Manhattan, the house in Palm Beach, and another in Aspen."

"That's ... nice." I tried to act like this was normal.

"But my house isn't what I wanted to show you." He took a step down on the stairway leading to the lake and held out his hand. "Are you coming or not?"

I nodded and took his hand in mine, heat rushing up my arm when we touched. He pulled me closer towards him so my body pressed against his, and I breathed in his warm scent that reminded me of the forest on a winter day. He wound his hand through my hair and I looked up at him, amazed by how much had changed since a week ago.

But Drew is still Chelsea's boyfriend, I reminded myself, even though it wasn't something I wanted to think about.

I took a step backward, breaking the spell between us. "What was it you wanted to show me?"

He blinked, surprised that I ended the short moment between us. "This way," he said, grabbing my hand again to head towards the dock. The wooden planks creaking beneath our feet were the only sound in the quiet night. I knew I should let go of his hand—Chelsea would be devastated if she saw the two of us right now—but we were already together in secret in the middle of the night. Holding hands wasn't as big of a deal in comparison.

I looked around to try figuring out what he wanted to show me. Then I caught sight of a small speedboat floating next to the dock. The boat was small; it looked like it could fit about four people. It bobbed in the water, completely unthreatening.

"You wanted to show me a boat?" I asked, looking around to see what else was in the area. There was nothing. I was surprised—he knew I hated speed.

"My dad and I used to go water-skiing and fishing when we came here over the summers," he explained. "But now it's just me and my mom, so I like taking it out when I need a break from everything."

"And you want me to go in it?" I crossed my arms over my chest, not happy about the idea.

"Tell me, Elizabeth," he said, like he knew where he was going with this. "Why don't you like speed?"

I took a moment to think. "I guess I don't want the car to slip off the road."

"Well, that can't happen in a boat," he said, lifting a leg and placing his foot on the side of the boat. "There's no road. Only water."

He squeezed my hand and waited for a response. I knew he was giving me a choice. I could say no, but this was something he enjoyed, and he wanted to share it with me. For weeks I'd wanted nothing more than to get to know him, and now I had my chance.

"Okay," I gave in. "I'll go. Just don't drive too fast."

A smile spread across his face. "I promise."

Drew's grip was firm as he lowered me into the boat, and I wondered why I doubted that he would let anything bad happen to me. My feet landed against the cushiony seat that wrapped around the back, and I nearly fell as I went to take a step down. His hands wrapped around my waist as he helped me step onto the floor, his face inches from mine.

"You'll be fine," he whispered in my ear, letting go so I could stand by myself. The boat was sturdier than I expected, and I smiled to let him know I was okay. Swinging the keys around his fingers, he walked backwards toward the captain's seat, never breaking eye contact with me the entire time.

I took a step forward, breathing steadier when the floor stayed sturdy under my feet. It wasn't much different from walking on the ground. Feeling more confident, I made my way over to the seat next to him.

He wrapped his hand around my forearm before I could sit down "Sit with me," he said, pulling me towards him. My body fit perfectly in the curve of his, and I brought my arms up around his neck. It was highly unlikely that I would fall over the edge, but I felt safer holding onto Drew.

He put the keys in the ignition and I leaned against his shoulders, closing my eyes as the engine revved to life. I didn't panic when the boat jolted forward. I felt calm, and I opted to enjoy the moment, focusing on the steady beat of Drew's heart beneath my ear and smiling to myself as it pumped faster when I wrapped my arms tighter around him.

"You can open your eyes now," he whispered in my ear after bringing the boat to a stop.

I opened them slowly. We were in the center of the lake, and I lifted my head to look at him, my breath catching in my chest as my nose brushed against his. Neither of us moved, and the boat bobbed on the lake, the water lapping against the sides the only sound in the night.

"I have to tell you something," he said, leaning back to look at me and taking my hand in his. "I broke up with Chelsea before I came to your house."

I stayed silent as I took in what he said. A part of me wanted to jump for joy at the fact that Drew and Chelsea were no longer together. The other half wanted to run to Chelsea with a pint of ice cream to help her feel better. Which of course I couldn't do, since I was sitting in a boat in the middle of a lake. With her ex-boyfriend. Who I was falling for more and more with each passing second.

"I want us to be together," he continued, pushing a strand of hair behind my ear that had been blown out of place during the boat ride, his fingers leaving a line of heat where they brushed against my skin. "I knew it could never work if I didn't do something about Chelsea. I never loved her. I could never love her, because I love you, Elizabeth. It's been you the entire time."

His lips connected with mine before I could respond, erasing all thoughts of Chelsea, Jeremy, or anything other than the two of us together on the lake. No one existed other than Drew, and I leaned into him, my body melting into his. The kiss was soft and tender, and I allowed the undeniable pull between us to take over, savoring the electricity that passed between us.

I wrapped my arms around him and he pulled me closer, pressing his body against mine as the kiss became more urgent. Being with Drew was the only thing that felt right since the beginning of the school year, and I knew that it was too late to turn back.

I opened my eyes, my lashes brushing against his cheeks. "Promise me everything won't go back to the way it was when school starts again on Monday," I asked, catching my breath as I tried to focus on what I was saying instead of on the array of emotions rushing through my veins. "I don't think I could handle it again."

He laughed like the notion was ridiculous. "Everything's changed now, Elizabeth," he said, leaning back to look at me. "We could never go back to the way things were before. You're everything to me—you always have been, and you always will be. Always and forever."

My head spun and I tried to gather my thoughts. "I just have so many questions," I started, unsure of where to begin. "The first time I saw you—that day in history class—I knew you were different from everyone else. But you seemed to know everything before me. You spoke French perfectly the first day in class, but it took weeks for it to come back to me. Am I super slow in picking up on things or something?"

"You're not slow," he said, smiling and shaking his head. "Two years ago I went on a family vacation to England to visit my grandparents. We toured the countryside and I saw a few things that caught my interest. One of the houses we visited seemed so familiar, and after we returned home I started dreaming about a girl with curly blonde hair and blue eyes. She was like an angel, so different from anyone I'd ever met in New York. I thought I was going crazy." He paused, his eyes darkening for a moment before continuing the story. "Some of my friends found girlfriends, but all I did was go from girl to girl, hoping one of them would live up to my expectations. None of them did. Then I saw you on the first day of school, and I think I went into shock. I knew we should be together, but I had this sinking feeling that all I would do was hurt you in the end.

"I tried keeping my distance," he continued. "But Chelsea was so insistent that I pay attention to her, and for some convoluted reason I decided that being with Chelsea would allow me to be close to you without being *with* you. That way I knew I couldn't hurt you. It was stupid, but you were all I could think about. Plus you were with Jeremy, and I didn't want to cause trouble between the two of you if you were happy with him."

"But it just made everything harder," I said, tears welling up in my eyes with the mention of my best friend and ex-boyfriend.

"I know." He pulled away, his eyes flashing with guilt. "If it's too much, we can stop now. This doesn't have to go any further."

"No." I didn't have to think about my response. "That would be even worse. It would hurt too much; it would be like losing a part of who I am."

He smiled, the golden flecks in his eyes shining like tiny sparkling lights. "I've wanted to hear that for so long."

"It'll be okay with Chelsea," I said, hoping it was true. "She's been my best friend since elementary school. We can get past this."

He looked away, and I worried that I'd said something wrong. "I promise I'll always be here for you," he said, confidence returning to his eyes as he wrapped his arms around my waist. "Even though I haven't done much in the past few months for you to believe me."

"You really haven't," I laughed, surprised by how at ease I was with him. Then a cold burst of wind blew through the air, and I moved closer to Drew to keep warm. "But everything's changed now."

He grabbed hold of the wheel again. "Let's go inside," he said, twisting the key and turning the boat back in the direction of his house. "You're cold, and I'll get to give you the tour I could see you wanted earlier."

The boat sped towards the dock, and I watched the house grow larger, aware of how little the speed was affecting me. I was beginning to enjoy the feeling of the wind running through my hair. He slowed down as we got closer, the engine lowering to a mere hum.

"Is it weird living in such a big house with just you and your mom?" I asked, hoping he didn't mind me asking about his personal life. So far we'd only talked about the two of us, but I wanted to know more about what his life was like before he met me.

"Sometimes." His voice was distant—it was clear he didn't talk much about the split between his parents. "It's been different without my dad around. My mom and I get along fine, but she's been emotional since the separation."

I scooted closer, feeling like a part of him wanted to share it with me. "What happened between them?"

"Their marriage just sort of fell apart." He paused, thinking about how to explain. "She didn't care much for the City or the people in New York society, and he started working longer hours. I think they just realized they weren't in love anymore. She offered to stay in New York for me, but I could tell it wasn't what she wanted. So I told her I didn't mind a change of scenery, and now we're here."

"You *chose* to move here?" I leaned back and looked at him, widening my eyes in shock. "I always thought you were forced."

"Don't be so surprised." He chuckled, bringing the boat to a stop when we reached the dock.

"I'm not surprised," I explained, shaking my head in amazement. "I'm just glad you told me. I loved you from the moment I saw you, but now I'm finally beginning to understand why."

"Because I left Manhattan for a town in the middle of nowhere?" he asked, the smile on his lips hinting that he knew what I meant. He just wanted to hear it from me.

"No." I laughed, shaking my head. "It's because as much as you try to hide it, you'll do anything for the people you love, even if it's not something you would choose to do yourself."

He walked over to the side of the boat to attach it to the dock. "I think you're forgetting how much I've hurt you for the past few months," he said, turning to face me when he was done.

"I didn't forget." I frowned, upset that he brought it back up. "I don't think I could forget. Every time you ignored me or told me we shouldn't be around each other tore me apart inside." I blinked away tears, trying to wipe the memories from my mind. "But I know you must have had some sort of reason, especially if it hurt you half as much as it did me." I paused, hoping I could get him to say whatever it was that he was holding back. "You can tell me, you know. It doesn't have to be now, but I want to understand."

"I already told you," he said, holding a hand out to help me out of the boat. "I don't know why we're here right now, but it didn't end well back then. All I know is that it was bad enough for me to not want you to have to go through all that pain again."

"We must be here because we have a second chance," I insisted. "Whatever happened then is over. All we have to worry about is what we have right here and now, and that's each other."

His dark eyes studied me so intensely that I had to remind myself to breathe. "You're the light of my life, Elizabeth." He reached his hand to touch mine, holding it protectively. "I love how much you trust people and want to believe in them. All I hope is that you can still trust me."

"I've always trusted you," I said without a second thought. "That's what made everything so hard. I felt how close we could be and didn't know how to handle dealing with the possibility that we would never have the opportunity to be together. It still feels so surreal ... I can't help but think that I'll wake up tomorrow and tonight will have been a dream."

"That's not going to happen." His eyes turned dark at the prospect. "I would say you should stay here tonight; that way you'll know the moment you wake up that you weren't dreaming, but I don't think your mom would be too happy to discover you gone in the morning."

"You're right," I agreed, imagining the horrified look on her face upon finding me missing. "She might think I was kidnapped."

"Kidnapped?" he questioned, his eyes sparkling with laughter. "I'm going to kidnap you inside."

In less than a second he lifted me in his arms and started to run towards the house. I wrapped my arms around his neck as he ran across the backyard and leaned into his jacket, inhaling the sweet smell of leather mixed with musky pine, capturing the moment in my mind to ensure that it would remain there for all eternity.

CHAPTER 26

The inside of the Carmichael house felt larger than the outside, if that was possible. It turned out that the part I saw walking in was only one "wing." Yes, the house had wings, like what you might read about in an old novel. The winding staircase in the foyer led to Drew's room on the second floor, and while the room was large, the decorations looked "normal" compared to all the others in the house. A set of French doors opened up to a large balcony overlooking the front yard, and there was a king sized bed on the opposite wall. All of the furniture was the same mahogany, and a sleek silver stereo system sat on the right of the window with a flat screen television above.

"I like your room," I said, adjusting my weight from one leg to the other as I looked around.

"Thanks." He shrugged like it was nothing special, walking across the floor towards a small door in the corner next to the stereo. I followed him, watching as he opened it to reveal the bottom of an iron spiral staircase that looked like something from an old Victorian home. "Now for the surprise I wanted to show you," he said, holding the door for me to enter. "Come on."

The stairs led up to a tower-like area in the shape of a hexagon above his room. It reminded me of a secret passage from a mystery book, except that instead of being dark and musty, windows filled three of the walls. A large flat-screen computer sat on a mahogany desk that looked out of one of the front windows, and a brown leather couch lined one wall across the room. On the other wall a built-in bookshelf stood tall enough to touch the ceiling, filled with titles ranging from old philosophy to the newest thrillers.

"I didn't know you liked to read," I mused, walking over to examine the spines of the books. "Have you read all of these?"

"Not even close." He laughed, scanning the length of the bookshelf. "I didn't have a lot of time to read in the City—there was always so much going on. But I've gotten through a bunch of them since moving here."

"I guess New Hampshire is kind of boring compared to New York," I said, smiling slightly.

He was silent for a moment. "Nothing's been boring since I met you."

I lowered my eyes, heat creeping up on my cheeks. "Yeah," I said, glancing back up at him. "I know exactly what you mean."

"I didn't bring you up here to show you the loft," he said after a few seconds. I nodded for him to continue, and he walked over to the desk and opened large drawer on the bottom, pulling out a square object and placing it next to the computer. "A woman at a store in England gave this to me when I was there two summers ago."

I went to get a closer look, standing inches away from Drew. His breathing slowed when I got close to him, and I smiled, happy to sense that he shared the same feelings while near me that I did with him.

I looked down at the box to see what it was. There was glass on the top and front sides, and the rest of it was a medium-colored wood. It was divided into two sections—the top was an inch tall and opened to reveal what appeared to be a miniature golden record player with small raised dots scattered on the disk. I kneeled to see what was inside the larger section, my lips parting in surprise at the scene inside.

Porcelain figures appeared to be dancing inside a miniature ballroom, and while they weren't actually moving, it looked like they were dancing to the imaginary music of a pianist in the corner. The yellow walls displayed elegant carvings, and the floor was an off-white marble, the lightness of the room making the space appear larger than it actually was. The women's flowing dresses created movement in the still piece. It was like the dioramas that I made in elementary school, only much more detailed and elegant.

"It's beautiful," I said, lifting my fingers to touch the glass, like I was trying to reach into the scene.

"That's not all." He moved his fingers to the back, winding a small handle that I hadn't noticed before. It clicked with each movement until it couldn't go any further. "Listen."

The gold plate on top started slowly spinning, sending clear notes through the otherwise silent room. A section of the floor inside the box rotated when the song began, making it look like the figures were dancing to the music.

"It's 'Minuet.'" I recognized the piece instantly.

He knelt on the floor beside me, watching the figures revolve inside the small room. "I knew it was important when I heard you playing it on the piano," he said, looking over at me. "It's our song."

The conversation I'd had with Jeremy in the beginning of the school year popped into my mind. At the time I didn't realize why I cared so much that Jeremy and I didn't have a song, but now I knew why. Music is powerful; it transforms emotions and experiences into something tangible. Every time you hear a familiar song, the feelings from it bubble to the surface, bringing back memories you might have otherwise forgotten.

We listened for a minute longer, the distance between the notes elongating and eventually coming to a stop.

"I can't believe you have this," I whispered. "It's too much of a coincidence. Don't you see that none of this would be here if we weren't meant to be together?"

"You're so optimistic, Elizabeth." He pushed himself off the desk to stand, holding out a hand to help me up. "I hope I don't disappoint you."

"You won't," I insisted. "I know you won't."

Doubt crossed his face, and I couldn't help but wonder what was so bad that he felt like he had to keep

MICHELLE MADOW

his distance to protect me. It was noble, yes, but I wanted to know more than what he'd told me so far.

I also didn't want to push it. Something about our relationship felt fragile, like if I touched it in the wrong way it would shatter into a million little pieces. It wasn't worth the risk to sacrifice losing how far we'd come this night because I was too impatient to wait for him to be ready to open up.

"The sun's rising," he said, interrupting my thoughts. "I should get you home."

"Right," I agreed, remembering that I wasn't even supposed to be there. I felt terrible about sneaking out, but I still didn't want to get in trouble. I also had no idea how I was going to be able to comfort Chelsea without feeling like a terrible friend, since I was the reason behind Drew's breaking up with her.

His eyes brimmed with concern. "Everything will be fine with you and Chelsea. She'll just need some time to adjust."

"How do you know?" I asked. "And how did you know I was thinking that?"

"It's because I know you, Elizabeth," he said, like the answer was so simple that I shouldn't have needed to ask. "I know how hard this is for you. If it helps, Chelsea talked a lot about what a great friend you are to her, especially when she needed you after her mom passed away. I loved when she talked about you. I want you to remember that whatever happens with you and Chelsea, I'm here for you. I'm not going anywhere, at least not anytime soon."

"I just don't know if I can do this to her," I said, trying to push the image out of my mind of the anger in Chelsea's eyes as I told her about Drew and I being together. "But we have to be together after we've come this far. I don't think I could take it any other way."

"You don't have to do anything yet," he said, his eyes softening in understanding. "This is a lot to handle at once. I've been trying to figure everything out since I met you—no, since I went on that vacation to England—and I still don't know what we're supposed to do. I'll figure out how to deal with whatever decision you make."

"And what do *you* want?" I asked, flashing back to when I asked him the same question in the hallway at school a few weeks ago.

"I want you," he said. "Just you. I used to go through every day without thinking about the future, but with you all I can see are the possibilities of the experiences we could have together." He paused, clasping my hands in his. "But remember that whatever you choose, I want you to do what will make you the happiest."

I nodded, deciding to take his advice and think about what to do before making anything final. It didn't seem possible to decide not to be together, but then I thought about why I had to make a decision in the first place. Chelsea would feel betrayed when she found out about me and Drew, and it would devastate Jeremy even more to know that Drew was the reason why I didn't put more effort into fixing our relationship.

The ride back was peaceful. Mellow music played in the background, and we watched the sun rise higher in the sky. When we arrived in front of my house, I didn't want to leave, still afraid I was dreaming and reality would slam down on me when I woke up. However, we eventually had to say bye, and Drew promised me again that he wouldn't discard what had happened that night and revert to the way he'd been acting towards me for the past few weeks. His words were consoling, and I believed him.

It was easy to sneak back inside, and despite knowing that I would have to deal with Chelsea the next day, it only took seconds to fall asleep.

CHAPTER 27

It was noon when I awoke, and I replayed the events from the night before in my mind, wondering again if it was a dream. It would have been a very realistic dream—but I wouldn't have woken up so late if none of it had happened.

Then I remembered about Drew breaking up with Chelsea. She was going to be devastated. My backpack still sat where my mom placed it the night before, and I walked over to it, dreading all of the missed calls that I was bound to see on my cell phone.

There were six—five from Chelsea and one from Drew. The voicemail box blinked on the top of the screen, and I stared at it for a few seconds before pressing send and raising the phone to my ear. The recorded voice told me that I had three new messages. I sat on the floor to listen, leaning against the wall as they began to play.

"Lizzie?" Chelsea's voice wavered, catching in her throat. "Call me when you get this. I need to talk to you."

There was no question about what she was referring to. She must have called right after Drew broke up with her.

The next was the click of a phone hanging up.

"Lizzie?" Chelsea sniffed on the third message. "It's 11 in the morning ... where are you? Did you forget to charge your phone again? I really need to talk to you. Call me back when you get this."

I deleted all of the messages, unable to listen to any more of Chelsea's crying. It was partly my fault that she was so upset. The second to last bar of the battery gage blinked and disappeared, and I walked over to my desk, plugging the nearby charger into the bottom of the phone. I stared at the lit screen, knowing I had to call Chelsea back. Drew wanted me to think through my decision, but I'd already made it. I wanted to be with him.

"Look who's finally up." My mom opened the door, poking her head into my room. "Chelsea called the house twice this morning. She sounded upset—you might want to call her back. Did you forget to charge your cell?"

"Yeah," I said, figuring that leaving it on silent was close enough. "I guess I stayed up reading longer than I realized." The excuse came easily, and while I felt awful for lying, I knew better than to tell her the real reason I slept so late.

"I ate breakfast without you," she apologized. "I couldn't wait any longer, and I didn't want to wake you up."

"That's okay," I said, smiling to let her know that I didn't mind. "I'm not that hungry, anyway."

She closed the door to let me get ready for the day and I grabbed my phone to call Chelsea back. It rang three times, and I hoped she wouldn't pick up. It was an awful thought to have, but at least it could buy me some time before dealing with the reality of the situation.

"Hey." She picked up mid-way through the fourth ring. "Where have you been? I've called you a million times."

"I forgot tot take my phone off silent," I explained. "What's going on?"

"Drew broke up with me." Her voice was flat as she told me what I already knew. "He said 'we weren't meant to be'—whatever that means."

I knew too well.

"Wow," I said, hoping it was enough to convince her that I was shocked at the news. "Are you okay?"

"I just don't get it," she continued, ignoring the question. It was obvious she wasn't okay—not that I expected otherwise. "He was the first guy I ever loved, and I thought he felt the same way. Then he just changed his mind."

I leaned my head against the wall. "Do you want me to come over?"

"Yeah," she answered, the waver I heard from the messages returning to her voice. "How about we watch a movie? Anything to get my mind off him."

"Okay," I agreed, forcing a smile even though she couldn't see it through the phone. "I'll be over in a bit."

"Thanks." She breathed a sigh of relief. "You're the best friend ever."

I said bye and stood to look in the full-length mirror on my wall. The guilt shined all over my face, even from a distance. There was no way I could fool Chelsea. The only thing I could hope for was that she was too upset about Drew breaking up with her to notice anything off about me.

I rushed to get ready, not bothering to change out of the sweatpants I'd thrown on after Drew dropped me back off at the house that morning. The walk down the stairs felt more like I was heading to a trial where I was the guilty defendant instead of about to go to my best friend's house, and I counted each step until reaching the bottom, somehow resisting the urge to run back up to my room.

"Going to Chelsea's?" my mom called from her office.

"Yeah," I answered, opening the closet doors to grab my coat. "Drew broke up with her."

"That's why she sounded so upset this morning," she said, nodding in understanding. "You're a great friend to her. I know you'll help her through this."

"Right." I cringed at the notion of me as a great friend, dreading how much I was about to have to lie to Chelsea. "I'll see you later."

The drive to Chelsea's felt shorter than normal. I sat in my car after pulling into the driveway, staring at her white wood paneled house that resembled a large cottage. I didn't have much time to think about what I was going to say, because the garage door started to open, grumbling like a dinosaur opening its mouth to capture its prey.

Chelsea stood inside of the garage, looking like she was recently run over by a piece of heavy machinery. Her jeans had large holes at the knees, and the red sweatshirt she wore was about three sizes too big for her. She looked like a giant cherry. Her shiny hair was in a messy bun on top of her head, and the rims of her eyes were pink, most likely from crying.

"Hey Chels," I said, stepping into her house, trying to pretend that everything was normal. "How're you feeling?"

"Fine." She shoved her hands into the back pockets of her jeans. "Do you want to watch a movie?"

"Okay," I said, looking down at the hardwood floor. "Your room?"

She nodded, spinning around and walking towards the steps without another word. There wasn't much to be said that hadn't been discussed over the phone, and I knew to wait until we were upstairs to talk about Drew and the breakup. Chelsea would bring it up when she was ready, but I doubted there was much I could say to make her feel better. With Hannah, I told her what an awful person Sheldon was and how she deserved better, but the idea of saying anything bad about Drew felt unnatural and wrong.

The first thing I noticed when we got to her room was that one of the light wood nightstands next to her bed was covered in used tissues. A few more scattered across her comforter. All her drapes were closed, and none of her lamps were on. Only the dim light in the overhead fan made it possible to see. Even though the room was huge, I felt like I'd just walked into a dungeon.

"I just can't believe this happened." She shook her head in disbelief, falling onto her bed like a Southern belle in a dramatic movie. "Everything was great and then suddenly ... we're not 'meant to be.'" She held up her fingers in makeshift quote signs.

I sat on the bed next to her, finding an area devoid of tissues. "If he said something like that to you, maybe you *weren't* meant to be," I suggested, worried that she might not be too happy to hear what I had to say. "Someone you were meant to be with would never treat you like that."

"No." She shook her head and crossed her arms over her chest. "We were perfect together. He was the gorgeous new guy from the city, and I always knew I wanted to move out of New Hampshire after high school. He also listened to me when I talked—which is more than I can say about any other guy I've dated. It was perfect."

"Maybe." I shrugged, bringing my feet up on the bed and scooting closer to her. "But you'll find someone, Chels. Every guy at school loves you."

"But none of them are Drew." She sniffed, grabbing another tissue out of the box and blowing her nose. "He was different, Lizzie. There was something special about him—something I can't explain."

I nodded in understanding. She didn't have to explain, because I already knew how enticing Drew Carmichael could be. She cried for a few seconds more and I tried conjuring up something helpful to say, but nothing came to mind.

"But I've been thinking about it," she continued, taking a deep breath and dropping the tissue on the bed next to her. "He might not like the idea of commitment, especially since he just moved here. Maybe he's thinking we jumped into the relationship too fast. He'll realize that breaking up with me was a mistake, and everything will be back to the way it was."

I fought back the urge to tell her that was impossible. "You can't count on that happening," I said, hugging my knees to my chest. "I don't mean to say it won't, but you shouldn't get your hopes up. Then it'll be even worse."

She shook her head, laughing. "My dad said the same thing."

"You talked with your dad about this?"

"You didn't pick up your phone," she said, sounding annoyed. "Tiffany's been busy at college and probably doesn't want to worry about her little sister's latest boy drama. I didn't want to bother Keelie about it, and our old friends would have been less than sympathetic."

"Knowing you, you'll be over him in a few days," I said, tilting my head and managing a half smile. "Aren't you the one always telling me how you never get attached in relationships?"

"It's different with Drew," she insisted. "He'll come around though. I know it."

I wanted to tell her she was wrong—Drew was mine and it was over between them. But it wasn't the right time.

I had a feeling there would never be a right time.

She reached to pick up the remote from her nightstand. "Let's just watch the movie," she said, turning the TV on. "There's no need to make myself more upset, especially since he'll come around soon."

"Right." I nodded, even though she had no idea how wrong she was. I had to tell her soon. If I didn't, it wouldn't be long until she discovered everything herself, and if that happened, it wasn't going to be pretty.

CHAPTER 28

Unlike the past few weeks when I arrived to school late to avoid Drew, I got there early on Monday morning to get a seat next to the door, placing my bag on the chair next to me to save it for Chelsea. I would have liked to sit next to Drew, but giving away any clues about what was going on between us would be a bad idea. Chelsea needed some cooling off time after the break-up. It would be hard to pretend like everything was the same between Drew and me as it had been a week ago, but it was best for everyone that way.

When Drew walked into the room, he winked when his eyes met mine, smirking at the unspoken secret between us. Only one other student was also there so early—Lindsey Newman—and she moved her head from me to him and back again, a quizzical look passing over her face. I lowered my eyes, pretending nothing happened.

The rustic smell of pinecones drifted by as Drew walked past me, and he placed a torn sheet of paper on my desk before continuing to his usual seat on the opposite side of the room. Once he passed, I brushed my fingers against the paper, inching it closer. His scratchy handwriting was in the center. A few strands of hair fell across my face as I read the note:

Our birth is but a sleep and a forgetting
The soul that rises with us, our life's star
Hath had elsewhere its setting
And cometh from afar.

I instantly recognized the Wordsworth poem we read a few weeks ago in English class. It was an excerpt from the "Intimations of Immortality" Ode. Wordsworth believed in reincarnation, and the stanza perfectly embodied the current situation. Underneath the poem was a short note:

The lake. Tonight.
I love you.
-Drew

I lifted my head to look at him, only to discover that he was watching me as I read it. Despite telling myself earlier that I wouldn't sneak out again, I nodded in affirmation, smiling at the idea of going out on the boat with him once more.

Of course, the sneaking out would only last until I gathered enough courage to tell Chelsea about Drew and me.

If I ever managed to do that.

A group of three girls entered and went to the opposite side of the room near Drew. Lara was in the center, and she looked at him, tilting her head and smiling to try getting his attention. I supposed that word of his and Chelsea's breakup was already out. He smirked and shook his head, glancing at me before reaching down to get his books from his bag. I folded the note and tucked it into an inner pocket of my bag since Chelsea would be there soon, zipping it shut for protection.

I sketched in the margins of my notebook while waiting for class to begin to keep my focus away from Drew, not wanting to clue anyone in to the fact that anything was going on between the two of us. The last thing I wanted was the entire school catching on before I mustered up the courage to tell Chelsea myself. If everyone already knew about Drew and Chelsea breaking up, I didn't want to know how short it would take for word to spread about how they broke up because Drew and I were now together.

Chelsea walked through the door and smiled when she saw me. She glanced at Drew, her eyes dimming at the sight of him, and walked over to remove my bag from where I'd placed it on the chair next to me. "Thanks for saving me a seat," she said, sitting down and looking around the room. She paused when she got to Drew, and a scowl formed on her face when he ignored her.

She tried to at unaffected by the exchange and turned back to face me.

"Of course," I said, glad that I hid the note before she arrived. It was illogical for me to think she would look inside my bag, but just the fact that it was there made me slightly paranoid. "I figured you wouldn't want to sit where you usually do."

"Yeah," she agreed, leaning back in the seat and crossing one leg over the other. "Everyone totally knows, and first period hasn't even started."

"Everyone doesn't know," I said, examining who was there. "I bet Katie doesn't." I lowered my voice so the dark-haired girl sitting by herself at the end of the table didn't overhear.

"That's because she has no friends." Chelsea didn't bother to lower her voice, and I cringed at her lack of sensitivity. "But I bet even she'll know by the end of the day."

I shrugged, knowing she was probably right. Mrs. Wilder arrived before I could reply, and the class quieted down from their discussions about what they'd done over the weekend as she started to lecture on Europe in the 1600's.

Chelsea paid a strange amount of attention to the lecture, taking three pages of notes in her boxy handwriting. She was a detailed note taker, but that was even extreme for her. However, it was an effective way to not look at Drew, so I tried to do the same thing, even though my notes weren't as detailed as hers.

Throughout class, I kept thinking of the night before, reciting the Wordsworth poem in my mind. There were so many questions I wanted to ask Drew, and I hoped that the poem he chose meant he would answer them. It took all of my strength to not lift my head and catch his eyes again, and when the bell rang, I shut my notebook in relief.

"That was awkward," Chelsea muttered, packing her books in her bag. "At least I have Jeremy to sit with in English, but chemistry will be like a torture chamber."

"You'll do fine." I tried to be encouraging.

"Maybe I'll accidentally blow something up in his face." She laughed, tossing her hair over her shoulder.

I scrunched my nose at the image.

"Chill out," she said. "I was just kidding. I'll see you later."

She walked to her next class with so much confidence that no one would have guessed that she'd just had her heart broken. Another pang of guilt swept through my chest. Lying to her was awful, but I didn't have another option at the moment.

I would tell her the truth soon—just not today.

"Are you okay sitting with Jeremy and the guys on the team?" Chelsea asked while we waited in the lunch line, taking a Diet Coke out of the refrigerator.

"That's fine," I agreed. "I guess Jeremy and I are still friends. We're not fighting or anything."

"Good." She smiled. "I still think you should consider getting back together with him."

I shook my head and reached inside the fridge to pull out a bottle of water. "That's not going to happen," I said, not wanting to discuss it any further.

"He thinks it will," she said playfully.

I paused, surprised at the arrogance of the statement. "He said that?"

"Yeah." She shrugged, twisting the top off the bottle and taking a sip. "He said you two are just on a break."

"A break?" I repeated, even though I knew I'd heard her right. Getting back together with Jeremy was a mutual decision that I in no way intended to make. "On second thought, maybe we should sit in the commons again."

"Chelsea! Lizzie!" Keelie called from the center of the cafeteria. "Come sit with us!"

Chelsea didn't acknowledge my comment, instead walking towards the packed table in the middle of the room. After making sure there were seats available that weren't near Jeremy, I followed her, focusing my tray as I walked.

Jeremy looked up and grinned when we got to the table. I managed a half-smile in return, scanning the area in hopes of locating Drew. He sat at a table in the corner with Garrett and Craig from his set design class and three sophomore girls I didn't know, appearing to only be half listening to their conversation. Chelsea pretended she didn't see him, and she slid into a seat next to Brad Carson, a member of the soccer team who happened to not be in a relationship. He was lanky with light brown hair; not Chelsea's type, but he sat in just the right to place to give Drew a perfect angle of her flirting. I chose an empty seat across from her, since it was far enough from Jeremy that it wouldn't be awkward between the two of us. Not that it looked like I would have to worry—Amber was sitting so close to him that if I didn't know better, I would think she was on his lap. She reminded me of Lydia from *Pride and Prejudice,* who threw herself all over the soldiers the same way that Amber was throwing herself at the guys on the soccer team. And just like Lydia, she looked and sounded ridiculous while doing it.

"What'd you all do over the weekend?" Keelie asked from her seat next to me, folding the ends of her taco before taking a small bite.

"Jeremy and I saw the new James Bond movie," Amber said with a smirk, making sure to look in my direction. "It was really good."

Jeremy glanced at me before turning his attention back to Amber. "Yeah it was," he agreed, looking around the table. "You should all see it."

"Maybe." I shrugged, looking down at the food on my plate.

For the rest of lunch I listened to everyone's conversations, adding a comment here or there so it sounded like I was interested in what they were talking about. Amber made an obvious effort to be as close to Jeremy as she could, scooting closer and touching his hand whenever possible. She seemed to enjoy throwing it in my face that she was with Jeremy, more than she seemed to enjoy being with Jeremy himself. To distract myself from their flirting, I focused on stabbing the pieces of lettuce on my plate.

I finished half of the salad before the bell rang at the end of lunch. Chelsea had a sour look on her face—I assumed Drew hadn't returned her not-so-subtle glances in his direction, and I somehow managed to not turn around and check.

"Time for chemistry," Chelsea said, not making an effort to stand. "This'll be just tons of fun."

"Why don't you just switch lab partners?" Shannon asked from her seat next to Warren. I was surprised at her sudden interest in Chelsea and Drew's breakup. She'd made it clear that she didn't like how we were now considered part of her group of friends, but I acted like her caring about our lives was normal and kept quiet. Maybe she was actually making an effort to be nice.

"Can't," Chelsea explained. "We're partners for the rest of the semester. Turns out my plan in the beginning of the year wasn't so brilliant after all."

"I never got what was so great about him." Shannon sighed, piling trash on her tray. "Obviously he's good-looking, but he hasn't even tried to make any friends here. It's like he thinks he's too good for us."

"I don't think having a million friends is important to him," I said without thinking, looking down at the table a moment later. "Maybe he just doesn't like being around people he doesn't know well."

"He seems more full of himself than shy." Shannon laughed, raising an eyebrow in interest. "And anyway, how would you know this?"

"Chelsea told me," I said, remembering how Chelsea said he wasn't a big partier when we went dress shopping earlier in the year.

Shannon laughed and got up to throw her trash away, the rest of the table following suit before leaving to go to their next classes. Drawing was right next to the cafeteria, but the door was still locked, so I leaned against the wall and watched people pass by. Most were too involved in their own conversations to be aware of much else going on around them, but I paused when I noticed Jeremy looking right at me. He sauntered to where I was standing and I lowered my eyes, hoping he got the hint that I wasn't in the mood to talk.

"So, Drew broke up with Chelsea." He leaned an elbow against the wall, turning his body to face mine.

"Yeah," I said, edging away from him. He leaned forward even more, towering over me.

"They sat as far away from each other as possible in English this morning," he continued, ignoring my discomfort.

"That makes sense," I said. "They just broke up."

"Right." He fidgeted and looked up at the ceiling, seeming to be at a loss for words. "Anyway, you're cool with Amber and me going to the movies last weekend, right?"

"Why wouldn't I be?" I asked, despite the fact that he was agitating me more and more by the second.

"I don't know." He shrugged, leaning inward. "It's just that you didn't seem very happy about us talking during lunch."

"I'm fine." The words sounded forced, even to me. "I'm glad you're happy with her."

He lowered his voice. "It's not the same as being with you."

"Jere," I said, frustrated. "We broke up."

"We can always get back together."

I shook my head. "I don't think so."

"Whatever, Liz." He lifted his elbow from the wall, giving me a little more space. "I'm going to class. But I'm not giving up on us."

He spun around, walking away without giving me time to respond. The sad thing was that Jeremy was right; we used to be good together. But he held nothing on Drew, and I hoped with every fiber of my being that we could make things work without hurting Jeremy or Chelsea.

Unfortunately, given the current circumstances, I doubted it was possible. At least I had the lake to look forward to later that night—the one place where Drew and I could be together without having to worry about anyone else besides two of us.

CHAPTER 29

"I wonder how long it'll stay warm like this," I asked, snuggling closer to Drew. The purple sweatshirt I wore was the only protection I needed against the abnormally warm weather, and it was nice to be able to go out with Drew on the boat and enjoy time away from the rest of the world.

He didn't answer the rhetorical question. Silence was never awkward between the two of us, and it was a nice change from Jeremy, who felt the need to fill every second with conversation.

"Have you remembered anything more from ... back then?" he asked, looking down at me in question.

"Not much," I said with a sigh. "But I kind of remember drawing in a field, and you were there with me. We would spend time together like we do now, but outside in the sunlight. Not at night on a lake."

He hugged me closer towards him. "This is something special in this lifetime," he said, his breath warm against my cheek.

"And I love that." I turned to look at him face-on. The light specks in his eyes stood out even more in the moonlight. "But I want to know more about 'back then.'"

"It's not as great as you think," he mumbled.

"Tell me a little, and I'll decide for myself."

He smirked. "Well, you were just as stubborn."

"But what were our lives like?" I asked, happy to be getting somewhere, even if it was only a small step. "How did we meet?"

"It was similar to how we met here," he said after a small pause. "My family moved to Hampshire when I was 17, in what I've narrowed down to around 1814."

"That was where Jane Austen lived," I said, remembering what Alistair had told me a few weeks ago. "Did we know her?"

"No." He shook his head, laughing. "She would have been about 15 years older than us. I think your parents knew her, but by the time we would have been able to meet her she stayed in her house most of the time. She rarely left until she died."

"That would have been cool if we had known her," I said, disappointed.

"I guess." He shrugged, not finding it as exciting as I did. "Anyway, my family lived in London before moving, and at first we didn't have much money. But my father was good at cards, and he spent years perfecting his methods. He created a team with a few of his friends—like those MIT students who beat Vegas—except using the card games of the time. When they were ready they took the gambling halls by storm, leaving as quickly as they arrived, but many times richer. They were already gone by the time people caught on, with more money than even they imagined they would make."

"What does your dad do now?" I asked.

"He's a lawyer."

"Oh." I laughed. "Funny."

"Catherine was the first person I met when we moved," he said, frowning. "Do you remember her? She was your closest friend."

"I don't remember anyone but you," I admitted.

"I think that's normal." His eyes darkened, like he was thinking about something he would rather forget. "I didn't start remembering anything apart from you until around a year after the trip to England."

"I hope it doesn't take me that long," I said. "But what was Catherine like?"

"Catherine was a bit of a gold-digger," he said with a laugh. "I didn't care though. She was hot, so I decided to court her."

I narrowed my eyes at him saying that about someone other than me.

"Not beautiful like you," he covered. "It's different. I didn't care about who she was—looks were all I cared about before I met you. Then my parents decided to throw a ball to meet everyone in town, and I saw you talking with Catherine. She must have said something about me, because you turned around and looked at me. When ours eyes met, I forgot about Catherine, or anyone else at the party but you. I was devastated when I found out you were engaged."

"Engaged?" I asked, sitting back in shock. "To who?"

"James." He sneered at the name. "But he was insignificant to me. You danced with me once—as friends, of course—to 'Minuet.' I spent a lot of time with you after that day, mostly in the field behind your house. You were an artist, which is something you brought into this life, and you liked using me as a model for your drawings. It gave us a reason to be together for extended periods of time. James was more of the active type—he didn't enjoy posing while you drew—and he was completely blind to what was going on. It was amusing.

"You tried teaching me how to draw, but I was never as good as you," he continued. "Mechanics were more of my thing, and I still remember how happy you were the day you came outside to find the swing that I'd built on the old tree in front of your house."

"I always did like swings," I said, an image of an old rope swing hanging from a tree filling my mind. "I guess that explains why."

"I tried to draw you on it once." He laughed. "It didn't turn out very well."

"I'm sure it wasn't as bad as you think."

"It was." He chuckled, shaking his head. "It always seemed like you were good at everything. You still are. Drawing, speaking French, playing the piano..."

"Only for the past month," I pointed out. "At least with the piano and French."

He smirked. "Do you sing as well?"

"No." I smiled, shaking my head. "Although if I did, I suppose I would fit Mr. Darcy's qualifications for an 'accomplished woman.' He was very picky."

"Those were just excuses," Drew said lazily.

"Excuses?" I raised an eyebrow. "For what?"

"So that he could have a reason to stay single until he met the one he truly loved."

I smiled, taking in what he'd said. "So, what happened next?" I asked, leaning forward, eager to hear the rest of the story.

"We saw each other in secret for a while," he continued. "Although we did dance together at the annual masked ball. It was only once—which didn't imply anything more than friendship—but that was enough to irritate Catherine, since the entire town thought I planned to propose to her. Her family had lost a lot of their money, but they were of high social status. Mine had no name of any importance, but we were rich because of my dad's schemes. To an outsider, we were the perfect match. But no one could ever compare to you."

"But you were still seeing Catherine?" I asked in distaste.

"Yes." He looked out towards the lake, guilt passing over his eyes. "My parents would never have supported you and me together, since it was more prestigious for my family to be connected with Catherine's. You were also still engaged to James, and I didn't take that too well."

I thought about what I knew of the era. "It wasn't easy to break engagements back then, was it?"

"You tried." He turned his eyes toward me again. "Your parents wouldn't allow it. Your family was middle class, and James's was well regarded in town—both in money and name. They said you weren't being sensible."

I scrunched my nose. "Sensible is boring. If I were sensible, I would still be with Jeremy. And that wouldn't be good."

"No, it wouldn't," he agreed. "I'm glad you're not sensible."

"So what did we do?" I asked, wanting to return to the story of the past.

"You refused to see me."

I jolted back in my seat. "What? Why?"

"I believe your words were that you 'couldn't handle the eminent doom of the relationship.'"

I tried not to laugh. "The 'eminent doom?' That doesn't sound like me at all."

"We're not the exact same as we were then," he explained. "I think it's because we've also lived a new life here, and that incorporates into who we are. But it's just a guess."

"So that was the end?" I asked.

"No," he said, a mischievous smile forming across his face. "I told Catherine we couldn't see each other anymore, and then I proposed to you."

I widened my eyes and leaned forward, liking where this was going. "But I thought I was engaged to James?"

"You were," he said. "Ours was a secret engagement. I still remember the ring—five garnets in a gold setting. It was simple, but it was perfect."

I looked down at my hand, envisioning what the ring would look like on my finger. An image popped into my mind of the five garnets, all the same size, lined up in a half moon shape along the golden setting.

"It sounds beautiful," I said, touching the part of my finger where the ring would have sat.

He reached down, brushing his finger against mine. "You remember it?"

"Yes." I nodded, smiling. "I think I do."

I waited for him to finish the story, figuring it didn't end there. There had to be a reason why he questioned trying to fix things this time around, and I wanted to find out.

"So?" I prodded, since it seemed like he wasn't going to continue without my encouragement. "Did the secret engagement work out?"

"No," he said, lifting his hand off mine.

"Why not?"

His body stiffened, and he turned his head to look across the lake. "It gets hazy at that point," he said, shrugging like it didn't matter. "All I remember was you saying that you wished you'd never met me. You were so upset, and that's why I thought it would be best to avoid all of those complications this time around."

"Why would I say that?" I asked. "Did we cause too many problems for our families?"

"Perhaps," he mused. "I only remember the pain in your voice. I knew I couldn't do that to you again."

"But everything's different now," I said, looking up at him in hope that he would agree. "We don't have all those issues with our families. The only people who will be upset about us being together are Chelsea and Jeremy, but we'll deal with that. It'll be a lot easier this time around, I promise."

He looked back down at me, his eyes shining with doubt. "You make it sound so easy."

"Because it *is* easy," I insisted, wishing he would understand. "Whatever problems we had back then don't exist anymore. It's why we have this second chance, and we can't throw it away. Besides, you were the one who said we're not exactly the same as we were back then. If we're not the same, then things can turn out differently."

He was silent for a moment. "I hope you're right," he said, although he still didn't sound convinced. "I just hate thinking I could lose you all over again."

I held my gaze with his. "I know I'm right."

He pulled me closer, and the next thing I knew his lips were on mine, and I had a feeling that everything would work out. I leaned into him, our bodies pressed against each other, and it was like everything he said swirled together in my mind. I was everywhere at once—in the ballroom seeing him for the first time, sitting in school on that first day when he walked into the classroom, at the Halloween dance when we were together for that one song, and on the lake with the gentle waves rocking the boat back and forth on the water.

"When will you tell Chelsea about us?" he asked, his breath warm against my cheek. "I don't know how much longer we can keep this up at school. I hate not being able to be near you, stuck watching Jeremy leering over you like he owns you."

"I don't like it, either," I said, leaning back to look at him. "But Chelsea's a mess. I've never seen her like this after any breakup, and she's had a lot of them. You broke her heart."

"And I feel bad about that," he said. "But it's you I love, not her. You believe me, right? Always and forever."

"Of course I believe you," I promised. "I'll tell her by the end of the week. She just needs a little more time."

He nodded. "Alright."

A light flicked off in the corner of my eye, and I looked over at a house almost as large as Drew's. I didn't know how late it was, but most of the lights were off in the neighborhood, minus the one shining from Drew's room. I glanced down at my watch, amazed by how much time had passed.

"It's getting late," he said, checking the time on his watch. "I should take you home."

Despite wanting to stay on the lake longer, I knew he was right. Plus, my mom would be awake soon, and I didn't want to get in trouble. The moonlight glimmered off his dark hair as he moved towards the captain's seat, and I replayed the events of the past few months in my mind, amazed by how much my life had changed in such a short amount of time.

Still, it was impossible to be completely happy knowing that every day I didn't tell Chelsea about Drew and me being together was a day closer she came to finding out from someone else.

CHAPTER 30

"My parents are going out of town this weekend, so I'm having a party at my house tomorrow night," Shannon announced that Thursday at lunch.

I nodded in acknowledgment, trying to keep my eyes open after the exhaustion of sneaking out every night. It felt like heavy weights hung from my eyelashes, and if I could have used toothpicks to prop up my lids without risking poking myself in the eye, I would have done it in an instant. I almost fell asleep in history that morning, and Chelsea had to hit me on the arm when I started to doze off.

"Lizzie." Chelsea snapped her fingers in front of my face, causing me to jump in my chair.

"Yeah?" I asked, turning my head to look at her, surprised by the annoyed look on her face.

"You're coming to Shannon's party tomorrow night, right?"

I wanted to say no, but the entire table went quiet, waiting for my answer. Chelsea watched me, her eyes begging me to say yes.

"Sure," I agreed, knowing I owed it to her. "It'll be fun."

"It will be now since you're coming," Jeremy said from his seat all the way on the other end of the table.

Amber leaned closer to Jeremy, shooting a death stare in my direction. I looked away, not wanting her to think I was trying to get in the way of whatever was going on between the two of them. If he wanted to be with her, then that was his decision.

"Thanks for agreeing to come," Chelsea whispered after everyone resumed their conversation. "You've been such a great friend these past few days."

"No problem," I said, forcing a small smile. "I want to go. It's been a stressful week."

She took a sip of her soda and placed it back on the table. "I bet it has."

"What do you mean?" I asked, confused by her sudden change of tone.

"Just the whole thing with Jeremy and Amber." She moved her head closer to mine to make sure he couldn't overhear. "I know you broke up with him, but it still must be hard to watch."

"I'm fine." I shrugged, knowing that there was only a small bit of truth in her statement. It wasn't so much that Jeremy seemed to be moving on that bothered me as much as the fact that it was with Amber, although I tried to not make a big deal about it. "He can do what he wants."

"I guess he can," she agreed. "But even though he's spending a lot of time with her, I still don't think he's over you."

I glanced at where he sat talking with Amber. "He looks pretty over it to me," I said, watching her lean closer to him and whisper something in his ear. "Besides, we broke up for a reason. It wasn't working between the two of us."

"Just checking," she said, resting her elbows on the table. "You're always so quiet about these things, and I wanted to make sure you weren't keeping things to yourself because you were worried about upsetting me after the whole thing with Drew. You've just been so nice since our breakup, and I really do appreciate it."

I nodded, dropping my fork on my plate, my food not looking appetizing anymore. At least there were only two more periods to go until the end of the school day.

"Any idea why Chelsea told me about Shannon's party tomorrow night?" Drew leaned against the locker next to mine as I packed my bag to go home, casting a shadow over the pile of books in my hand.

My first instinct was to look around the hallway to make sure Chelsea, Jeremy, or even worse—Shannon— weren't in the area. After seeing that no one from our close group of friends was around, I allowed myself to breathe normally. My muscles relaxed when I looked back at Drew and I smiled at my slight bit of paranoia. Refocusing, I allowed what he said to sink in.

"Chelsea invited you?" I asked, making sure I'd heard right.

"In chemistry today." He cocked his head to the side, curious to see my reaction. "I believe she said something about how you and Jeremy were going, and how it would be fun for all of us to be friends again."

"We weren't exactly all friends to begin with," I said in confusion, trying to figure out what Chelsea was up to.

"It was weird," he agreed. "I said I had plans already, since I'm guessing being around Chelsea and Jeremy isn't on the top of our 'fun things we want to do' list."

I put my books into my bag and shut my locker. "I did tell her I'd go," I said, wincing as I spoke, still annoyed at myself for agreeing. "Everyone was talking about it at lunch, and she guilted me into it."

"I guess that means you're waiting until Saturday to tell her about us?" He leaned his back against the locker, crossing his arms over his chest.

"We said I should wait until the end of the week." I shrugged. "Saturday's still the end of the week. So I'm sticking with the plan to tell her by then."

He leaned closer to me, reaching forward and stopping himself a moment later. "I just don't want this to be even worse because you kept it from her for so long," he said. "On that day in class—when we had to read what we wrote about the most important moment in our lives—it was obvious how much your friendship means to both of you."

"I'll talk to her on Saturday," I said, knowing he was right. "I just don't want to ruin her entire weekend.

He nodded once, locking his eyes on mine and resisting moving any closer. "The lake tonight?" he said softly, making sure no one else would hear.

"I want to," I said, running my hands through my hair. "But I need sleep. And I haven't even started studying for my genetics test tomorrow, which I need to do so I don't fail."

"You won't fail," he said, edging his hand towards mine until I felt his fingers graze my palm. A warm tingling sensation traveled up my arm, and I didn't move my hand away. "I think I'll go to the party tomorrow night. I heard Shannon's parties are wild, and I'm curious to see how it compares to the ones in the City."

"You do know that Manhattan isn't the only city in the world, right?" I joked.

"Sorry." He laughed. "But if you're not having fun tomorrow night, let me know and I'll take you home. Alright?"

"I'm going to try to have fun," I said, hoping it would be possible. "But if it's that awful, of course I'll let you know."

"Good." He drew his hand back, satisfied with my answer. "I just want you to know you can trust me."

"Of course I trust you," I said, smiling. "What we have is strong enough to transcend time. I've never trusted anything more in my life."

His eyes shone with sadness, and I wondered what I'd said wrong.

"Is everything okay?" I asked, momentarily forgetting about trying to keep our relationship secret.

"Yeah," he said, relaxing his face into a smile. "But it'll be better next week in school when we can finally stop hiding the fact that we're together."

"It will," I agreed. "Just be patient."

"You know I'm not the patient type."

I laughed. "I know. But two days isn't that long."

"Compared to how long we waited to be together, I guess you have a point," he said, smirking.

"So I'll see you tomorrow then," I said, upset that we wouldn't be going to the lake that night. It was a good decision though. All those nights sneaking out meant I barely got any studying done. Or sleep.

"I guess you will." He leaned closer to me until there were only inches between us. "I love you, Elizabeth."

"Always and forever," I repeated the same words he spoke earlier that week on the boat. It was impossible to imagine being without him. The roots of our relationship were deeper than anyone could ever understand, and they were wound so tightly together that they were impossible to break apart.

If we were strong enough to make it this far, then one party wouldn't be a big deal at all.

CHAPTER 31

Apparently the light makeup I'd put on before driving to Chelsea's house wasn't sufficient, and she insisted on sitting me down in the armchair in the corner of her room to "work her magic" before we headed to Shannon's party. I studied my face in the mirror to see what she did to it with all of her shadows and blush. She'd used three different liners—coal, black, and super black—going as far as peeling back my lower lid to line the inside of my eye. Dark purple shadow covered my top lids, and black "wings" stuck out of the sides of both eyes, making me look like an exotic cat. I tried to wipe some of it off when she went into her closet to try on a dress, but it didn't make much of a difference.

"How's this one?" Chelsea asked, emerging from the closet.

I looked at the white terrycloth dress, wondering if she was serious. The light color contrasted her bronzed skin from the tanning beds, but it had no straps and ended halfway down her thigh, resembling a beach cover-up instead of something worn in the middle of November in New Hampshire. She looked in the full-length mirror in the corner of her room and struck a pose before turning around again, waiting for an answer.

"It's cute," I said, trying to figure out if she had a higher percentage of skin showing than clothing. "But won't you be cold?"

"We'll only be outside for like, two minutes." She looked in the mirror again and smiled, placing her hands on her hips. "Besides, this is sure to catch his attention."

"Who's attention?" I asked, hoping she meant Brad, or even Jeremy. Anyone but Drew.

She turned and looked at me, her eyes glinting with mischief "Drew's, of course," she said, turning one side of her lips up to form a half-smile.

I pulled my sleeves over my hands, reminding myself that Chelsea had no idea she was hurting me when she said that. She wanted what she couldn't have. She didn't love him—she probably saw Drew breaking up with her as a challenge to try winning him back.

I paused, not wanting the anger I felt to reflect in my voice. "What about Brad?" I asked. "He's cute, and he seemed happy when you sat next to him at lunch the other day."

"He's not bad." She paused to apply bright red gloss to her lips. "But I've been talking with Drew in chemistry, and I don't feel like it's over between us. I knew it was a good thing that I made sure we were partners on that first day of class. He even said he was glad I invited him to Shannon's party." She turned around to face me again, not giving me time to respond. "What do you think of this color?" she asked. "Is it too red?"

"It looks good," I said, even though it looked like there was blood covering her lips.

"What're you wearing to the party?" she asked, throwing the gloss into her tiny saddlebag with the designer's name in light blue covering every square inch of it.

I looked down at my dark jeans and black long sleeved shirt with a white tank peeking out underneath. "I'm wearing this."

She did a once-over of my outfit, pursing her lips in disapproval. "Okay," she said, not caring enough to try to force me to wear one of her barely-there dresses. "We have to go. I'm sure Jeremy won't care what you're wearing." She paused. "You know, Lizzie, he really does love you."

"I'm not going for Jeremy," I insisted, getting up and grabbing my bag from the floor. "I'm going for you."

"Whatever, Lizzie." She strutted across the room, her white stilettos digging into the plush carpet as she walked. "Are you ready?"

I looked at myself in the mirror before following her, bringing my hair over my shoulders and wondering if the guilt in my eyes was as obvious to her as it was to me.

Shannon's house was two away from Drew's, and the entire ride there was like déjà vu. The only difference was that instead of talking with Drew as he drove with light music in the background, Chelsea blasted the top forty radio station at full volume, rolling down all of the windows when we pulled into the circular driveway to make sure everyone heard us arrive. Freezing air from outside blew into the car, and there was a bright flash of light in the sky, followed by the booming of thunder.

"Let's get inside before it starts raining," I said, looking up at the clouds swirling overhead, so thick that they blocked the moon. Thunderstorms weren't in the forecast, but the coal black clouds looked like they could dump rain on us in a moments notice. Goosebumps rose over my skin, and I rubbed my arms to try to warm them up as I waited for Chelsea to lock the car. She ran past me, most likely attempting to avoid getting a case of hypothermia from wearing practically no clothing in thirty-degree weather.

Shannon's house was nowhere near the size of Drew's, but was still way nicer than anything found in my neighborhood. Chelsea rang the bell and a girl with short brown hair who I didn't know opened the door for us, revealing the spacious two-story entranceway with a single curved staircase. Dark hardwood floors traveled all the way into the great room, and the large windows in the back had a perfect view of the lake that I'd been out on with Drew nearly every night this past week.

"Let's get some drinks," Chelsea said, grabbing my hand and pushing through a group of senior girls standing in the entrance. We walked through the hallway and turned right to go towards the kitchen. Another roar of thunder boomed through the air, followed by the pattering of raindrops outside. I looked at the windows to see small droplets of ice pelting on the glass, forming crystalline shapes on the surface. It must have been a freak storm—I'd learned in my middle school science class that thundersleet was rare, but I was learning to expect anything.

Shannon stood at the end of the kitchen talking with Warren, who was pouring drinks into red plastic cups and entertaining a cluster of girls. She waved Chelsea over when she spotted us. "You made it." She beamed at Chelsea first, and then at me like we were old friends. "I love your dress," she told Chelsea, glancing at my outfit a second later. "You look cute also, Lizzie."

"Thanks," I said, looking over her outfit. "I really like your dress, too." The black dress with silver straps looked like it would fit in better at a cocktail event than a house party, but she smiled thanks and looked back at Chelsea. I scanned the area to look for Drew, but didn't spot his familiar dark hair and leather jacket anywhere in the crowd.

"Liz!" I heard someone call my name from across the kitchen. I looked up and saw Jeremy waving his hands in the air to catch my attention. Despite everything that had happened in the past few months, it was nice to see a familiar face in the crowd of seniors that I didn't know too well.

"Hey Jere." I tried to speak loudly so he could hear me over the blaring music.

"Come play darts!" he yelled.

"You should play," Chelsea said to me before I could respond. "You'll have fun."

I looked at her in shock. She knew to keep me away from anything involving hand-eye coordination, especially one that revolved around throwing sharp objects at a wall.

"I'm not good at darts," I said, annoyed that she wasn't giving up on her project to get Jeremy and me back together. "Remember when we tried playing in sixth grade and I couldn't even get them on the board?"

She laughed. "That was forever ago. Maybe you'll do better this time." She took my hand and pulled me across the kitchen to where Jeremy waited, not giving me a choice.

As we walked down the hall I looked around to see if Drew had arrived yet, wondering what was taking him so long. I finally spotted him sitting around a coffee table in the great room with Danielle, Brandon, and a few other seniors playing a game involving a deck of cards laid out in a circle on the table. He leaned back into the couch, watching them play. My steps slowed as I walked by and he looked up, pausing when his eyes met mine. I didn't want to wave with Chelsea behind me, but there was a mutual understanding between the two of us before he returned his attention to the game.

"Drew's here," Chelsea whispered as Jeremy opened the door leading to the game room. "Did you see him?"

I contemplated telling her that I didn't, but there was no need to lie about something as simple as spotting someone at a party. "Yeah," I said, figuring it was best to say as little as possible. Chelsea was already acting weird, and the more she talked about Drew, the guiltier I felt. "Just ignore him. Let's go play."

CHAPTER 32

Members of the soccer team and groups senior girls crowded inside of the game room. The dark hardwood floors and billiard table looking more conducive to businessmen then high school students—not like that made anyone act more mature than usual. At the billiard table, Steven Ericson, the goalie of the soccer team, took a shot and landed two striped balls in separate pockets. A cluster of girls in the back cheered over Warren and Brad battling it out in a game of foosball on the side of the room, and a few other people stood in small circles chatting and sipping on drinks in red plastic cups. Amber stood in front of the dartboard, yanking the darts out to prepare for another game.

"Liz, you're Keelie's partner," Jeremy said, spinning a dart in his hands as he walked to stand next to Amber.

"Maybe it would be better if I just watched," I said in an attempt of getting out of having to play, not wanting to embarrass myself in front of everyone in the room, or worse, injure someone with a dart.

"You'll do fine." Chelsea pushed my shoulder, forcing me to take a step towards where Keelie stood gathering the white darts.

"Don't worry," Keelie said, smiling in encouragement. "It's not hard, and no one's even watching."

Apparently she'd never witnessed the atrocity of me trying to do something that involved catching or throwing. "Right," I answered, testing the end of the dart on my finger to see how sharp it was. I pulled my hand away after touching it, hoping for everyone's sake in the room that my aim wasn't as bad as I'd remembered.

Jeremy explained how the game worked before we started, since it had been a while since I'd last played. It didn't sound complicated.

"You can start," Keelie said, handing three darts to me, all with white feathers on the end.

The first dart didn't stick on the board, and the other two didn't land in the right triangles. Amber gathered the darts and handed them to Keelie, not bothering to call a score. It went unsaid that I didn't get any points.

Keelie's first shot hit the wrong triangle, but she got the next two in.

"Two points," Jeremy called, twisting the darts out of the board. He handed them to Amber. "Ladies first, of course."

She spun around herself to look at me, a triumphant smile plastered on her face. Only one of her darts made it into the right section, but it was in an area that gave them three points. Jeremy got three more on his turn.

"Awesome job!" Amber congratulated him, throwing herself into his arms. She probably expected him to pick her up and spin her around like he did for me at the Derryfield soccer game after he scored the winning goal. Instead, he wrapped an arm around her for a second, letting go a moment later. She looked annoyed, but she shook it off.

By the beginning of the ninth inning, Jeremy and Amber were beating us by a significant amount.

"Is the game over after this?" I asked, preparing to take a shot at the sixteenth triangle. I missed.

"Nope," Jeremy answered, watching as I missed the second shot as well. "There are three sets in a game."

The next set passed quickly, and I was surprised to discover that while I wasn't going to be a professional dart player anytime soon, it was fun to play. Amber and Jeremy won, but it wasn't by as many points as the first time.

I looked around the room to find Chelsea, but she must have left sometime in the middle of the second set. "Do you know where Chelsea went?" I asked Keelie, even though she had been just as absorbed in the game as I was. She shook her head no. I did another glance around the room to make sure I didn't miss her, but she definitely wasn't there.

"She left a few minutes ago," Jeremy answered, glancing at his cell phone and putting it in his front pocket. "I'll help you find her."

"That's okay." I shook my head. "I can go by myself. But thanks for offering."

"I don't mind," he said, walking to my side. "We'll find her faster if we both look."

"What about the game?" Amber whined, crossing her arms over her chest and pouting in a way that she must have thought looked endearing. "We still have one set left."

"I'll fill in," Steven volunteered from behind us. He flashed a huge smile and rushed to Amber's side before she could respond. I had no idea where he came from, but apparently he'd finished his game of pool and had been watching us play. "Just until Jeremy gets back."

Amber narrowed her eyes at me like I'd arranged the entire thing to get Jeremy away from her. A girl I didn't know offered to fill in for me, and Jeremy led the way out of the room. He seemed intent on helping me find Chelsea, and it wasn't worth it to cause a scene by arguing.

"Thanks for letting me come with you," Jeremy said as we walked through the hall. "I needed an excuse to get out of there. Amber's cool and all, but she's kind of … smothering."

"I can see that." I laughed, surprised at how easy it was to talk with Jeremy after everything that had happened. "So, did you let us do better on the second set?" I asked. "I know I'm not *that* good at darts."

"Maybe a little." He shrugged and turned to look at me. He wasn't acting arrogant, or angry like the time in the French classroom. He seemed happy. "It was fun hanging out with you," he said. "Like how we used to be."

I looked down at the ground, not knowing how to respond. "It's good that we can still be friends," I said, pulling my sleeves over my hands. "But we should find Chelsea. I think she wanted me to stick with her, especially since Drew's here."

He nodded and navigated through Shannon's house, trying to ignore my dismissal of his hint that he wanted to get back together. As we passed the great room I glanced inside to see if Drew was still playing cards, but while the same group from earlier was still there, the couch where he sat before was empty. Perhaps he went to get a drink.

Jeremy stopped in front of carved double doors that looked like they led into a library, or some room that was equally as fancy. "Maybe she's in there," he suggested, moving to the side so I could walk by.

The room seemed quiet. "Maybe," I said. It wasn't likely, but I was interested to see the rest of Shannon's house. A peek couldn't hurt.

I turned the brass handle and opened the door, gasping in surprise at what I saw, freezing in place as I tried to make sense of the scene in front of me.

CHAPTER 33

Not only was Chelsea lounging on top of the mahogany desk at the end of the room, but Drew was there too, leaning against the bookshelf closest to her. He was only a foot away from Chelsea, who looked at him like he was an expensive chocolate she wanted to eat right up. She leaned forward, her hair cascading in front of her shoulders, and he listened to whatever it was that she was saying.

Then I saw what it was that Drew didn't want me to remember.

The scene in front of me was replaced by a flash of a party long past, except the inside of the room was lit with candles instead of electricity. An orchestra played in the background, and the women's dresses covered up much more of their bodies than most of the tiny ones the girls wore at Shannon's party. I walked into the library and saw Drew and Catherine standing close to each other—closer than he was with Chelsea, while

Chelsea was doing what she said she was going to do all night—getting Drew back. Catherine was as near to him as her large party dress allowed, and by the time they spotted me it was too late. I had already seen her kiss him, and him not move away.

Tears blurred my vision, and I fell against the heavy door, leaning against it for support. I felt like I was about to be sick. Catherine—no, Chelsea turned to look at me, and a smile formed across her face. She must have somehow found out about Drew and me. The worst part of it was that even though she knew I had feelings for him, she still tried to get him back.

I couldn't even look at Drew. He promised me that everything was going to change and we would be together like we were supposed to. But he lied.

He opened his mouth to speak, and I slammed the door shut, the echo traveling through the foyer. Unable to hold it back any longer, I allowed myself to cry, not bothering to wipe the tears off my cheeks.

"Liz?" Jeremy asked from somewhere far away. "Are you okay?"

I shook my head no, burying my face in my hands to prevent myself from crying even harder, hoping that the darkness would erase the scene from my memory. Everything from the past blended with the present, and I couldn't separate them anymore.

"I need to get out of here," I said to Jeremy, gasping for air through the tears. "Take me home."

Not waiting for his response, I rushed towards the front door and stepped into the cold, trying to focus on the icy rain hitting my skin as it froze the tears running down my face. Jeremy slammed the front doors shut so Drew and Chelsea couldn't follow. I looked around for the familiar red Jeep, my thoughts drifting to the last time I was stuck in the rain when Drew drove me home after the soccer game.

Don't think about him, I told myself as I hurried towards the car, yanking the handle to open the door. The vents blew freezing air onto my face and the tires screeched against the icy pavement as Jeremy weaved the car through the others parked in front of Shannon's house. Sleet pelted against the windshield and he pressed his foot harder on the pedal, jerking the wheel to the side. The tires squealed again as he wound along the twisting street, the high-pitched noise sharp in the air.

"Slow down," I told him, my voice cracking through the tears.

"You're the one who said you wanted to get out of there." He laughed, speeding up even more. "So that's what I'm doing—getting you out of there. You see, Liz, I'm doing you a favor. Chelsea was right, but I'm giving you another chance. You should be grateful."

I turned to look at him, gasping at the rage shining in his ice-blue eyes. "Right about what?" I whispered, not wanting to know the answer.

He turned to look at me, breaking his eyes from the road. "About you and Drew. Don't play stupid, Liz. I know you too well to fall for that."

I leaned back in the seat at the mention of Drew's name, unable to believe he would cheat on me. I trusted him; I loved him with everything I had. His voice, deep and reassuring, played through my head again. *You're everything to me. Always and forever.* All lies.

The car squealed around another corner, slamming my body into the door and sending a sharp pain through my head. That was when it came back to me. The memories filled my mind too fast, spinning in a blur of images I couldn't piece together. I tried to push them away—I didn't want to remember any more of my past life with Drew, but they forced their way to the forefront of my mind, too strong for me to control.

The car, the speed, the rain. This had happened before.

I heard the clatter of the horses' hooves pounding on the ground in a steady rhythm, the whip slapping against their backs as a gruff voice that I vaguely placed as James's screamed at them to run faster through the storm. I yelled through the open window in the front, telling him to slow down—he was going too fast for the winding road. He didn't listen to me, instead pushing the horses faster each time I tried to speak. I eventually stopped trying, closing my eyes so I couldn't see the trees rushing by as the carriage bumped along the road. Drew had to be following, so perhaps the speed was good. I didn't want him to gain on us. I didn't want to see him again for as long as I lived—not with the image of Catherine and him kissing in the library burning in my mind.

I saw the bend in the road before James reacted, and he yanked the reins to the right, but it was too late. The wheels lifted off the ground, tilting further and further up until the carriage felt like it was floating through the air. Seconds slowed, and for a moment it felt like I was flying. Then the side of the carriage crashed to the ground, everything speeding up as it rolled over more times than I could count, slamming my head into the glass window. I closed my eyes, wishing it to stop. Finally it did.

Cold mud pressed against the side of my face, the rocks wedged into my cheek. Broken glass from the windows scattered across the ground. I raised my left hand to feel the back of my neck, pulling out a shard of glass piercing my skin and holding it in front of my eyes to see how bad it was. It should have hurt, but my skin was tingling, numb. The rain washed away the blood coating the glass that was as big as my finger, and I watched the red rivulets trickle down my hand, dropping to the ground.

The world grew hazy and started spinning around me, so I closed my eyes, not wanting to feel the pain anymore.

CHAPTER 34

My eyes snapped open and I jumped in my seat, grabbing the armrest as I took a few deep breaths to calm my heart pounding in my chest. I looked around, taking in my surroundings to re-orient myself into the present. There was no carriage or horses. I was in Jeremy's Jeep, the windows protecting me from the pounding rain outside that was impossible to drown out, even with the music blaring through the car.

I focused on breathing evenly to push the images of the crash out of my thoughts. Each breath was forced, and the lack of oxygen made everything hazy, like I was watching my life through someone else's eyes and not living it myself. I tried to calm myself, attempting to forget the feeling of lying helpless in the cold, surrounded by rain, ice, and blood. What I had just experienced was all in my mind—I was okay.

But what I'd seen was more than my fear of speed. It was a flash of the past, and I had to stop it from repeating itself. I tried to remember what had happened after the crash, but it felt like I was slamming myself into a brick wall. There was nothing more to see.

This must be what Drew meant, I thought. He wasn't referring to what had happened with Catherine—although I didn't know which was worse—seeing the two of them together, or a fatal accident in the freezing rain. At least the lies about what he'd remembered were to save me. I suppose it made him somewhat of a martyr.

I tried to push the thought out of my mind. He could have stayed away from her if he'd wanted to—he promised that he wouldn't let history repeat itself. At this point, it would be easiest to let fate take its course. It would be better than seeing Drew and Chelsea together again, and maybe he'd feel guilty about hurting me so deeply.

This was too much to handle. All I wanted to do was curl up in a ball, close my eyes, and make it go away.

The car shifted gears, and I looked at the speedometer passing the sixty mph line, which was too fast for the icy, winding road. Jeremy swerved around another curve and I shut my eyes in preparation for the crash, waiting for the car to start rolling over itself until coming to a stop in the mud, but he made it around the bend. I opened my eyes when I realized that the car wasn't about to go spinning out of control and looked ahead at the upcoming hill, knowing it would be impossible to get Jeremy to stop the car before we reached the top.

A bolt of lighting illuminated the sky, and I allowed myself to realize what I was about to let happen.

Everything would be over if I didn't try to stop the accident, and I wasn't so stupid as to throw my whole life away in the heat of one moment. I didn't know if I would ever be able to make peace with Chelsea or find someone that I shared as deep of a connection with that I did with Drew, but I would never find out if I let events continue on their current path. It would lead to my death.

There was no evidence I could do anything to change destiny, but I owed it to myself to try.

"Jeremy." My voice was surprisingly calm. "Stop the car."

"In the middle of nowhere?" A cruel laugh escaped his lips. "Don't tell me you're about to crawl back to Drew and beg for his forgiveness." Thunder rumbled through the air and he sped up even faster, soaring towards the clouds that seemed to be getting darker by the second. "Don't you see that I love you, Liz?" he said, his eyes burning with rage as he looked over at me, turning back to face the road a moment later. "It wasn't until we broke up that I realized how much I was lost without you. Then Chelsea came to me with this crazy idea. She claimed that you cheated on me with Drew, saying that Shannon saw the two of you out in his boat on the lake in the middle of the night. I said that Shannon must have seen wrong, but Chelsea promised she could prove it, so I let her. I just wasn't expecting..." He turned to look at me again, his eyes flashing with pain as he searched for the words. "I wasn't expecting her to be right."

"She wasn't right," I cried, another tear rolling down my cheek. "I never cheated on you. I promise."

"So you and Drew were never together?"

"Not exactly." I shook my head, unable to look at him. "We were. It was just... after I broke up with you. And after Drew broke up with Chelsea."

"That just makes it so much better." He pressed his foot harder on the pedal, forcing the car to seventy miles per hour. "I trusted you, Liz. I don't see how you could do this—to me or to Chelsea. It doesn't make sense."

"I know, Jere," I whispered, realizing for the first time how deeply I'd hurt him. We'd known each other for so long, and while the relationship felt over for me, it wasn't the same for him.

The only way I could get out of the car alive was to use Jeremy's weakness to my advantage. The thought made me sick. It was awful to lie to him, but I couldn't think of another option. While my feelings for Jeremy weren't the same as with Drew, I still cared for him, and didn't want to add more lies to the twisted situation. But I had no other choice.

"I don't love Drew," I forced out, the words feeling like sandpaper in my throat. I looked over to gage his reaction, relieved to see his hands loosen around the steering wheel and some color return to his knuckles. But the car continued flying up the pavement, and his face remained hard and focused on the road. "I promise you, Jere," I continued, "everything that happened between Drew and me was a mistake. He means nothing to me. I was upset because of our breakup, and I couldn't talk to you, or Chelsea, or even my mom. He was there for me, but the whole time, you were the only one I thought about."

My head pounded from the lie combined with the speed, and I directed the vent towards my face for some fresh air, hoping I didn't get sick all over Jeremy's leather seats. He slowed the car as it climbed the hill, the speedometer falling below sixty.

He was silent for a moment, thinking. "I don't believe you," he said, pushing the car faster, the gears begging him to slow down. "You never were a good liar."

I leaned back on the headrest, trying to drown out the sound of the wind rushing past the car. I would have to try harder. We were almost to the hill—it wouldn't be long until we got to the top, and then it would be too late.

"You need to trust me," I begged, hoping he would listen. "Stop the car. Please."

"In the middle of the road?" He sneered. "You're not making any sense."

The crest of the hill quickly approached, and I knew what I had to say if I wanted to get through this alive. I crossed my fingers behind my back, knowing the superstition was silly, but hoping that whatever was up there looking down on us would understand why I had to lie to him.

"I love you, Jeremy," I choked out, my eyes filling with tears at how much this was going to hurt him later. I leaned in his direction and brushed my fingers against his hand that gripped the steering wheel. His fist loosened, and a surge of hope rushed through my body that my plan might work. "I've always loved you, even before we started dating in eighth grade, and you've been here for me through everything," I said, my voice trembling. "You're the only one I can trust. Drew means nothing to me." I leaned closer towards him and he lifted his right hand off the wheel, intertwining his fingers with mine. "You're the only one I've ever loved," I said, the lie feeling like rusted metal on my lips. "It's always been you."

He swerved to the right and my hand tightened around his as I squeezed my eyes together, preparing to crash against the window as the car rolled to the side, unable to stop because of the ice and the drop on the side of the road. At least I wouldn't be alone when I died. Despite everything that had happened between Jeremy and me, it was comforting to know that he would be with me in those last few seconds.

CHAPTER 35

I held my breath as I braced myself for the crash, but the only noise I heard was thunder booming through the air and ice pounding on the glass. I opened my eyes, allowing myself to breathe when I realized that instead of slipping off the pavement, he'd parked on the side of the hill.

I unhooked my seatbelt to get out of the car, but Jeremy pulled me towards him before I could move, lifting me over the center section of the car and onto his lap. His lips collided with mine with so much force that my back hit the steering wheel behind me. There would be a bruise there the next morning, but at least I'd *have* a next morning.

As hard as I tried, I felt nothing when kissing Jeremy back. All I could see was the disgusted look that I imagined on Drew's face if he ever were to see the two of us together. It hit me again that Drew wouldn't care, and I kissed Jeremy with more force, willing myself to feel something for him again and forget about Drew. It would be easier to continue with how things were with Jeremy before Drew came to town, but the feelings that I once had for Jeremy were gone. His lips were familiar and his hair as soft as I'd remembered, but when I closed my eyes, it was Drew's face that flashed into my mind.

Another car squealed to the side of the road and I looked up, recognizing Drew's black Hummer through the back window of the Jeep. "He followed us," I said, happy that he'd cared enough to come after me. Then I reminded myself of what he'd done with Chelsea and the hurt hit me all over again. I jumped out of Jeremy's lap, hoping Drew wouldn't catch on to what had just happened between us. I knew I should want to make him jealous, but I couldn't ever cause him that sort of devastation.

"Elizabeth!" a muffled voice called from outside of the car, followed by a pounding on the window. "Come out. I need to talk to you. Please." His fist pressed against the glass, and I focused on my hands in my lap to make sure that I didn't look at him. It would hurt too much.

"What's *he* doing here?" Jeremy hissed, rolling down the window. He looked at Drew and draped an arm around me, like he was trying to prove that he owned me. It might have been sweet if what I said to him a few minutes ago was true. "If you can't tell, Liz is fine." His eyes narrowed; an unspoken threat that if Drew came closer, there would be hell to pay. But I couldn't stay in the car with Jeremy anymore. Even though the worst was over, I couldn't be sure that the crash still wouldn't happen if he drove me home.

"Stay here," I told him, looking him in the eyes and hoping he wouldn't give me a hard time. "I'm going out to talk to Drew. I'll be back in a second."

He grabbed my wrist, not allowing me to leave. "Let's just drive away," he insisted. "Leave him in the dust. You told me he means nothing to you. Prove it."

"No." I widened my eyes in shock "You know me, Jere. I can't do that. Just let me talk to him and explain everything, and then we'll go. Okay?"

His grip around my wrist loosened. "Fine. Just a second, then we're out of here."

I pulled my arm back towards my body, worried that Jeremy might change his mind and drive off before I could open the door. But he stayed put, and I stepped out of the car, immediately assaulted by the ice blowing into my face with more force than earlier.

"Elizabeth," Drew said, walking towards me and running his thumbs under my eyes to wipe away the tears I'd forgotten were still there. I closed my eyes, pretending that what I'd seen in the library had never happened. "You're okay. Thank God—I was so worried about you. All I could think about while driving after you was how it was about to happen all over again and that I would never be able to feel your warm skin under my hands or look into your beautiful blue eyes, or tell you how much I love you. I thought I would find you like I did before." He grimaced in pain at the thought. "But you're alright. You're here with me now, and that's all that matters."

I took a deep breath and opened my eyes, forcing myself to remember what had just happened in the library. "Stop," I said, taking a step back. The image of Drew and Chelsea together flashed through my mind, except it wasn't of him with Chelsea—it was of him with Catherine. Not that it mattered; everything merged together into a mess of confusion. A huge lump formed in my throat, and I didn't know if I could speak through it. "I can't believe you could do something like that to me," I cried, wiping away the tears that started to run down my face again. "I trusted you. I *loved* you. Then I had to see the two of you together." His hand started to move towards mine, but I stepped back. "Don't touch me." The words came out harsher than I'd expected, and his eyes darkened to the hard stare that I hadn't seen since the time in the music room at school.

Unable to look at him any longer, I turned away and took my cell phone out of my back pocket, trying to figure out who to call. I had to get out of here. There was no way I was going to let Jeremy drive me, and I couldn't handle being alone with Drew—I would never be able to be around Drew without feeling like my heart was breaking over and over again.

"What's going on?" Jeremy shouted through the wind, slamming the door of the Jeep behind him. "Come on, Liz. Let's get out of here."

The wind made it easy to drown them out, and I scrolled through the address book in my phone to figure out who to call. Obviously Chelsea wasn't an option. I didn't want to wake my mom up and worry her, and I doubted that Hannah's parents would allow her to drive in the storm since she just got her license. Halfway down my list of contacts I figured there was one person I could try, and I pressed send, waiting for her to pick up.

"Lizzie?" Keelie asked, answering after the first ring. "What happened? Everyone's saying something about you running out with Jeremy and Drew following you two. Shannon's with Chelsea right now and I think she's crying in the bathroom ... what's going on?"

"Can you come get me?" I asked through the tears, trying as hard as possible to control my voice. "I'm on Woodland Road, right at the top of the hill. I promise I'll tell you everything in the car."

Not everything, I thought, even though Keelie didn't have to know that. It's not like she would believe the truth.

"Okay," she said, not needing time to think about it. "I'll be there in five minutes."

"Thanks, Kee," I said, closing the phone and shoving it back into my pocket.

Jeremy grabbed my arm before I could turn around. "What was that about?" he asked, his breath hot against my ear. "I thought you were coming home with me."

"No, Jeremy," I said, turning to face him. "I'm not."

He looked sad, and the guilt set in immediately. "What about everything you said in the car?"

I shook my head in apology. "I'm so sorry Jere. I had to get you to stop driving. It was too dangerous—you were angry and you were going so fast. I didn't want us to get into an accident ... it could have been really bad."

He was silent as he took it in, and I turned to look at Drew standing five feet away from me. His eyebrows were scrunched together, and I wondered what was going on in his mind. A spark of hope flashed through my chest that maybe he did love me after all, but I extinguished it immediately. If he loved me, we wouldn't be in this situation in the first place.

"Elizabeth." His voice was hollow when he said my name. Perhaps he felt like he'd lost a part of himself, too. "I'm so sorry."

"You should be," I said, surprised again by the anger in my tone. Another flash of lighting lit up the sky, like the weather was reacting to my words. "I just can't believe you let everything happen again."

"Again?" Jeremy looked back and forth between Drew and me in confusion. I ignored him.

"That's the thing," Drew said, taking a few tentative steps towards me. "Chelsea tried, but all we did was talk. She wanted more, but I told her no. The past didn't repeat itself. That's what I was trying to tell you, but then you got in the car with Jeremy and all I could think about was how no matter what I did differently, there was no way to change what was going to happen. Feeling like I had to lose you for the second time..." He shook his head, and I thought I saw tears under his eyes. "I don't think I could bear it. You're everything to me, Elizabeth."

My breath caught in my chest, and everything I saw in the library started spinning in my mind. I didn't want Drew to be lying, but he'd always known the full story of our past, and he'd kept some pretty important parts to himself. I didn't know for sure what went on with Chelsea and him, but the image of Catherine and Drew together was so sharp in my mind that it may as well have just happened again. It was too much to handle in such a short amount of time.

The sound of another car coming up the hill interrupted my thoughts, and I looked at the headlights shining as they curved around the bend, hoping it was Keelie. I couldn't think clearly, and I didn't know how much longer I could deal with being around Drew. It hurt too much. It felt like my entire body was about to turn into ice and break into a million tiny pieces. The car sped past us and I turned around to look over the edge of the hill, about to burst into tears again when I saw the lake where Drew and I had spent the last few nights together.

"Come home with me," Drew insisted, walking around so he could look at me. "I'll explain everything in the car. I should have told you the truth from the beginning, but I didn't want to hurt you. I promise you that this time I'll tell you everything I know." He held his hand out, and I lifted mine to take it.

"Lizzie!" Keelie screamed my name, honking the horn as loudly as she could. I jumped, pulling my hand away from where it was just about to touch Drew's. "I got here as fast as I could—come in before you freeze to death!"

I motioned to her that I would be there in a minute and turned back around to face Drew. "I don't know what to believe anymore," I told him, watching his eyes drop with the realization that I wasn't going home with him. "All I see right now is you with her ... and it hurts too much.

"And Jeremy," I said, turning to look at Jeremy, who was standing to the side listening to the entire conversation, looking thoroughly confused. He was so different from Drew—broad and blonde—but in that moment his eyes held the same emotion, like he had the biggest let down of his life, and it was all because of me. "I'm so sorry. You deserve more than what I'll ever be able to give you. I'll always love you. I hope that one day we can be friends, if you're ever okay with that. If not, I understand."

His mouth formed into an angry line, and I doubted he would ever be okay with only being friends.

"I'm riding home with Keelie," I told them both, holding up a hand to stop them before either of them could speak. "I need some time to figure everything out." I lifted my eyes up to meet Drew's, hopeful that whatever explanation he had was somewhat believable. But I couldn't hear it right now. If I let my guard down, it wouldn't matter what he said. My emotions were too strong to allow me to think rationally. All I'd done so far was follow my instinct, and it left me standing in the freezing cold with Jeremy and Drew, unable to trust either of them.

I looked at both of them in apology and turned to walk towards Keelie's car, escaping into the warmth inside. I told her what had happened—leaving out everything regarding my past life—but there was nothing she could say to help. All I wanted to do was get home and curl up in my bed to give myself time to think. It was the only way I would be able to see everything clearly.

I hoped that after a full night's sleep I would be able to fit the pieces together, but in the car ride back my thoughts were jumbled in my mind. Chelsea hated me, Jeremy had no reason to ever trust me again, and Drew had lied to me.

It was a huge mess, and there was nothing I could do to fix it.

CHAPTER 36

I woke up the next morning and replayed the events of the night before, hoping it was all a nightmare and that everything would go back to the way it was before the party. Then I saw the pile of crumpled clothes in the middle of my room—the jeans and black shirt I'd changed out of before snuggling into my pajamas and passing out on my bed—and I knew it wasn't a dream. It was real, all of it, and it was a total disaster.

The images returned in a rush, and I rolled over onto my stomach, burying my head in the pillow. Drew cheated on me in our past life with Catherine. I couldn't say for sure that he cheated on me with Chelsea at Shannon's party, but if he remembered what had happened in the past and wanted to change it, why would he be alone in a room with Chelsea to begin with? And even if what he'd said was true and nothing had happened between them, it didn't erase the fact that he'd cheated on me before, even though it was a lifetime ago. I kept thinking about how he said that he loved me and wanted us to be together. He was so hypnotizing, and it would have been so easy to believe every word he said and drive off with him into the moonlight like a scene from a fairy tale. But I wasn't meant for happily ever after in my past life, and it was starting to seem like this one wouldn't be any different.

I lifted my head, seeing the three volumes of *Pride and Prejudice* still sitting on my nightstand. They looked like they were ripped out of another time and traveled through a magic portal to arrive in my bedroom. I reached over and ran my fingers along the cover of the first book, feeling the scratchy material against my skin. I almost picked it up to read but decided against it, not wanting to think about that time period more than necessary.

Maybe Alistair can help, I thought. He had a connection to what was going on. Perhaps he would give me the answers that I needed if I went to see him at the store. It wasn't like I had another option—everyone else would think I was crazy if I asked them about past lives and reincarnation.

Apparently my mom went out to dinner the night before, because there was some leftover Italian food in the fridge that I reheated for lunch. I took a quick shower and threw on jeans and a long-sleeved shirt before driving to the mall to see Alistair. The sun shone in the clear sky, but the roads were slick from the ice storm the night before. I walked into the store and smiled when I saw Alistair sitting behind the antique desk.

"Elizabeth." He smiled, setting down a small box he was inspecting. "I was hoping to see you soon."

I walked towards the back of the store, running my hand across a wooden table as I walked by. "Hi," I said, not knowing where to start. "I love the books. Thank you so much for letting me have them."

"I knew you would enjoy them," he said with a twinkle in his eye. "And I must say, I'm glad to see you here today, alive and well."

That was it. He knew.

"I actually wanted to talk with you about some things" I said, deciding it was time to trust my instincts.

"Yes?" he asked, leading me to continue. He got up and walked towards a round table with four velvet chairs around it, sitting down in the one closest to the back of the room. "Please, take a seat." He motioned to one of the other chairs at the table, and I knew there was no backing out now.

"This might sound crazy," I began, sitting down and holding onto one of the armrests for support. "But do you believe people can have past lives?"

He nodded, a knowing smile creeping onto his wrinkled features. "Very much so."

"I think I might have one." I looked down at my hands, embarrassed to talk about it with someone other than Drew. "Actually, I know I do."

"Of course you do," he said, like he knew it all along. "I was wondering how long it would take you to ask. I gave you enough hints, don't you think?" He chuckled, not in a demeaning way, but like he was glad I was coming to him. "I'm just happy I was able to help guide you in the right direction."

"Guide me?" I asked, wondering what he meant.

"I suppose I can tell you now," he said, leaning back in the chair. "I don't think the spirits up there will be upset, since you came to the conclusion yourself."

"Okay..." I urged him on, curious to hear about his role in all of this.

"I'm your Memory Guide," he said, like I should know what that was without further explanation. "It's my duty to help you come to terms with your past life so you can stop history from repeating itself in this one. I've been waiting a long time to meet you, Elizabeth."

Judging by his age, it appeared so. I was terrible at guessing the ages of anyone over thirty-five, but he appeared to be around seventy, possibly older. I nodded, waiting for him to continue.

"I too had a past life, and had the opportunity to fix what I did wrong." His expression went distant as he remembered his own experiences. "My Memory Guide helped me recall my past life, and I was able to fix my mistake the second time around. Afterwards I was given the choice to either live forever in a place of peace—what some call Nirvana—or return to Earth to help someone just as my Guide helped me."

"When was your past life?" I asked, resting my elbows on the table. It was nice to know that there were others like me, and that some of them were successful in changing what went wrong the first time. Perhaps it wasn't too late for me to make everything right again.

"I grew up in 'Medieval England,' in the late part of the twelfth century," he replied, sitting back and waiting for my reaction.

My lips widened into a circle of surprise. It felt like the Regency Era was far in the past; I couldn't imagine growing up in a time that long ago.

He smiled at my shock, and continued, "It was the time of the Third Crusade, which was full of great peril and war. I was part of the English army invading the Holy Land, and I fought alongside my twin brother Tristan. He was badly wounded in the siege. I still remember the arrow hitting his chest, and the look of shock on his face as he crumpled to the ground. The arrow didn't hit a vital organ, so he remained alive, twitching and looking up at me with his eyes that mirrored my own. Even though I wasn't injured, I could feel the pain in the same place where the arrow entered his skin. It was like it had hit me as well.

"I knelt down to try to save him, but a close friend of mine grabbed my arm. He told me that Tristan was a lost cause, and that I needed to keep running in order to not be hit myself. The battle became worse, and soldiers from my infantry urged me to continue, saying that I had to be there to help. I was unable to bring myself to look back at where my brother had collapsed on the field. The image of him laying there dying and begging for my help haunted me for the rest of my life."

"Wow," I said, my eyes wide in shock.

"I know." He nodded in agreement, his lips forming into a scowl at the memory. "I was a selfish person in the past. Then I was given another opportunity."

"You were reincarnated," I said, still amazed all of this was possible.

"Yes." He smiled, the twinkle returning to his eyes. "I was given a second chance."

"But can we really change who we are?" I asked, thinking of Drew. "I know we're given a second chance, but aren't we still similar to who we were in the past?"

He contemplated the question. "I believe we can change," he said, nodding at his response. "And that's precisely what I did."

"How?" I asked, his answer giving me a surge of hope.

"In my second life, I was a Union soldier in the Civil War," he started, his eyes becoming distant again as he remembered his past. "Only some people can remember their past lives, and reincarnated lives always parallel the ones of the past. Those who are reincarnated can try fixing what went wrong the first time as long as they're given a trigger of some sort, which can be a person, place, or thing. Others can go their entire lives and remember nothing—many believe it's because they're not supposed to.

"My past life started to come back to me when the war began. The Battle of Gettysburg had the highest number of casualties during the war, and as the events unfolded I remembered what I did in the past and was determined to not desert Tristan the second time around, even if it meant risking my own life."

"You were able to change," I said, feeling like I knew the ending to his story.

"Yes," he replied. "Not only did I save my brother, but we both survived the battle."

"And you both lived to see the end of the war?" I asked, hoping he got his happily ever after.

"Not quite." He leaned back in his chair. "My brother passed in the last battle of the war, but I did everything I could to save him."

I played with the sleeves of my shirt, not knowing how to reply. "I'm so sorry," I finally said, knowing that there was nothing I could do to help.

"It's okay." He smiled in understanding. "I chose to return to Earth as a Memory Guide. I couldn't save my brother, but I can do whatever's in my power to help you. So tell me—what happened to bring you back here?"

I explained everything that had happened since the beginning of the school year, starting with when I first met Drew and ending with the events leading up to the crash. Alistair was silent as he listened, allowing me to tell the story without any interruptions.

"What did you see at Shannon's house in the library?" he asked when I finished. "When we get flashbacks, it's sometimes hard to separate the past memories from what's going on in the present. It sounds like you remembered Drew with Catherine at the same time that you saw Drew and Chelsea. Try to separate the emotions of the past from the facts of the present—I know this can be difficult because of the strength of the flashes, especially when they're about something painful, but really think about what it was that you saw."

I closed my eyes, bringing myself back to the time right before opening the door to the library. It was easy to remember the flashes and not reality, but I focused on what was in front of me instead of the overwhelming emotions of the past memories.

Drew and Chelsea stood about two feet away from each other, talking. The flashes consumed my mind after that point, but I pushed the images of the past out of my head and focused on what actually occurred in the present. Drew's expression was cold and uncaring, and he looked at Chelsea like she meant no more to him than a stranger passing by on the street. Then he turned to look at me and Chelsea reached out to him, grabbing his arm to stop him from leaving. That was the last thing I saw before turning around. Since Drew arrived at the side of the hill moments after Jeremy pulled over, he must have pushed Chelsea away before chasing after me.

"You might be right," I said, explaining the revelation to Alistair. "I was focused more on the flash than what was happening in front of me. I'm still not positive about what really happened, but even so, it's hard to forget that Drew cheated on me in the past."

"People can change, Elizabeth," he told me gently. "The two of you wouldn't be here today if you couldn't. Drew made a mistake in the past—there's no denying that—but the love between the two of you is strong enough to transcend time."

"So you think I should give him another chance?"

"I think you should do whatever you think is right." He leaned back in his chair, satisfied with the answer.

It took less than a second for me to make up my mind. I grabbed my bag from the floor and rose from the chair, knowing who I needed to speak with to sort out my emotions.

"Thank you so much," I said to Alistair, eager to start mending my mistakes. "I'll let you know how everything turns out."

"You do that," he said, "and good luck."

CHAPTER 37

I'd never felt so much dread before approaching Chelsea's house—not even a week ago when I went to comfort her after Drew broke up with her. I still couldn't believe she'd known about Drew and me for almost a week and didn't say anything. She must have felt the same anger that Caroline Bingley dealt with in *Pride and Prejudice* when she realized Mr. Darcy preferred Lizzy to herself. The big difference was that Lizzy and Caroline weren't best friends, so Lizzy never had to feel like she betrayed Caroline by marrying Mr. Darcy.

"What are you doing here?" Chelsea snarled when she opened the door. She crossed her arms over her chest, clearly not about to offer me to come in. I don't know what I expected. From her perspective, Drew and I lied to her and were seeing each other behind her back. She had no reason to be welcoming.

I shuffled my feet on the doorstep, watching out for a patch of ice. "I wanted to talk about what happened at

Shannon's," I said, looking down at my feet and then back at her, hoping she would at least talk to me.

She was solid as a statue as she stood in the doorway. Her lips were set in a straight line of distaste, and she glared at me like she was about to take a gun out of her jacket and shoot me on the spot.

Another pair of footsteps sounded from inside, and Chelsea's dad walked down the hall, smiling when he saw me. He was good looking for an older man, his hair dark red like Chelsea's, although some grey streaks were starting to form above his ears.

"Lizzie," he said through his toothy grin. "It's so good to see you! There's some leftover Italian food from Alfonzo's in the kitchen if you're hungry."

"Thanks," I said, putting my hands in the pockets of my jacket to protect them from the cold. "But I already ate."

"Alright." He looked from Chelsea to me and back again, realizing something wasn't right. "Well, I'll leave you two alone. You know where the food is if you get hungry."

"Thanks, Dad," Chelsea said, turning her attention back to me.

"Can we go upstairs to talk?" I asked, hoping she would invite me inside. My hands felt like they would turn into icicles if she left me standing on the steps for much longer.

"Fine," she huffed, stepping aside and standing next to the door. I squeezed by her, making sure to stay as far away as possible. The last thing I wanted to do was make her madder than she already was, and I had a feeling that anything could set her off.

She stayed silent as we went up the stairs, and I heard each step creek beneath my feet as I walked. When we entered her room she dropped onto the side of her bed, leaning on her palms behind her for balance. I sat down on the armchair where she'd done my makeup the night before and pulled my legs up to my knees, hugging them to my chest like they could protect me from whatever came next.

"You and Drew were seeing each other behind my back," she finally said, her voice so cold that it gave me chills. "I can't believe you, Lizzie. Going after my boyfriend when you were seeing Jeremy? Now I see what he meant when he said you'd changed. I don't even know you anymore."

The truth of her words stung. "I'm so sorry, Chels," I apologized, knowing it wouldn't be enough. "I promise that Drew never cheated on you, and I never cheated on Jeremy. I wouldn't do that."

Her eyes filled with tears, but she blinked them back, not wanting to show weakness. "So the two of you broke up with us so you could be together. How *nice* of you. But it doesn't make a difference; you stole my boyfriend. How could you do that to me?"

I flinched at the accusation. It sounded terrible when she said it, but I knew she was right. I considered telling her everything—about our past lives and how we couldn't help it; how I loved Drew from the moment I saw him. But it sounded crazy, and there was no way she would believe me. I wouldn't have believed it either—except that I'd experienced it myself.

"I don't know." I shrugged, knowing she deserved a better reason. "It wasn't intentional. It just sort of ... happened."

"It 'just sort of happened?'" she repeated, looking at me in shock. "Going behind my back with my boyfriend doesn't 'just sort of happen.'"

I decided to try my best to explain. "Do you believe there's one person in the world who you're meant to be with?" I asked, holding my breath as I waited for her answer. "That people are connected to each other from a life other than the one in the present?"

"No." Her answer was solid; she didn't even need a moment to think. "There's no one person out there who's perfect for us. That's stuff from fairy tales." She paused to examine me, crossing her arms when I remained serious. "Please don't tell me you think you and Drew are 'meant to be.' If you think you're making me feel better, you're not."

I looked down at the ground, unable to meet her eyes. "I don't know," I said, sitting back in the chair. "But can I ask you a question?"

She blinked, and I took her silence as a yes.

"What was going on between you and Drew in the library?" I took a deep breath after asking. It wasn't my place to expect her to explain herself, but I had to know the truth.

"Oh yes. That." She laughed, tossing her head back so that her dark red hair flew behind her shoulders. "I'm sure Jeremy told you everything. It almost worked perfectly, don't you think?"

"Almost?" I asked, the word catching in my throat.

"If it worked, Drew and I would be back together," she continued. "Not that it mattered; from the way you freaked out in there you would think that you walked in on us doing more than just talking. All it took was that devastated look on your face to make me realize that what Shannon told me was right. You and Drew were sneaking around behind my back. And then there was the way you ran out of there, like some sad heroine in a movie when she realizes that the love of her life cheated on her." She paused to collect herself. "I just can't believe you could do that to me."

I widened my eyes, taking in everything she'd told me. "You mean nothing happened between the two of you? Besides just talking?"

"I tried." Her lips formed into a snarl. "But Drew didn't go for it. He acted like everything between us didn't mean anything. He's the most cold-hearted person ever. I would watch out with him if I were you—you think you're special now, but just wait until he moves onto his next 'challenge.' He'll leave you in the dust, and don't expect Jeremy or me to care."

I barely registered what she'd said other than that nothing had happened with Drew and Chelsea. Alistair was right—I couldn't separate the past from the present. We had the chance to change, and Drew did it right this time. It still stung that he was alone with Chelsea in the first place, but she could be manipulative when she wanted to. All that mattered was that he didn't repeat the same mistake he'd made in the past. Maybe he *had* changed. I wanted so badly to believe it was possible.

"You really think you're different, don't you?" she hissed. "Well, you're not." She wiped a tear from beneath her eye and stood up to walk over to the desk on the other side of her room, starting to shuffle papers that didn't need re-organizing. "I have a lot of homework," she said, glancing at her planner. "I think you should leave now."

"Okay," I said softly. Chelsea needed space, and I could tell that being around me was only hurting her more. "I'll see you in school on Monday."

"Right." She didn't bother looking at me.

I stood up, watching her hovering over her planner like she was studying something more important than what assignments she had due in the upcoming week. I walked towards the door and waited for her to say something more, but she remained in place, saying nothing as I shut the door behind me.

I opened my bag to get my cell phone, realizing a moment later that I had turned it off and thrown it in the corner of my room after the events of last night. It would be a waste of time to backtrack to my house, and I pulled out of Chelsea's driveway, my heart pounding as I started on the familiar route to Lakeside Circle.

CHAPTER 38

There was nothing to say to Drew to make up for the way I'd acted last night.

So instead of worrying myself further, I turned the music up louder. A contemporary version of the song "Hallelujah" filled the car, and I focused on the music, trying to feel it traveling through every part of my body. The song was one I'd heard played in many movies during a dramatic scene, and the experience of driving to Drew's felt so surreal. I didn't know how I could fix everything between us, and it felt like I was an observer of my own life instead of actually living it.

I inched up the driveway leading to his house, the columns around the double doors resembling the mouth of a giant about to swallow me whole. The multitude of windows stared at me like large eyes, and I wondered if he was standing in front of one, watching me approach.

I hated arriving unannounced, but I had to talk with him. I was the only one who could make everything right, and if he felt even half as awful as I did, then it couldn't wait. My head pounded as I walked up the steps leading to the entrance, and I rang the bell, waiting for someone to answer.

The door swung open, and Drew stood completely still when he saw me. I stared blankly at him, trying to think of what to say, but came up with nothing.

"Elizabeth," he said my name slowly, like he was convincing himself I was really there. He opened the door wider and stepped to the side, motioning me to come in. I kept my eyes focused on the ground as I entered the foyer and heard the door shut behind me, the sound echoing throughout the room. I finally looked up, the guilt setting in again when I saw him under the light. He looked like he hadn't slept all night—but judging from the small smile on his lips, he was happy to see me.

"I hope you don't mind that I came over," I said, stumbling over my words. "I was already out and was about to call, but then I realized I left my phone at home."

"Of course I don't mind." He started to take a step towards me. Then he stopped, like he was afraid I would turn and leave if he got any closer. "Do you want to come up to my room to talk?" he asked. "My mom's been hovering over the divorce papers all day, and she freaks out at the drop of a pin."

I nodded and followed him up the curved staircase, trying to be as quiet as possible. He didn't turn to look at me until we were both inside his room.

"I'm sorry for not listening to you last night," I said, shaking my head in apology. "I talked to Chelsea and she told me nothing happened. She hates me, but at least she was honest. I just..." I paused, gathering my thoughts. "I saw you two together, and the memories of you with Catherine returned so quickly—all of the images rushed through my mind and blended together. Seeing you with her again hurt, but I finally separated the past from the present, and I realized that what matters is that nothing happened between you and Chelsea this time around. The present is what's important; not the past."

He kept his gaze focused on mine, like he was afraid I was about to disappear in front of him. "I thought I was too late," he said, sadness shining in his eyes. "I figured you'd gotten in the car with Jeremy and I expected..." His face twisted in pain, and he shook the thought out of his head. "I'm just glad you're alright."

I stepped forward and reached my hand towards him, the same way he did last night out in the rain. He didn't move, allowing my fingers to wrap around his. "I just wish you'd told me everything from the beginning," I said sadly. "Why didn't you?"

"I didn't want to scare you." His answer was simple. "I wanted to prevent you from remembering that night. I didn't want you to have to re-live..."

"My own death," I finished his sentence.

"Exactly."

I took another step closer to him, leaving almost no space between us. His arms wrapped around me and pulled me closer, and I leaned my head against his shoulder, closing my eyes and thinking about nothing but the two of us together. It might have been easier if he had told me everything from the beginning, but as much as I thought I would have wanted to know, I understood why he didn't. I couldn't imagine living through all of those weeks afraid it would be impossible to stop my own death.

His hands cupped my face, and I looked up at him, hoping that he could forgive me for what I'd said last night. "About everything that happened ... back then," he said, pausing for a moment. "You know I'm a different person now. I would never do anything with Chelsea. I love you, Elizabeth. I believe what you said earlier—if we weren't supposed to be together, we wouldn't have this second chance."

"*Now* you believe me." I said, glad that everything was finally coming together.

His lips curved into a small smile. "I've always believed you."

"But if you believed me ... then why didn't you tell me everything?" I asked. "Then we could have worked on fixing all of it together."

"I guess I wasn't convinced it could be fixed." He shrugged, looking down at me in apology. "I was afraid if I told myself it could be changed and I was wrong, it would be harder when everything happened all over again. I thought it would be easiest to just stay away from you; then you could live a long life without me in it and never know any differently. But we both know how that worked out." He paused, and I could tell what he was about to say next was hard for him. "If you don't want to be with me after I kept so much from you, I understand."

"Of course I want to be with you." I laughed, unable to imagine Drew and I not being together after everything we'd been through. "If you remember, the first time Mr. Darcy asked Lizzy to marry him in *Pride and Prejudice*, he went about it all wrong," I started, smiling at the connection I'd just made in my mind. "He insulted her and her family. But after her refusal, he made a conscious effort to change for the better, and everything worked out for them the second time he proposed. It's the same with us. You learned from your past mistakes, and everything's different now. Just as Lizzy gave Mr. Darcy a second chance, I'm going to do the same for you."

"I'm glad that Lizzy gave Mr. Darcy a second chance." He smiled at the comparison. "She was the only one for him. He would have been miserable without her."

"And she would have been miserable without him." I laughed. "Even though she might not have admitted it."

He leaned back, his hands remaining in mine. "I have something for you," he said, the light returning to his eyes.

"And what's that?" I asked, intrigued.

He walked to the mahogany nightstand next to his bed, rummaging around for something buried in there and pulling a small light green cardboard box out of the drawer. I walked towards him, sitting on the side of his bed. He sat next to me and lifted the top open, revealing a silver chain bracelet with a heart charm, each link slightly smaller than the tip of my pinkie finger. It was modern—unlike anything produced in the early nineteenth century—but it was perfect.

"I got this for the day we could finally be together," he said, lifting it from the box. "It's something current, since we're not quite the same as we were back then." The metal glimmered in the light, and I realized there were words engraved on the heart.

"Lizzie & Drew," I read the words aloud, brushing my fingers against the charm and turning it over. "Always and Forever."

"Do you like it?" he asked, his eyes sparkling like he already knew the answer.

"Like it?" I was amazed he even had to ask. "I love it."

"I'm glad." He smiled and put it around my wrist, leaving a trail of warmth where his fingers brushed my skin. It fit perfectly. I played with the heart, reading the inscription again. "What's wrong?" he asked, cupping my chin with his hand.

"I was just thinking," I began, unsure if I should even bring it up. "Since my memories of the past ended with what happened that night, then what comes next?"

"I have no idea," he answered. "But the hard part's over. You're here and we're together. That's all that matters."

"You're right," I agreed, deciding it wasn't worth worrying about. "Now I need to figure out how to patch things up with Chelsea and Jeremy."

"They'll get over it," Drew said without a second thought. "Whatever happens next, we'll deal with it together." He paused, his eyes turning serious again. "You know I'll always be here for you, right?"

"Yes," I said confidently. I had never been so sure of anything in my life. "Always and forever."

ABOUT THE AUTHOR

In the fall of 2009, Michelle saw Taylor Swift's "Love Story" music video for the first time. She thought up a story to go along with the video, and decided to write the beginning of this story as a homework assignment for class. Her classmates and teacher loved it so much that they wanted to know what happened next, so Michelle continued writing, and that story eventually became her first novel, *Remembrance*. She's so happy to be able to share this novel with you, and hopes you enjoyed reading it as much as she loved writing it!

Check out her website, www.michellemadow.com, to add her on Twitter, Facebook, YouTube, and her many other social networking sites ☺

Michelle is currently studying creative writing at Johns Hopkins University, and is hard at work writing more novels for young adults.